Threshold

Threshold

An Anthology of
Contemporary Writing
from Alberta

Editcd by
Srdja Pavlovic

The University of Alberta Press

Published by

The University of Alberta Press

Ring House 2

Edmonton, Alberta T6G 2E2

Threshold: An Anthology of Contemporary Writing from Alberta is published for the book trade.
A volume in *(currents)*, an interdisciplinary series. Jonathan Hart, series editor.

ISBN 0-88864-338-1

Printed in Canada 5 4 3 2 1

Canadian Cataloguing in Publication Data

Main entry under title:

Threshold

  ISBN 0-88864-338-1

  1. Canadian literature (English)–Alberta.* 2. Canadian literature
(English)–20th century.* I. Pavlovic, Srdja, 1961-
PS8255.A4T57 1999   C810.8'097123   C99-910887-5
PR9198.2.A42T57 1999

∞ Printed on acid-free paper.
Printed and bound in Canada by Transcontinental Printing Inc.

Cover image: "Canada Classic: Frosted Morning" (detail) by Robert Sinclair, 1986.
Acrylic on canvas, 127.8 cm x 152.6 cm. From the University of Alberta Art and Artifact
Collection, Museums and Collections Services. Used by permission of the artist.

The University of Alberta Press acknowledges the financial support of the Government of
Canada through the Book Publishing Industry Development Program for its publishing
activities, and the support received for its program from the Canada Council for the Arts.
The Press also gratefully acknowledges support received for this project from Syncrude.

THE CANADA COUNCIL | LE CONSEIL DES ARTS
FOR THE ARTS | DU CANADA
SINCE 1957 | DEPUIS 1957

Foreword

I am pleased to introduce this fine collection of work from Alberta writers, the first of its kind in many years. In the pages that follow, thirty-six authors explore diverse themes through their fiction, essays, poetry, and short stories. This body of work suggests that Alberta's literary community is indeed healthy, giving the province a strong and distinct voice. Importantly, this collection includes work by new, emerging, and established writers, making it a text well suited for the study of Canadian literature in high school, college, and university classrooms.

On behalf of Syncrude Canada, I want to thank everyone who played a role in making this anthology possible. Our company is proud to support artistic expression in its many forms and is especially pleased to have formed this new link with Alberta writers.

Eric P. Newell
Chairman and Chief Executive Officer
Syncrude Canada

Contents

Acknowledgements

I would like to express my gratitude to many people who supported me in working on this project. I wish to make particular mention of the kindness of E.D. Blodgett, without whose expertise, support, and encouragement this anthology would not have seen the light of day. I am grateful to Rudy Wiebe for bringing his critical judgement and refined taste to our discussions of the content. To Douglas Barbour, George Melnyk, Fred Wah, Robert Hilles, Claire Harris, and many other authors for giving me unpublished material for my collection. To Myrna Kostash, Kristjana Gunnars, and Roberta Rees for their generous and invaluable advice. To my wife, Darka, for believing in me. To Miki Andrejevic and his colleagues at the Writers Guild of Alberta for being there whenever I needed their help. To Syncrude Canada Ltd. for providing much-needed financial support. I would also like to thank Mr. Glenn Rollans, Director of the University of Alberta Press, for his benevolence towards me and his belief in the importance of this project. Finally, I would like to thank Mr. Robert Kroetsch, a master craftsman, whose extravagance of words has inspired me for all these years.

–Srdja Pavlovic

Srdja Pavlovic

Introduction
The Intimacy of Ink

I first encountered Alberta literature through *Seed Catalogue*, a collection of poems by Robert Kroetsch. The book was a present for my eighteenth birthday from my uncle, a sailor, who had just returned from one of his frequent exotic *viaggi* across the ocean. At the time, because of my limited English, I was not able to make out much of Kroetsch's poetry. The verses sounded distant and complicated. But the book sat on my shelf for years and its dreamprints helped me imagine a distant place and wonder about the people living there. I was young and dreamed the symmetry of the world.

> No trees
> around the house.
> Only the wind.
> Only the January snow.
> Only the summer sun.
> The home place:
> a terrible symmetry. (Kroetsch, *Seed Catalogue*.)

Some twenty years and a few host countries later, I began to understand this "terrible symmetry." Yugoslavia dissolved, my English improved, and it was time to replace broken dreams with the refuge of distant places.

I wanted to live in a place far away from the mainstream. The centres of culture have become too self-absorbed, harried, imploding to madness and soot and broken bottles. The periphery is more attractive. That is why I chose

Alberta. At the time, I was not aware of its cultural profile. I was told that people here are calm and friendly, that they drive carefully and obey the traffic signals. And most important of all: no one asks where you came from. Only your speech betrays its origins.

But I was in for a big and pleasant surprise. Having come from a different cultural, social, and political framework – and having grown up within the European and Slavic frame of reference – to encounter such versatility and opulence of literary life and, at the same time, to learn about the transparency and the absorbent nature of Alberta's literary landscape was a fascinating process. Here, there still exists an open-ended communication with the environment: animals and natural phenomena have their characteristics, histories, and personalities too. Even when the surroundings are hostile, one can fit in and not be isolated. As a typical exile who struggles against all forms of loneliness, I knew that I had finally found a refuge for the soul.

Wanting to learn more and participate in the process of cultural interaction, I began to translate the works of Alberta writers into Serbo-Croatian for readers in the former Yugoslavia. While translating the writings of E.D. Blodgett, Fred Wah, Douglas Barbour, George Melnyk, Monty Reid, and Myrna Kostash, I realized that writing in Alberta is not a mirror image of foreign influences but a living organism that creates at its own pace for the outside world. The works of these authors bring memory to the surface and then modify the meandering remembrance. I felt that the writers from Alberta were opening doors to rooms, letting me have a good look around and then saying – now, let's move on, since what you have just seen is all yours. What an experience!

I understand that Alberta literature is often perceived as an isolated house, standing alone in the prairies, largely shielded by its geographical remoteness from new artistic trends and influences that occasionally make their way across the ocean and the province's southern border. Contrary to such a notion, however, it is obvious that those literary innovations continuously meet and are absorbed here, and that their forces are employed in a different manner. They are tools for experiencing and analyzing urban living, questions of time, space, and the meaning of life; for exploring one's identity and the sense of home and belonging.

The effort of Alberta writers to reshape the influences they encounter appears to have the same purpose: to define various senses of identity and explore the traditional knowledge of history through the prism of a post-modern literary approach. This often entails writing about intimate, even sordid, everyday rituals. It means being able to walk through the outer regions of awareness, consciously off-centre, along the edges of experience. All of it has to do with the lyric intensity of a narrative consciousness that refuses to be limited to a single identity or a single form of expression.

To paraphrase George Melnyk, one should see Alberta as the crossroads where opposites meet, each adding its own touch of spice and colour, thus creating a distinct reality. This intersection of various cultural circles with their multitude of voices is what makes Alberta literature, the product of which is by no means accidental: it is the author's response to the environment, to the vacancy and stillness of the Alberta landscape.

The central purpose of this anthology is to present these characteristics of Alberta writing. *Threshold* offers a substantial sampling of current work in several genres – fiction, poetry, essays, and short stories – by Alberta's major authors. It also attempts to include the material of less-known writers whose significance derives from their uncommon sensibility or from their promise of future development. In this book, I have tried to recognize the vitality of interest in the roots of Alberta's literary tradition and the search for new forms of expression. For each piece presented here, five or six others came immediately to mind; the result, of course, is no more than a hint of what the literary community in Alberta produces at present. My intention has been to supplement the known and to stimulate exploration. Bio-bibliographical notes on contributors have been added, in the hope that readers will be encouraged to pursue an interest in those authors whose work most appeals.

This selection is not genre bound, nor does it attempt to follow a particular literary style or form. I realize that such an approach is something of a departure from the usual sense of what an anthology represents. What I have tried to do in this book is to free the authors from the limitations imposed by genre, literary style, form, or topic. There are two main reasons for this choice.

First, I truly believe that today's standards of literary excellence could not sufficiently prepare a reader for the complexity of responses the writings in this book will evoke. Each piece is unique in the sense of the author's perception of reality and the meaning of life, thus engaging a reader on more than one level.

My second reason is defined by the need to portray a literary community whose members are continually crossing the boundaries of a cultural circle and are reaching across political, ethnic, gender, social, religious, linguistic, and stylistic division lines. They are trying to put holes in the fences of their own literary backyard.

By including works that, some more than others, correspond to the rules imposed by various "isms," I have tried to stress the artificial nature of such categories, to blur the boundaries between them, and to point out the common thread that runs through many of the works included in this anthology – redefining oneself within the framework of postmodernism. Each author, in a sense, is going back to where it all started – to the prairies and the people living there, to the horizon where, in Robert Hilles' words, "the moon is spying on their lives." Only this time, the voyage is taking different twists and turns, and the landscape is seen through a different kind lens.

The content of *Threshold* may appear to some to demonstrate a rather eclectic literary taste. I must say that this selection reflects my perception and understanding of the Alberta literary landscape within which I reside. Reaching out for the "imaginary Alberta" (Goyette) of writers meant discovering the real Alberta as a vibrant and ever-changing literary community. This community is not a sand-castle, but the prairie sound-castle, filled with different voices – its walls resonate with the cadences of many languages. These omnipotent voices carry an enormous healing power and mark the ethnicities that are "transplanted like immortelles to a boreal forest" (Darbasie).

This book is a journey from Budapest and Venice, through the heat and dust of Dar es Salaam and the serenity of Guadalajara, to the disappearing stones near Stanley Point, across Two Coyotes Crossing, and all the way to the spiritual world of the Medicine Wheel on the Bow River. The curious fencing and marking of geographic and mental landscapes, where the vertical and horizontal winds meet, represent homecomings. In this anthology, I have tried to lend my eyes and ears to my fellow travellers, to share their excitement, to learn from their experience, and to enjoy their curiosity.

The present volume represents some of the range of literary work produced by Alberta writers during the past three years. It includes those born in Alberta as well as those who choose to call it their home. The authors are arranged not chronologically but rather according to the topics and notions they explore. Many of the pieces included herein have not yet been published, but publication notices are included, where applicable, in the notes on contributors.

No anthologist can hope to win approval for all his inclusions and exclusions, but I hope this book will offer readers the possibility of finding new loves and will stimulate further exploration.

Linda Goyette

Imaginary Alberta
Is It a More Appealing Place?

When you run out of gas, you have to find a filling station.

I ran out of writing fuel at the end of the winter. This happens all the time to newspaper writers, and it's quite a nuisance. You walk along the side of the highway with an empty jerry can, watching the stories whizz past, and you mutter to yourself: "There must be more to this province than anti-deficit campaigns and airport conundrums and homophobia and hockey stadium financing and Young Offendermania and welfare scapegoating and Steve West-ism and half-time kindergarten and Ken Kowalski-itus and Percy Wickman's drunk-driving charge. Why can't I write about a more appealing Alberta?"

Anyway, sometimes you get lucky. Dead tired and dusty, you find the self-serve pump. I found it in the first issue of a rough, little magazine called *Filling Station*, published in Calgary, with an appealing introduction:

> You know the sort of place, that little gas station in the middle
> of nowhere, out between Heisler and Donalda, between Red Deer
> and Calgary. On long trips, or short ones, you can buy snacks,
> cigarettes and coffee to keep you going. You stop between these
> fixed points on the map to get an injection of something new,
> something fresh that's gonna get you from point to point. You stop,
> talk, fill up — maybe learn to appreciate things you have not
> noticed or paid much attention to before.

The upstart magazine offers new Alberta writing – premium, unleaded – as a "connection between polarities, a link." Browsing through its pages, I began to wonder about differences in perception between Alberta's creative writers and journalists. Both are interpreters of place, but they see, hear, and tell stories differently. What are the poets and short-story writers discovering this year as they sift through life in a harsher province? Do they even live in the same Alberta? Do they like it better?

To find out, I scooped up five fiction magazines, one anthology of Alberta short stories, and hit an imaginary highway to new destinations. My only rule was that the stuff had to be new. I passed by established writers to pick up neglected newcomers with their thumbs out. The speed limit was not respected.

What a place! I could barely keep my eyes on the road. As I started out, R&all Thomas, a weird Calgary guy I met at *Filling Station* who calls himself "an image text manipulator," recommended that I "run from anything that reduces to a label or a category." Diane Mirosh, goodbye! Hello...absinthe?

Absinthe is another small magazine from Calgary with the subtitle "writing from the margins." It is the successor to *Secrets from the Orange Couch*, a sadly missed publication from that great literary capital of the world, Killam, Alta. *Secrets* recently ran out of...ooh, this metaphor is tiresome...steam. Southern Alberta writers in the collective regrouped to publish *Absinthe*. You get an idea of the unpretentiousness of the magazine when you read the preface thanking somebody "for donating the proceeds from the sale of her pool table, and for everyone else who made the garage sale a success." This mag is no *New Yorker*, but it's fun to read.

Here's Weyman Chan on a Canadian kid tasting his own culture: "Years ago/inside uncle's pocket were plum candies/into China writing on the wrapper/then White Rabbit toffees their lucent rice paper/melt on tongue we spoke better Chinese then/the tongue in one place sailed up and down soft sweet/palate, roof of heaven, these opened words."

Here's Paul Therrien finding beauty in unlikely places: " A ditch outside of town, check it out, South on the 22, the gasplant crossing, there's a discarded tire filled with dandelion, wild rose, thistle and vetch, those big purple Canadian thistle flowerheads will blow you away. I wanted to fall to my knees."

Here's r. rickey with a torrent of words about parched Calgary: "there is no see there is no sea high above in a wind in a storm watch glenmore reservoir push the waves a little faster to the shore the image of water strikes the heart of a prairie boy if this is our sea how small we are this is not an expanse not a lake but a reservoir cannot replace sea on a cold crisp calgary just before the chinook rolls in from the coast the warm warm coast."

Journalism is always about now. This imaginative Alberta has a past and a future, not just a present. Ghosts stick around. Every year, for example, the *Absinthe* collective invites writers to a retreat in Blairmore, then takes them exploring to the sites of the Frank slide and the Hillcrest mine disaster. Some of the writing appeared in a special Crowsnest Pass edition last winter, and it's evocative. "The mountain fed the town with coal," wrote Debra Dudek in a fragment about the Frank slide. "Every day the men marched into its mouth and stumbled home dipped in the black juice of her tongue."

Creative writers, unlike journalists, concentrate on personal rather than public issues. They prefer to explore the universe of the interior. No wonder their Alberta seems like a bigger place.

Noisier, too. This Alberta has three million voices, a cacophony of opinions, instead of that single, cranky voice you hear on Alberta's open-line radio shows. These imaginary Albertans – or are they the real ones? – come from all over the world. They speak foreign languages, aboriginal languages, and even the dreaded Other Official Language without complaint. They love to travel. They don't seem as fearful, hostile or single-minded as their often-quoted cabinet ministers. They seem more introspective, yet at the same time, eager to look beyond their borders. They are definitely smarter and funnier, not so earnest and puritanical.

How often would you expect to find aboriginal rights and great sex in the same column of newsprint? Michael Paul Martin, a native poet, makes the earth move for the First Nations in a hilarious poem in *Absinthe* called "Oh Tipi Crawlin' Visions." Was it good for you? It was good for me.

This is the Alberta you want to call home. People move away, sometimes in a huff, but they usually come back. They share a refreshing sense of humour about the place.

A Calgary snowplow driver in Bruce Hunter's "Country Music Country" jokes constantly about the city and the province. ("During Stampede week, you could feel dumb two ways, if you dressed Western or if you didn't... Here, if there's four corners, there's a gas station on one and churches on the other three. The twins in this town: God and Gasoline...there never was a shortage here of religious nuts nor bad taste.")

Sounds like he hates Alberta, doesn't it? But then the snowplow driver and his friend drive up to what sounds like Rocky Mountain House to go fishing, and on the way, they see men guiding horses through an alpine meadow.

> It was something you didn't see much anymore even out here, and
> the smell of pine on the dry air and even the dust kicking up under
> the truck smelled good in the mountain air. This was the West none
> of us dealt with well. Now I drive it. Deb keeps taking pictures,
> lining them all up on the table until she's got ten in a row showing
> the whole horizon. Then she realizes she didn't get the sky in.

Jacqueline Larson, a poet published in *Absinthe*, would understand the snowplow driver's ambiguous feelings. She finds a "devil in the heart's house for each girl born in Red Deer," but she's resigned. Coming back from Vancouver, she writes: "A delight/comes sudden on my heart and I am glad/my dad's a redneck reform party type and my/Mom's oblivious as hell. If not for the/ Boom and bust I'd never have left."

These writers are not oblivious to the unforgiving politics, the intolerance, and the hard times of Alberta in 1994. They just tackle them differently.

Some, like poet Danielle Holloman, lash out at a dominant white society that embraces Caribbean culture while remaining suspicious of black immigrants. ("You perm your hair so it could be full, buoyant, not unlike my hair/You pay to sit in a human microwave/to tan your body to a/soft/nubian/bronzed brown/not quite unlike my own hue...You do not make sense. I vie for the same job as the tanned/leather skinned/underqualified/perm-wearing/bird nested hair/non-degreed white girl./To my dismay she gets the position/OK, I tell myself to start all over/here goes my culture out of context blowing up black.)

The Calgarians in Rick Bowers' "At the Trailer Park" are similarly irate about the double standards of Alberta's managerial class. A clerk complains that she works for the cheapest (unprintable) lawyer in Calgary. "'He said that everybody has to be prepared to tighten their belts these days.' She rolled her eyes just as the toaster popped. 'Can you believe it? I don't imagine that he has to do much tightening.'"

You read about Alberta's conflict in the newspapers every day but you rarely read about meeting places. In contrast, the best local fiction and poetry find the intersecting points for people who disagree.

My favourite story in the NeWest anthology, *Boundless Alberta*, is called "Texas Two-Step," by Barbara Mulcahy of North Star. (For culture-vultures with a map, North Star is a literary hotbed somewhere south of Manning.) In the story, a rural woman is infuriated after losing an environmental battle at a northern Alberta pulpmill hearing. To cheer up, she joins a country dance class. She ends up with her arms around a stubborn feller-buncher operator who opposed her at the hearings. Anger dances with forgiveness. "He leaves a comfortable distance but still holds me so that I know he's holding me. And he smells nice. Like a person."

Connections like that are reassuring. So are familiar places. Journalists do their best to give you the feel of a place but they don't linger on the scenery. Reading Alberta's fiction, there is so much pleasure in recognition.

In Astrid Blodgett's "The Color of Fidelity" – published in the local literary magazine *Other Voices* – you ride along with a psychiatric outpatient from Whyte Avenue to Alberta Hospital. He's confused but you know every bus stop is the right one. In Anna Mioduchowska's beautiful story "Over Here, Over There: Sacking Byzantium," you eavesdrop in an Edmonton living room as a traveller packs a suitcase full of WEM treasures for the old country. You can practically smell the cabbage rolls in the oven.

Oh, yes, and in Gail Helgason's "The East Face of Sorrow Peak" – published in the latest issue of *Grain* – not only do you scramble all over your favourite hiking trails in Jasper, you find yourself in your very own newsroom, talking to a suspiciously familiar copy editor in a cardigan he still wears!

"There'll be football polls and publisher's dinners and the odd downed plane or constitutional crisis to keep things lively, and the years will just go by." And so they do.

You know what's so compelling about the best homegrown poetry and fiction? It's true to the place. In a year of rapid change, it's instructive and comforting. "When the centre's hold loosens, do things fall apart or do they really come together?" ask the *Absinthe* editors in a provocative challenge to Albertans on the margins. Well, you think, why shouldn't they come together?

To a newspaper writer, standing at the edge of a frantic highway with her empty jerry can, poet Abe Deyto whispers: "Go and find those mountains… go and search for altitude." That's what Alberta's imaginative writers are telling the rest of us about this province. When life on the ground becomes a little discouraging, you can always look up.

Alice Major

Tales for an urban sky

If...
an amnesiac was set down in a few square blocks of a northern city
and felt the need of a mythology, what kind of stories might she
make up?

She might start by noticing the sky. All around the world, tribes
of human beings have noticed how, in a year, the moon cycles
through the sky twelve times and a bit. They have named each moon
for the natural objects important to them.

A northern people might call a spring moon "The Moon of New
Reindeer Calves." A tropical people might call it "The Moon of
Frogs." In a city, it might be...

5. The moon of tricycles

circles like the slip-slowing wheel
of a toy left on its side on the asphalt –
the rider called inside to bed. The moon rocks
in the nursery twilight, knits up apricot
and rosy-pink sky-fluff, thinks how it would be
to have another child, now the youngest
is trumbling up and down the pavement
on a third-hand tricycle. Another baby to hold
in her thin, crescent arms.
                          Then wonders
where the little one would sleep.
Or play. The older ones are toughening
already, only the apartment parking lot
to run in, shouting the foreign words she thinks
are curses. She feels them grow away from
her, take on the unfamiliar constellations
of this hard-paved land. But still – to have
one more small face to brighten at her curved
smile, to give back light. Perhaps this would be
the one to stay and love her, growing older,
an immigrant among these alien stars.

7. The moon of magpies quarrelling

shimmers in the pale sky of early morning
like a court reporter's screen. It records
the magpies' proceedings – litigious birds
with ermine draped across their glossy shoulders,
their bellies drooped in prosperous curves.
They introduce their offspring to the court's
attention in harsh, good-natured voices.
They teach their fledglings legalese, the value
of bright shiny objects and their importance
in the scheme of branches.
                        They do not mean to be
so handsome, so much bigger than the other
birds, or to have such clever eyes. It's just
the way things are, they tell
judiciously brightening skies.

10. The moon of strippers

snaps her garter like a first taste of frost
against summer's warm thigh. She illuminates
crude paintings on the walls outside
Pierre's – Exotic Dancers Nitely.
Women squatting with top hats on their heads;
women in chaps and stetsons, their breasts
and asses bare; and one, a woman walking
naked on a Polynesian shore with the round moon
a hole in the lampblack sky beyond her shoulder.

The painted girls arrive, bored or business-like,
tired or tart-tongued. The customers arrive
ready to appraise – like so much real estate –
the beachfront bosoms, the size and tilt of nipples.

And all the while, the moon of strippers leans
against her sky tree full of ripening apples.
Her vulva shines, a slit in the perfumed heaven,
a luminous wedge of fruit. The crescent widens –
                              all that juice
painting the town, spilling on the little men below
who dance about and poke up measuring sticks.
She laughs at them, so arrogant they are. So cock
sure.

12. The moon of fur coats

wears ermine, turns the backs of foxes white
where they glimmer in the furriers' windows
behind bars. The street is strewn with leaflets
passed out by anti-trapping protesters and roughly thrust
aside by passers-by. They could not afford garments
like these, anyway – these sleek-sewn, fluid
draperies, these rich pelissons.
      The moon pauses to scan
graffiti soaped on shop windows. "*Stop the
pain...*" She reads slowly, but with no
comprehension, taps the words with pearly, tapered
fingertips. Moves on. From the white-furred
pavement, frost snaps futile jaws at her lucent,
affluent heels.
      Those not clad in fur lie outside
her circle. Like the man who walks and walks, pacing
some cage the size of the city. His legs straw-thin,
his loose and flapping trousers sucked empty
by the wind. Or the girls in their short skirts, thighs
pale as moonlight, boots black as sky, who wait
on the corner – wait and wait in their leg-hold traps
circling small, desperate spaces.

Roberta Rees

Hoar Frost

Plain prose, today I want to write plain prose. I want to write, "Yesterday the sun didn't come up & hoar frost clung to the trees." I read the newspaper, *Teenage Girl Lived in Fear, Stabbed to Death by Boyfriend.* I want to write comfort, not sorrow. I want to write hot milk in the belly. The belly of my arm lying beside the headline, *Women Struggle to End Violence Against Women.* Trees wearing hoar frost, white & heavy. Trees wearing hoar frost in the fog. *Woman Murdered by Ex-Husband, Neighbours Say She Was a Wonderful Person.* I want to write plain prose about the surprise of trees coming out of the fog wearing hoar frost all day. On CBC a male announcer's voice, "Tomorrow's question on Cross-Country Check-Up – now that we have a female astronaut in space, has feminism outlived its purpose?" Plain accessible prose. I want to make it plain.

Ow chut writes my friend Weyman Chan. Seed growing. Seeds growing. Into trees wearing hoar frost, surprised out of the fog. Plain prose of seeds growing, starting with "plain prose, today want to write." So many seeds. The boyfriend saying, "I'd sooner kill her than see her with someone else." Four people he tells & they walk around with this seed, thinking who knows what, maybe hoping, but not telling, not arranging protection. Prosaic as the words "protection" or "political will." And the girl, fear sending roots down into her intestines, hard branches up her lungs, carries a knife just in case. Or "seed of doubt," we say, "is there a seed of doubt?" But wanting to write plain prose about the trees heavy & beautiful & surprising out of the fog, not the pain eating up my back & neck & shoulders. Plain as 1:50 when a friend phones, "I'm coming to you." Accessible as five orange oranges with green leaves & stems, sticky, red bean rice cake, red tin of Oolong Tea, sesame red bean balls she pulls out of her pack. "I'm thinking about writing," I say, "I am thinking about quitting." Her eyes behind her glasses, "You're not going to die, are you?"

Oranges, I want to write. Not the blade of a knife. Oranges. Sweet and seedy-segmented. Orange seeds on my tongue. How often I write "tongue." How my friend and husband and I go together to *Miss Saigon*, but wrong, the words so American, so simple my friend says. Hoar frost on the trees, trees coming out of the fog. We are laughing in the car, laughing, oranges on our breath, oranges on our fingers. Fog on the river, hoar frost on the trees. To our friend's house. "Come in," she says, "come say hello to my sister and brother-in-law and nieces and nephew. Try some Vietnamese food." "We don't want you to go to any trouble." "No, no trouble, a little food." Into the kitchen. A pot of boiling broth, rice wraps, noodles, thin squid, beef slices, lettuce, cucumber, & coriander & mint & beer. "Happy New Year, Happy Vietnamese New Year, one week early." Into clink of glasses. Against knives. Knives my friend's brother-in-law carried when he went to tell the farmers what crops & how, knives because he worked for the government, knives even though friends. A degree in horticulture, & knives. "Two jobs," he says, "I must work two jobs here. Maybe when my kids grow up I can go back to school." Two jobs, my friend's sister works, two jobs seven days a week. A rice wrap, lettuce, cucumber, noodles, squid, mint, & roll it up. Happy New Year. Plain as generosity, aromatic as oranges.

Today I want to. Plain prose about the coffee pot on the table, half-full, and the choice of words. Luxury like coffee. Choice of "I want" or "half-full" or "today." Focus on the coffee. Bean. Being. Grounds. Floating half-way. The newspaper beside my cup, *Woman Abducted from Store in Small Town, Feared Dead*. The lightness of coffee ground in a machine in a shop, floating on the surface. *Family Waits in Fear as Police Search for Missing Woman*. Weight of the plunger pushing the grounds to the bottom of the pot. Ground into, or on the. *Body Found in Field*. Predictability of the grounds sinking, coffee bubbling up.

"Things like this just don't happen in small towns," says a resident, "women here haven't had to fear the way they do in cities. Now we all have to fear." The way coffee smells better than it tastes. "I thought he was joking," says a neighbour, "you know how some guys like to brag. I never thought he actually killed someone. He was a quiet kinda guy." Plain as the grit at the bottom of the cup, grit in my teeth.

How I want to write "seeds spun from the Poplar tree, spun down and around, landed in the new snow." Or hoar frost on the crab apples outside my window. "Heavy and hoary." Plain as that, as the ache in my tongue, behind my teeth when I think "frost" and "apples." Plain as the lit street where a man attacked my friend, knocked her down, kicked her head, broke her nose. Plain as "I just can't read or write or think about that stuff" or "help me, please somebody help." Plain as the woman stopped on her way home from work, shot twice in the head, buried in the field. Or my mother when she was eleven, dragged out of town beside the river, beaten and raped. The sound, the impact of boots and bullets when we are inside or out of our heads. With fear, we say, "I was out of my head with fear." Or not. Plain as that. Where we sit over coffee, my friends and I, lift foamy milk to our lips, laugh at the warmth on our tongues, our teeth, in our bellies. And coffee, not because it's coffee, but just because.

Accessible as the coffee pot on the table or "Would you like a cup of coffee?" Common as "hello." Prose plain as the period at the end of the sentence, the comma in the middle. Today I want to write plain plain prose. Except for the coffee beans and where they come from and how we rarely talk with people who have no choice but to burn their forests for coffee trees and even then can they make enough to live on. Today I want to focus on the coffee pot. On the beans. Already sliding into "being." And ground. The grounds at the bottom of the pot, the ground under the soldier's boot on the front page of the newspaper. A Rwandan soldier lifting the corpse of a child. A girl. Her arms up stiff. I want to write about hiking through cow parsnip and magenta paintbrushes and wild strawberries, up the trail between rocky cliffs, to the lake nestled among the peaks. "Nestled," I want to write "nestled." Or "Here at the lake a gold-eye duck swims with her three chicks, and the chicks are fluffy and downy and climb onto their mother's back." But the child on the front page. A girl. Children fall down. But down, grounded. A soldier helping her up, but she is dead. Three downy chicks behind the rock in the middle of the lake. Water, millions of children men women without water. How the yellow flowers keep living on the bottom of the lake. And you can't bring her back. Bring her up, arms stiff, head back. Coffee pot lake child dead politicians women soldiers guns run ribs tongue stuck to stuck to. Mud so clear through the water, all the water.

Richard Stevenson

Wait till you see her

Wait till you see her. My muse is so
lovely in her bones, is a dancer who prances.
Wait till you see her. You won't believe
the ache her hesitancy inspires. The fire
in the loins, the heart to see her part
her hair. Wait till you see, She is
every note I could hope to play. Every
note I'd ever want to hold out to love,
the whole bouquet. Wait till you see her,
then you'll really hear me play! I'll stay
the crease in every rose and give you such
a whiff of grace in every permutation and fold.
Wait till you see her ghostly presence glide
down from the blue halo of smoke
in this room. She holds the air like a balustrade.
An ingenue of impossible beauty and grace.
Wait till I make her appear and disappear.
You will never fear your loneliness again.

That Mournful Ballad Sound

1. "Baby Won't You Please Come Home"
First Victor tickles the trickle
of rain water from the eaves
then comes that mournful
harmon mute and Miles
clean as mist evaporating
from the leaves of grass
before the foot falls anywhere
on this pristine lawn and you
know your baby's gone for good
this time and though that muted
horn sounds like a begging fool
you know the admission of failure
in those notes is just another
cool rebuke and the sadness
is the sadness of the bell of a flower
heavy with its drink and no hurt
can slake the thirst like that
first cool drink of memory.

2. "Once upon a summertime"

Once upon a summertime it was
before there was the ache of success
or the need to drink from sad Elysian streams.
Once upon a summertime when there were horses
high upon a ridgetop and cattle lowing,
the only mournful creatures on the farm;
once upon a summertime when the raindrops
were prisms of the heart and broke the world
into colours no one knew the names of
and there were rabbits – dozens – on the lawn
and you picked up that trumpet of fate
and eased those doeskin notes out of the bell
and they tumbled and slurred and fumbled
for the labial folds of the rose with such an ache;
once upon a summertime before Irene
teen pregnancy and even newspapers delivered
door to door there was no floor or ceiling
to the notes and you bent them with such
dexterity once upon a summertime upon a time
there was summer and all the leaves
and the birds and the bees were singing to themselves.

Claire Harris

Correspondence

Dear Jasmine

this past week bedraggled as a cat caught in rainstorm
today a khaki sky sprawls pungent over Calgary twisting
the traffic's white hum to grind and jar   greasing
flyovers tagging the hazed purse-lipped iron bridges with
ragged promise   the river refusing this nicotine light retires
into skin which here and there creases where trout slide by
and winged water things tremble and feed
our north side modest villages   time's cul-de-sacs still
touched with the gentle ungentle   huddle under
wait a drunken boot   in the trees' flattened tops even
the jays are silent   and visible   even from this tight bed
where the steel gleams from caring smiles   our glasshenge
pride and rue   altars hushed sanctuaries grey-suited nuns
monks acolytes strange ceremonies where we worship   market
eagles nesting noisily   remember don't you   how above law
the buskers seductive private music how energy shapes   power
dims hallways and byways whisper to gossip   hush   money
even so   behind that musty bruising sky the spirits of those
denied set up lodge poles forage hunt love and are
loved in a clear perpetual blue
                                                well   why not?

who absorbs only
         what you call
         'the dark'?
                  miss
               under
            standing
who playing at gardens ignores
            the devil in the hedges?

   here
   there is
   this

   Jas
         after all
               my truth searches the blank spaces
yours   the web and tangle of your life
                        consider me
         if at all
               an enabler

meanwhile despite narrow room   high window   that scent that
seeps into nightmare sharp pinch of in(re)jections careful
nagging a constant swallowing of pills and saccharin soothing
today   eyes sealed   i limbo
                  in the green-stirring
                     poplars
                  net of topmost branches
         under my lids   i curve i bend
      the blue rinsed Bow   i shimmy
         the circling gulls   in the topmost branches
         small boys hoot   among mango leaves sibilance
the blue crowned motmot   i move to the tamboo bamboo

even so

      my soles cling to crabgrass my toes opening to
        small stones worm casts heel into mole hills
   the fruitfull invisible life's faint signals squashed

  …is groan yuh groaning…

     yet how is it

i write to you of painful whirling falls into momentary
silence   into blankness   you write back
            'silence is not such a bad thing'?
an exile i think of 'home'   sky/ earth/ wind-forested hills
circling green and tangled valley
               lesser hills struggling towards
our road its bright roofs   its light pregnant curtains
its old men their lancing eyes their hard-scabbed dry-wrinkled
hands
        and i think   'safe'
          think   'net'   though knowing
today mcdonald's oozed into those clefts
    and hills into our green life-haunted tropical womb
      needing to   i think 'nosy but caring   warmth
soft airs and breezes'
     …sheesh 'saft air an breeze' is
     sun like bull pistle an' days ha' no wind…
  and now my sister writes 'you should rejoice at your gift
for escaping the world'!!!
            (damnnnnn…oh oh shhh)

    …Listen girl   is dead i almost dead
       this not time for mamaguy me
    i ain't come to you for back chat nor
  for squeeze either   this is true-true stuff

come scary   rise from your ease   and get with it
you know what doctor here can't figure mus' be in your head

(sigh oh sigh sigh)
ggg good night Jass
(oh oh God ooohhh)

...well sisters of brave mettle
   we have lifted the moon out of her sphere...

...katie you worse than She   you know that....
         now do we not shake or pare the moments
                        of this our victory...
...Victory! is look at my crosses now!...
   Feda, wait!
            here pale butterflies and dark
                              swooping far sky
            ichthyornis
      spirit wheels laughing

...Katie, you finish? I could talk?

Dear Feda!

Is a horspital.

Anne Le Dressay

Another story altogether

Not my story, but the other one
that was there all along, tangled with mine
and utterly separate, breathing at night
in the bed across the room, while I lived
my own story. My own. Small, centred,
mine, that talked my words and saw
through my eyes.

This other story sees it through her eyes,
and they are 3 years younger and a different
colour. It's not the same family and not the same
traumas. The family is 3 years older when she
starts remembering, and there are more people in it.

Two stories, two worlds barely touching,
the light hitting the same things at such
different angles they are not the same things
at all. To her, I am part of the world outside of
her, in which she must find or make a place.
To me, she is outside.

You'd think it would be the same house at least,
the same bedroom. But she was afraid of the dark
and I wasn't. We had a fair and equal arrangement:
one night, the door closed tightly for me, the next
night, left open a crack for her.

Only now does it occur to me to wonder
if, every second night when the door was closed
to spare me the small distraction of that
shaft of light, she lay awake, facing alone
the terrors of the dark,
while I slept.

Just Darkness

My soul has gotten
thinner
in these last lean years
of huddled seclusion.

It has sat too long
in a dark corner
alone, has forgotten

that darkness is not often
the dark of God, is not
often the black night of the soul
where God waits

but rather just
darkness.

It is baffled
by the glow and bustle
of the lives
around me that do not
touch mine.

Its hands hang
empty.

Rosemary Nixon

Kiala

Fairy tales always have a happy ending.
He leaned back in his chair. That depends.
On what?
On whether you are Rumplestiltskein or the Queen.

— Jane Yolen, *Briar Rose*

Allegra careens her tricycle past the house, bony knees pumping, elbows laced in wind, she feels so light. Wind blows into her private parts, she's whipped her panties off because she peed them, can't stop, she's an engineer, driving a freight train, whoo-whoooooo, she's a fast car speeding down a highway, whistling wind, slicing sunshine, great blue sky, zips back behind the fuel tanks, fill 'er up! she drives a tanker. June! Marigold! Valerie! Rose! Vroomvroom! Her sisters have lost interest, have stopped riding their bikes.

Rose has ridden over Allegra's soggy panties.

Her sisters are disgusted.

Allegra sails right by her sisters scratching their eczema. The wind blows her down behind the barn where cowpies hang heavy with summer flies. Allegra slams off her trike, pops the wire that holds the barnyard fence shut, wheels inside. She cackles over cows' hoof prints, bounces the ruts, the cats parade from the barn's dark interior to stare at this dust-raising girl. A mouse hangs from Sunset's teeth, stuck-out stiff tail.

Ships ahoy! yells Allegra. Against the fence, a calf bunts its mother's teats for milk.

June hasn't been out riding today.

June! Allegra cried this morning, but her mother says June won't be coming. Why?

Personal reasons.

June didn't pee her pants; she bled them. Allegra knows a thing or two. A wet stain low on her backside. Allegra saw it at breakfast, yelled, June's bloody! and June cried, was excused from breakfast dishes, and has spent the morning in her room.

Allegra rides till she breaks free of her sisters altogether, wheels out to the back pasture, Bouncing to the rotten ocean, Where the people can be seen! Allegra wails into the wind. Where buildings go five stories up, And I will be the Queen! From here she can see the pasture with its willow clump, the wheat field, the Boettger farm. But when she sees the creek, full to over-flowing, she pulls a U-ie, remembers the time she nearly tipped in, doesn't want her backside paddled with Dad's shoe. Allegra squints up to the sailing clouds, the yawning sky, her bum so cold stuck to the metal seat. The farm-yard is a magnet, or maybe it's the big fat eye of God, because something pulls her back to her sisters' voices, rising on the wind.

Allegra's knees coated in grime, Mom's wash floats the wash line as Allegra rattles round behind the shanty, skids her trike up to the back door, enters a house of female smells.

In the afternoon, Allegra sets up her dolls, Betty pin-poked through her thick rubber skin to hold her diaper on. Sets Margaret, Hazel, Monica, Theresa, Betty, Sylvia in the doll carriage, on the grass, propped against the rose bushes, in the petunias bordering the lawn. The sky clouds over, brightens, clouds again. Allegra hisses for silence. Begins to teach. She's the only one not yet in school. School holds endless pleasures: lunch pails, the fruity smell of books, fountain pens, homework, girlfriends, daily excursions off the farm.

Allegra starts with spelling.

Her dolls, stuffed in too many clothes, regard her suspiciously. Some have forgotten pencils. Allegra's voice goes harsh and raspy. She warns of spankings, detentions, the writing out of lines if work is not finished for tomorrow, if silence is not maintained. Hazel throws a spitball, Allegra sends Hazel to the corner.

There is no corner.

Hazel, always the class clown, flops over on her face. Well, then, those students who misbehave will be forced on their faces, their noses rubbed in dirt.

Allegra's sisters move in and out of her school world. Race through her classroom, play catch over it, don't apologize, make freshie popsicles, suck them on the back step, a happy crowd, don't, won't fetch Allegra one, shout, Teachers aren't allowed to eat in school.

Allegra has a tantrum. The wind blows away her papers, her dress-up scarves, by now all her dolls have sagged or flopped face down. Hazel keeps giggling. Allegra spanks her. That quiets the classroom down. She'll punish them all again tomorrow. Her mother comes out and announces it's the teacher who'll be punished if the lawn is not cleaned up immediately.

Allegra's sisters refuse to carry in her dolls, push in the carriage, gather her dress-up clothes or teaching supplies. Allegra weeps, but her mother has already gone inside to start supper.

Allegra's legs ache, her nose feels snotty, she makes three glowering trips inside past her popsicle-slurping sisters. Her mother tells her she is very dirty, feeds her early, and pours pot after pot of steaming water into the large tin bathtub, water they will all share. It's Saturday, everyone will bathe tonight, starting with Allegra, because she's the littlest. She has to bathe quick so the water isn't too cold for the next one. Allegra pulls off her dress, her mother discovers she has no panties, the dress is yanked back on, and Allegra sent out into the yard to find the smelly things. The wind has had great fun with Allegra's panties. She finds them stuck against the barnyard fence. She undresses all over again.

Hurry, Allie, Hurry, I'm next, I'm next, I'm next, her sisters cry.

Allegra sinks into the warm grey water. Hey, she forgot to pee. Allegra lies back, hears her sisters playing Parcheesi without her, opens her knobby knees, and, ahhhh, lets a stream, a sweet release, into the foamy suds.

I will sing a new song. I will lift up mine eyes. I will lean not unto mine own understanding. I will trust and not be afraid.

She is afraid. Head wet with her mother's blood.

The baby wakes to the whistle of nerves, motor wind, light's pulse. Her knowing builds. She is not meant for this place. She stays the night, does not recognize the night, buried in brightness. The world ends. It begins.

We call upon you, O Redeemer God
You who did not abandon Israel in exile
You who gave hope to them that call your name
You comforted them when your coming was not what they expected.

Her coming is not what she expected
she waits in a singing tunnel
strains against the swabs of cloth that tie her to this place.

What did you go out to see? A reed shaken in the wind?

She has material, a texture, colour. A body. It has a smell. She flutters, skin blue like water.

Send the child for whom we long to live among us.

Allegra sits in Foothills Neonatal Intensive Care Unit, and imagines a daughter. Fluorescent lights stare down, a worker vacuums. Ninety machines hum. Her baby. Her girl. The baby next to Kiala's isolette was born last night without a brain. His eyes stare out. *There's nothing in there.* Allegra has to look away. The mother sits beside his isolette. Unmoving. Iceberg face. Allegra feels choked up laughter. *You look just like your baby.* Looks down at Kiala. Her eyes are closed, legs splayed, blue diaper dwarfing. Her daughter. Inside burning. She will be reckless, this daughter, Kiala. She will play hard, be a tomboy, scrape shins, throw a football, throw herself into her history.

Throw away this picture, Allegra.

A friend of Allegra's sister is sitting on a hard bench in the waiting room. Allegra hardly knows her. The husband left her two, three months ago. Allegra has seen the woman, Judith, on occasion, at the grocery store, at church. Has never talked to her. What would one say? This morning Judith showed up at the hospital. She wears a dark coat, no earrings.

You can't stay, Allegra said. They only allow family. You can't stay. Even my sisters have trouble getting in.

Two hours now. There she sits, on a bench in the waiting room. Offering no words.

Allegra looks over at the arctic mother.

Dr. Norton enters the nursery. The one doctor who never dresses like a doctor, who neglects to take on that identity. Dr. Norton will not last the month. Today she's wearing a floral print dress, it shows beneath her lab coat. She carries a chart, moves to the isolette next to Kiala's. Her sleeve touches that mother cast in ice.

Good morning, Mrs. Angonata. The woman doesn't answer. The doctor pulls up a stool, sits down beside her. Expels a breath. There's not a lot we can do for your son. This is hard. He's being kept warm and safe.

A twitch. The woman begins shaking. A shimmer. She shimmers in this cold blue-lit neonatal nursery.

We don't know how long. Some hours? Perhaps several days. No, you don't have to hold him. No, some mothers choose not to. I can offer you little more than honesty. We're here for you. Please, call me any time. Wait, no it's not too hard. It's just the cords get caught. I'll help you lift him out. Of course it's good. This baby needs you. She lifts the empty baby, empty dangling legs, stare fixed on nothing. Lifts him from the mess of wires into a frozen mother's arms. Mother. Doctor. Allegra. Judith on a hard bench. Under fluorescent lights, four women without a language stare into the present.

October 8

524010

Draeger, Girl

Diagnosis

Problem List:

1. Respiratory distress

2. Dysmorphic features

3. Auditory evoked responses show abnormal

4. Draeger, girl has decreased calcium and magnesium

5. Has feeding difficulties acquiring a gastrostomy tube

6. Was put on digoxin 0.1 mg p.o. bid, and is being followed by Doctor Vanioc

7. Draeger, girl kept on 38% oxygen. Goes off colour during feeds.

Dr. Vanioc finishes the list, undoes his shoe laces, leans back in his chair, raises his arms to ease his backache, and begins to study the child's charts.

The baby came in yesterday, transferred from the Holy. She has everything wrong with her, and no reason that he can see. He can give no name to her problems. He reviews the particulars. Three weeks early. Normal delivery, although the mother was induced due to toxemia. The right side of the child's mouth shows evidence of facial paralysis. She has excessive mucous secretions from her nose and throat. Dr. Vanioc is a scientific man; he dislikes cases he can't understand. The baby's on 35-40% oxygen. Her feedings are resulting in coughing and choking and vomiting. She already has developed an upper lobe aspiration pneumonia as a result. The ductus is still open. The doctor makes notes on his pad. He will suggest lasix, have her put on digoxin. He checks nurses' reports. The babe developed hypocalcemia and was given an IV of calcium gluconate. Feedings started again 12 hours ago. The doctor takes off his glasses and rubs his eyes. The infant sucks moderately well. But according to this morning's flow chart, her pulmonary signs are becoming worse. Likely more aspiration. And then there is the problem of the parents. Young, but not so young. Mid-late twenties. The wife a case for the textbooks – high anxiety, intense.

Dr. Vanioc thinks of his own wife, at this moment angrily spooning mushed peas and puréed squash into his small son's mouth. Angry he is never home. Angry he gives sixteen hours a day to these sick babies who will probably die anyway, and neglects his own. Turbulent emotions possess his wife, concerning their child, concerning him.

Dr. Vanioc thinks of his wife's angry back, the fine curve of the spine where it reaches her buttocks, thinks of this for a moment, then pushes it into the headache that climbs his neck. He turns back to the charts.

Mobius's syndrome? he scribbles.

They're going to have to feed her through gastrostomy.

When you were born you were very sick.

Was I going to die?

I didn't want to think about that.

They sit in silence on the lip of Nose Hill looking over Calgary's glass skyline, rushed wind reflecting air and sunshine.

She soothes the child's neck. Brushes against the child's translucent skin. The child snuggles against her.

Tell me the story.

I don't know if I can.

The news is like staring into an eclipse of the sun. Look at it straight and you'll go blind.

Richard prepared. He prepared for this child to be born.

He has not prepared for this child to die.

Richard stands at the window of his physics classroom and looks out past his plants. He can see down to the smoking door. Kids huddled in bunches without their coats. Their breath rising, even cloudy spirals.

Roses. He must bring Allegra roses. For a moment, shifting through papers on his desk, hunting for a missing wire, Richard forgot. Forgot he has a baby. This baby. But remembrance caught him, scorched his stomach, and he dragged his breath and bent into his chair. His physics students sit quiet in their desks. Some are looking at him, others look away. Richard says, When a wave passes from deep water into shallow, the ray refracts toward the normal. Sixteen years you have survived, he wants to say. The students go about their work, filling water tables, generating waves. They haven't noticed they've turned sixteen, have functioning kidneys, breathe. When water rolls from deep to shallow, he says, it can create a tidal wave.

Miraculously, the day ends.

Richard packs his satchel with student lab reports, drives to a florist. Asks for a dozen roses. The young woman behind the counter winks, says, Oooh, have we got hopes tonight! then gets glum when Richard doesn't answer.

At the hospital, Richard steps off on fifth floor. Wonders how he got here.

Neonatal Intensive Care Flow Sheet
Oct.11: 3:30 a.m.: Babe received on 40% oxygen. Colour dusky. Passed large sticky meconium. Appears jaundiced. Coffee ground-like material in white mucus. Not tolerating oral feeds. IV restarted in scalp vein. Babe dusky and apneac. Two bradys. Respiration very shallow. Jittery when disturbed.
Parents in to visit. Apprehensive.

✣

Three sculptured ivory heads sit on the woman's desk. Two have their eyes closed. One stares at Allegra. Allegra stares back. Beside them a booklet. *Perinatal Bereavement. The Unique Nature and Factors Surrounding the Death or Acute Illness of a Child.* Allegra hears food trolleys roll down the hall. Smells well-done roast beef. The swish of footsteps. Quick flick of fingertips. The woman, the social worker, flips the pages of Allegra's file. Allegra leans back against the brocade chair. Tries to relax. The flipping stops. The social worker, like Allegra's dog on point, makes no movement. Caught on a page. *Hysterical mother. Inability to face reality.* The button on the woman's suit jacket sleeve gleams metallic.

Let me start with the situation, the social worker says.

Needles stab Allegra's thighs.

This morning, in neonatal care.

The wary nurse herding Allegra out, the doctor's turned back, professional reserve.

Allegra says, Oh, God. She smells the baby on her skin. Wipes salty moisture from her hands. The social worker taps her fingers against the desk. She wears six rings. Allegra says, I've seen their attitude. Ever since I came to neonatal.

The social worker says nothing. Waits for Allegra to carry on.

She's just a number to them. Just another...

The social worker scratches on her paper. *Hostile. Bitter.*

Allegra presses her lips together. She was asked here. She didn't volunteer. Let the woman do the talking. Tap. Tap. Tap. Let her fingers do the walking. Allegra's on trial. The silence stretches.

Are you sleeping well? the woman says. Because there are pills.

I had a peculiar dream. My budgie, Dicky, I had him as a child, every night I said, Pretty bird, Dicky, pretty bird, pretty bird, before I covered his cage. He was a talking budgie, but he never talked to me.

So what was the dream?

That was it. Right there. I never had a budgie. I was at his cage with the blanket in my hands, saying, Pretty bird, Dicky, pretty bird. Then I cover his cage. And I can't see him anymore.

Do you want to talk about this morning?

No.

The woman takes a statue by the head and rearranges it. One high heeled blue shoe dangles off her foot.

Mrs. Draeger.

It's Gillis. Allegra Gillis.

The doctors, the nurses on fifth, they're worried about you. They think you aren't coping well. You need to talk to someone.

I do talk. My husband. My sisters. I have friends. Did she unplug the iron this morning? Did Richard attach his seat belt as he backed from the driveway? Allegra's milk is leaking. A stain grows at her breast.

I didn't mean to imply you don't. The woman writes. *Neurotic.*

The rumble of trolley carts heading back. Smell of caramel pudding. The woman's stomach growls.

Your baby has been on the unit two weeks now?

Eleven days.

When have the doctors last spoken to you of her prognosis?

Pain splashes up Allegra's legs, her groin, intestines, rides her esophagus. There are words no one must say. How dare this woman make her say them. Allegra stony on her chair. Never again the humiliation of this morning's whooping grief. The tight faces of the nursing staff. The grim posturing of the head nurse, her pull-yourself-together-woman look. The hall outside is silent for the moment. A silence that mirrors the sudden quiet on the neonatal unit when that first surprising sweep of sobs slid out Allegra's ribs: the other mothers' panicked, averted faces. Like Allegra had thrown up or soiled her underwear. Breaching the code of behaviour in neonatal, Allegra is learning, has consequences. She's been sent to the office.

Tightness seizes the muscles of her upper arms. It's hot in here. The social worker watches.

You've been in shock. The woman sits back in her chair. Numb? The numbness is a buffer. It helps you cope with this pain you feel. Don't blame yourself.

Allegra hadn't known she should.

The woman actually reaches out and pats Allegra's arm. An awkward, unfamiliar gesture. Withdraws it quickly.

Allegra closes her eyes, transports herself out of this woman's perfect office, pushes her hands through the arm holes of Kiala's world, skin against skin, the tiny fingernails.

…moving out of avoidance…

Allegra reaching for the baby's shaved head. The needles. So many silver needles. Acupuncture gone crazy.

Here your grief will be…

The baby opens her mouth to cry. Only one side goes down.

…emotional extremes. Fear. Anger. Anxiety…

Breathe from the diaphragm.

…common at this stage.

Breathe. Huuuuuu. Breathe. Huuuuu.

Oh, dear...perhaps not a good time. Let's bring you back when you feel more comfortable. The social worker is searching in her day book. Allegra's body a river: mucous and blood and breast milk. A week from Friday...get yourself together...Pat. Pat. Of course...this Kleenex, no, of course we know it's hard.

Lady. You have no idea.

I read the nurses' reports. I sneaked glances when I could. I didn't know anything. No one told me anything. I was so afraid for you.

The dog runs in crazy loops around them, barking.

What did they say? What things?

The chinook arch, a painted line, sails sky from sky. A thick white line of cloud rolls back from stone wash blue.

Mostly I didn't understand. They used words I couldn't understand. Angiocath removed when retaping for packed cells infusion. Today no bradycardia.

The child bursts into laughter. I don't understand it.

She smiles. I didn't either. Hand in the child's hair.

The child's fingers tease her small scared ankle.

About them gusts the wind.

The words spring unbidden from the social worker's office door. Allegra, heading past, sees feet. The social worker's violet pumps. A mother's sneakers.

Well, it was my husband, crawling over me in the middle of the night, and it was like he was throwing up, you know, only he wasn't, he was sobbing. Well, you can't you couldn't describe, it was like. Words don't even come. All I feel is my chest when you ask me to describe it, like you know. I can't describe it.

A woman's fractured voice. A social worker scratching at her paper.

Allegra keeps on walking.

She walks through the hospital, down the parking lot, drives home, phones Marigold, whose answering machine comes on. Then, in the midst of her recorded message, Marigold's breathless voice.

Hello? Hello?

Allegra begins to cry and Marigold feels shame that she only just walked in the door from taking her two bouncy girls skating at the Olympic Oval. Shame she's been out in sunshine. Shame the hospital won't let her see her sister's baby. Shame she has normal children. Shame she hasn't called Allegra yet today.

Everything will work out, Allie, Marigold says soothingly. These things take time. She has to stick the pot roast in. It's going to take three hours. Things will work out fine. They always do.

Allegra and Marigold are writing stories. The day is warm. A Saskatchewan wind shifts over the lawn, stirs Mom's petunias, morning glory, phlox, the yellow roses burning up their stems. The girls sit in the basement on the old cupboard stacked with rejected sheets of Dad's accounting records. They have finished playing secretary, have begun to write. Allegra is using her Grade 2 spelling notebook. Marigold has the bigger notebooks with rings that Allegra covets. Share, says Allegra, but Marigold sniffs and turns her back. Selfish witch.

The basement window is ajar and the breeze slides through, strong with zinnia and caragana. Marigold is crouched on top of the cupboard, tongue curling from her mouth. In the adjoining room, separated from them, not by walls, but joists, sits their father's barber chair. The neighbour boys file in for hair cuts Thursday nights and Allegra watches Marigold eyeballing Harris Shantz as their father snips away, and buzzes the razor up his tanned neck. When the chair is not in use, Allegra and Marigold pump themselves up, then shove on the handle, shhhhhh, their own amusement park, and ride the seat back down. Allegra scribbles on.

And the mother gaspt and flinged herself on the cradel of her dead baby. Then she sobd histarikly. Then she took a shovl and climbd the hill. The wind was cold tears flung from her eyes. Then she took the shovl and dug a hole and dropt her baby in it. then she planted a cros on the hill and waled and wakt weerily back to tend to her sevn reemaneing childran.

Allegra can feel the welcoming womanly swoop of tears even as she writes. Marigold is grinning. Marigold writes stupid stories. A lovely young woman with slim ankles named Ferris, or Maxine, or Crystal sits gracefully on a riverbank, or the side of a mountain, and she will have windswept hair. Allegra yawns. Her wildly handsome lover, Rolph or Allister, will row her to the centre of the lake, or threaten to throw himself off a cliff, and ask her to marry him in a husky voice. Ferris, Maxine, or Crystal will breathe, Oh darling! Yes! and they will kiss. Allegra cannot abide this. Allegra cannot believe that Marigold is in Grade 5 and has no imagination.

Mom calls, Gi-irls. Marigold. Yoo-hoo.

It's time to fetch the cow. Marigold's job, but sometimes Allegra trots along. Sometimes Marigold makes her. Sometimes Marigold won't let her. Today Marigold is living in her dull old story and she doesn't notice either way. So they set off down the road after Ida Ruby. Sometimes they change Ida Ruby's name to Fern, or Ethel Mary, Jacinth, or Esther, depending on what time in history they're pretending. The cow ignores all her names, just lumbers along the road from the quarter mile where she lives in the pasture, chewing her cud, switching her tail. Sometimes she stops to eat grass in the ditch. Then she won't move and the only way to get her going again is for Allegra and Marigold to dig their heels into the spongy ditch and shove their backs against her big behind. Eventually the cow gives a snort deep in her nostrils and takes off at an irritated trot.

A car turns at the mile, dust swirls behind it. Marigold and Allegra stand against the ditch and wait as it barrels towards them.

Allegra looks at Marigold, skirt swiped between her legs, bony knees facing the wind, hand raised in a two-finger salute just like their dad's. Marigold is starting to bug Allegra. Acting hoity-toity grown up. Putting on airs. It's Harris Shantz. He's travelling hell bent for leather. As he whizzes by he answers Marigold's wave, and Marigold's face stains red in the wind, and she hop-skips along the road's edge toward the cow who is looking forlornly through the dust over the barbed wire fence. Allegra runs to keep up to Marigold's sudden energy where she now fast steps along the road's edge, feet turned out slightly, thin nose in the air. Too good for the likes of Allegra.

Yoo-hoo, oh, Harris, darling, Allegra singsongs.

Marigold throws a rock into the pasture.

So your next stupid story will be about a stupid farm boy called Harris, Allegra shouts against the wind. Hair-res, with stringy nose hairs.

Marigold's own nose lifts a smidgen.

They're getting duller, your stories, Allegra yells, if that's possible.

Marigold whirls, grabs hold of Allegra's ponytail. Allegra twists out of her grasp and dances backwards.

Marigold loves that nosed-haired Harris

Hey laudi laudi lo

If I was her I'd be embarrassed

Hey laudi laudi lo.

Marigold marches on. There's a pit filled with junk down in the pasture. Rusted pails, a few glass jars, an old pair of tennis shoes, a brass bed stand, bed springs pitched against the earth, the teeth and skull of a coyote. Marigold yanks the elongated wire that the fence pole fits into. As she drags the barbed wire gate laced with poles in a wide arc to rest against the fence, Ida Ruby, far across the pasture, lifts her head and begins a slow amble over. Allegra darts across, shouting, Marigold! Marigold's in lo-ove! Above them, blue sky yawns.

Marigold drops the poles and lunges. Allegra pitches forward, snorting giggles as her heels hit the dirt. She sprints away. Thud-thud, thud-thud. Marigold's wheezy breath whipping behind her.

Ha-ar-is! Allegra, laughing so hard she can hardly run.

They hurl toward the sprawling poplar grove at the pit's edge, feet churning dust.

Ha-a...

Whap!

Marigold emits a wail.

Allegra slammed with sickness. The ground rising to meet her, Good Lord, she's nailed to a two by four. It lifts slow motion as if it were a shoe. She's crucified! Marigold throws herself screaming at Allegra's foot, and yanks. The nail sucks out, and from the hole in Allegra's brown foot spurts a high arc of blood, a dark red geyser shooting Marigold's legs and dress with each beat of

Allegra's heart. Marigold grabs Allegra, hoists her onto the back of startled Ida Ruby who has mozied over for a look and now takes off lowing. Allegra sprawls along the cow, arms strapped against its sides, Marigold running behind, punching the cow on the buttocks, snot-faced, sobbing. They shoot into the yard all bawling, Allegra, Marigold, and Ida Ruby, just as their father emerges from the barn. The procession wheels past the barnyard toward the house. Their father stares at his daughter's blood spraying the ground like a water pistol, and yells, Halt, in a terrible voice. Allegra does, but Ida Ruby doesn't. Allegra's father scoops her from the hard ground, throws her unceremoniously in the back of the station wagon. Her mother races from the house, mouth a horrified O, wraps the bleeding in a towel. Allegra and her father head for town. Allegra peers out the back as the station wagon roars onto the road, catching a last glimpse of Marigold, open-mouthed, howling, clumped round by her for-once speechless sisters, all staring into disappearing dust.

It was probably rusty, the doctor says. He makes a wick out of the tiniest piece of rope, soaks it in a solution and shoves it right up the hole in her foot. Allegra hollers. She has not yet recovered from this indignity when the doctor orders her to pull her pantics down. Allegra's head spins toward her dad. Her father says do what the doctor says and before she can protest, he reaches around and gives her a tetanus shot in the bum. Allegra snivels against the examining table with its stupid crumpled paper sheet, like a giant paper towel, and imagines what she would do to the doctor if she had the chance. While her father says, Thank you, looking meaningfully at Allegra, Allegra stares at the red poke mark on the top of her foot. She'll kill one off in her next story. That's what she'll do.

On the way home, Allegra's father shakes his head, says, I don't know, girlie. What were you thinking? Thinking? She was hurtling from Marigold's wrath! Her father drives the red station wagon into the shed, lifts her in his strong arms and carries her from the car. He smells of sen-sen. She feels his neck against her skin. Over the barnyard fence, Ida Ruby regards her morosely, her side cracked with rivulets of dried blood.

That evening Allegra's sisters vie for position to examine the bruised foot with the hole in it with a wick in it. Just like a candle, Valerie says, delighted.

Let's light it! says Rose. Marigold tells and retells the story, which she concocts in order to leave out her responsibility in the affair. Allegra's too sleepy to correct her. Anyway, for once Marigold's telling Allegra's kind of story. Allegra's foot throbs. Her mother fries her doughnuts. Her sisters with sugar-coated mouths curl up around Dad's big chair in the living room while her father sits in it, lifts Allegra on his lap, and reads to them all from the story of *Rumpelstiltskin.*

As soon as the girl was left alone, the little man appeared for the third time, and said,

What will you give me if I spin the straw for you this time?

I have nothing left to give, answered the girl.

Then you must promise me the first child you have after you are queen, said the little man.

Marigold outdoes herself, carrying doughnuts to Allegra, asking if she needs more sugar, taking back to the kitchen her empty cocoa cup. Giving Allegra meaningful glances: alternately menacing and pleading.

In the meantime she brought a fine child into the world and thought no more of the little man; but one day he came suddenly to her room and said,

Now give me what you promised me.

The queen was terrified greatly, and offered the little man all the riches of the kingdom if only he would leave the child; but the little man said,

No, I would rather have something living than all the treasures of the world.

The window lets in dark and light. Shadow skims her father's page.

Then the queen began to lament and to weep, so that the little man had pity on her.

I will give you three days, said he, and if at the end of that time you cannot tell me my name, you must give up the child to me.

Allegra ignores hovering Marigold, who says at the story's beginning and at the story's end, She'll be all right, Allegra's all right. Allegra says nothing. Silence is power. She snuggles into her father's generous lap, and listens to the story. Stories make everything better. She holds this knowledge for another time.

※

Foothills Neonatal ICU breathes story. Stories weave the isolettes, suction machines, heart monitors, the oxygen tubes, the heaving ventilators. They cling to the hems of nursing uniforms and ride the lapels of doctors' lab coats. They smell, these stories, these angry prayers.

Allegra holds Kiala on her lap. An intravenous needle stuck in the baby's head. Yellow bruises crisscross the shaved scalp where intravenous needles went interstitial. Even needles fail her baby. When Allegra was a child, farm boys caught frogs, cut off their legs and let them go. The frenetic gyrate of legs, the bulging eyes. Stop it! I hate you! Allegra crying. The boys laughing.

Just being boys.

Kiala fights like that when the nurses suction her. Her fists punch out, head wheels from side to side. Allegra conserves strength for those suction episodes – fifteen, twenty times a day. A tube inserted up Kiala's nose, mouth open in a gag, push farther, farther, Kiala's frog legs jerking, a nurse hauling tubing like a hose snaked down a drain hole. White green gunk sucking up the hose, spastic limbs, her baby's face a caricature of anguish. Allegra sobs quietly beside the isolette, hand pressed into her face. The nurses step around her, doing their job.

Dr. Summers enters. One of the boys. The head nurse is also one of the boys. This is an old boys' club and Allegra has crashed it. Nobody likes her here. Nobody likes her baby. Allegra asks permission to bathe Kiala. To lift Kiala into a warm water basin. The surprise of skin on skin. Baby, you exist. We're really touching. Allegra knows to arrange the gastrostomy tube inserted in Kiala's stomach, to keep hold of it five inches down the tube so gravity doesn't pressure and pull it free, to arrange the oxygen tube, the heart monitor attachment tubes, her intravenous lines. Allegra's fingers support the baby at the small of her neck. Kiala finds herself in water, her expression is surprise. Allegra laps water against her belly, the soles of her feet. Cheek against the baby's head until Kiala's features lose their tenseness, her head moves to touch cheek to her mother and she kicks. For one strange moment the institution smell lifts, and Allegra is a live whole mom holding a live whole baby.

No bath. Nurse says no time this morning. Beepers are going off. Babies are trying to die. The nurse has filled a basin with water, then abandons it when the baby next to Kiala goes into cardiac arrest. The nurse moves fast, her elbow catches Kiala's foot which hits the basin, knocks it to the floor, and now the cleaning staff have been called in – more bodies, more equipment.

Allegra hums. It's an act of rebellion. Hums to Kiala who ignores her bath water sweeping across the neonatal floor.

Allegra, standing before Kiala's isolette, sees Kiala's life here at Foothills Hospital as one big awful song. Ninety-nine bottles of beer on the wall. Ninety-nine bottles of beer. Fragments. Bleak and rhythmic. The sickening repetitive pattern. Pass one down. Hand it around. Same tune, same words. Fewer bottles.

Anna Mioduchowska

Singing in the Garden

I will search for a warm den
my child
when your time to be has arrived
I will search in the softest
the blackest soil I can find
plant you knee-deep my child
as I would any rose bush
or an apricot tree

I will build an enormous fence
my child
to shield you from the north
from the wicked Arctic winds
their fury shocking
no matter how regularly
and how often they come
I will build an impenetrable fence
to the north
maybe to the west as well

night and day I will watch over you
my child
day and night especially
to lay traps for seductive moths
dragons who with their flashy wares
distract the most vigilant of souls
with cockatrice eyes
will I watch over you day and night

then
one sunny morning in late summer
that ruby-studded morning
I'll try not to wail
when you sprint
to the top of the wicked fence
to the north
maybe to the west
your eyes into the gale
I'll try not to claw my face
when you wave good-bye
when you wave good-bye

Small Island

According to the inhabitants of the Trobriand Islands, "*a remarkable thing happens to the spirit immediately after its exodus from the body...the baloma (which is the main form of the dead man's spirit) goes to Tuma, a small island....*"
— from Bronislaw Malinowski's *Magic, Science and Religion*

I hope my turn to leave comes in July
and there's someone willing to launch the scuffed canoe
loon barking in alarm at the sudden shadow
cast over its territory, annoyed ducks
nattering

let it be at the moment
the lake's precisely balanced – the sun holding it
by one end the moon by the other, water thick, shiny
crepuscular cream insects slurp
with a terrible greed

for incense, juniper will do
sweetened with fermenting leaves, an aroma
that follows from the shore, lingers on the skin
like old memories, fades with each stroke
of the paddle

the island – a black pincushion
cormorant and heron nests up and down dried-up spruce trees
reclining fledglings, sleek Buddhist monks
in calm contemplation of sticks they've plucked
from the floor, the wall

until the next fish is flown in
and then the jostling, the squawking, the island lifting
quivering, cries of triumph and self-pity such perfect
cacophony against the deepening
silence —

let it be that island
let it be an old spruce trunk, even a clump
of reeds nearby, I could do worse than spend eternity
in the company of birds

In Bed with a Book

in bed with a book
you are light years away from me
the here and now dissolved in desert heat
sheltered by pointed shadows, the Sphinx
panting by your feet, you turn the pages
your hands deceptively calm
a cursory glance at the skin stretched
over the intricate structure underneath
fails to reveal the extent of their longing
to coax truth out of weathered stones

I too long, for your hands
to stray to my side of the bed the way
my thoughts stray from the labour camp
in the hills of northern China
where I've been herding sheep
all winter their dumb eyes my only mirror
uncomprehending bleating the only answer
to questions burning holes in a mind
I have managed, just, to keep
from forgetting its human origins

listen, the night is still young
and we're at ease and liberty, our bed
neither a jealous rock nor beaten down
earth covered with moldy straw but a supple cocoon
woven of yarn we've spun with our fingers
over the years –
what do you say we take a break?

I'll put my book away
if you do

Norman Sacuta

Soft Shoe

Before Victoria Day my dad walks, his body
limping chronicles of winter falls,
his slow movements memories
of black ice beneath snowfalls –

as if his garden this spring weekend
might be a rug on linoleum,
the soil is tested, turned on and
to be sure the cool earth absorbs sun.

By late summer his stride
has grown to match the rows of beans,
a garden too big for his wife –
my mom watches through the backdoor screen

one foot lift, then the other
as he spreads blankets over cucumber vines.
She hopes the heavy cover
will save nothing from the coming rime.

But by autumn his gait is enormous,
heavy, sure thuds to the kitchen;
arms laden he climbs the back steps,
the sink soon full of pickling.

She stands confined to his lead:
at the counter her feet ache with a coming winter
full of memory's need –
his youth is their larder.

They'll walk the crescent before first snow
dad three strides ahead like some scout;
mom out of practice, summer-slow,
waiting for winter and his doubt

to rise again with each falling degree,
as the larder shelves begin to empty.

Death of a Scuba Diver
at West Edmonton Mall

Aura is the unique phenomenon of a distance no matter how
close the object might be.

—Walter Benjamin, "The Work of Art in
the Age of Mechanical Reproduction"

The fish need to be imagined
around him, finning
clear shadows along panes of glass.
He sees people talking where
sharks whiff their tails,
palms pressed like mimes against glass –
the walls he can see through
enclose them in a shaped cave
of air.

His own is running out.
Even if he struggles, wet suit and tank
pinched in the filters he's come to service,
they'll wonder at the hydraulics
that make his movements so lifelike.
But no one is watching, anyway –
the sharks are real and closer.

His head tilts upward
to the bridge where shoppers
check reflections on smooth water;
their wishes flutter down to him
like tin foil.

They imagine their coins are
the cause of occasional bubbles

that stop.

His is a better death than most –
that same day children
tumble down slides to a man-made lake,
burn under a false sun stronger than
the tilted earth provides
this northern city;
                          everywhere
girls turn they see
themselves in mirrors and know
the thin mannequins are better dressed.
And on Bourbon Street, the bronze
hooker holds her clenched fist
forever failing to scare a cop.

The diver will be found
a day later,
and will not happen again.

Peter Prest

Drawers

The whole purpose of a drawer
is to remain out of sight,
to hang suspended just below
the daily working surface.

I am alarmed how organized people
will set things at right angles,
sort rubber bands, paper clips
and pins in trays,
clean out pens that have dried out,
pencil stubs, hardened erasers.

There has to be a place for these remains –
opened cough candies, name tags,
bent business cards, crumbling aspirins,
a single button, eleven thumb tacks,
a confiscated water pistol –

but if I do not return on Monday
waste no time in sorting and picking;
take the drawer out and turn it over.

Start fresh with the new occupant;
I'd do the same for you.

Sunday Nights in the Early '50s

We tried to sleep on the way home
wrapped up in a blanket in the back
of the old Hudson, head to feet.
The fumes made me light-headed,
queasy, aware of the pitted surface
we drove on endlessly, every Sunday.

Our parents up front, outlined by
the dash light and my mother's
lit cigarette swinging back and
forth gracefully between them,
punctuating quiet sporadic talk.
Miles separate comments about
some dark landmark, a sag-roofed
shed or a tree split by lightning.

I used to think of them as pilots
on those long drives back, one
hundred miles in a car that creaked
and threatened weekly to leave us
stranded. Sometimes the spartan
talk was of the services, listless
reviews of sermons practised during
the week, or her cutting comments
about one of the country women.

We travelled through time this way
for less than a full year, nearly fifty
years ago. Now, with both parents
dead, I still feel the bumps as we drive
through the night, and my eyes burn
    that I keep them squeezed shut.

Caterina Edwards

Where The Heart Is
An Essay

The city becomes a packed raft about to capsize, to sink under the weight of the bodies and the volume of the human wastes. In the evening, the tourists retreat to the mainland, abandoning their debris: plastic bottles and bags, sandwich wrappers, papers scattered over the ancient stones. At night, the cleaners sweep up the mountains of garbage and carry it off in barges. Morning, and again, the tour buses pour over the causeway, disgorging the groups – French school children, American seniors, German honeymooners, the entire First World, it seems. Most of the eastern Europeans arrive dazed; they have travelled a day or more on their buses to arrive in this fabled city, this wonder of the world, once beyond their reach. It seems they cannot afford even the coffee and shade of a café. But the sights are free, and they are free to gaze upon them and litter.

The last time I visited Venice, we (husband, two daughters, and I) avoided the tourists, renting an apartment in Castello, a working-class neighbourhood. The stone stairs to the attic apartment were cracked or tilted alarmingly. We sweated at each step. The air was heavy with humidity and heat. At night, since we didn't have a fan, we closed the shutters, but not the windows. There was a *pizzeria* a few doors down, the equivalent of a neighbourhood pub. The patrons' laughter, the buzz of their conversations, kept us awake late into the night. At dawn, the neighbours began hailing each other in the street, calling from window to window; the woman opposite screeched at her three-year-old son. In Edmonton, we were buffered by trees and lawns, protected by space. Here, everything and everyone was closer, louder, brighter.

I was happy, comfortable, connected to the city by history and family. Two elderly aunts, a multitude of first and second cousins lived here: the conductor on the *vaporetto*, the girl behind the bar, the manager of a leather store, the seamstress, the fish farmer, the bank clerk, sprinkled from one end of the lagoon to the other. I knew the city, not as tourist does, as a series of 'sights'; I knew its daily rhythms, its hidden life. In those labyrinthian streets, I was at home.

Yet – I am not Venetian.

Despite many summers I spent there, despite my affectionate, extended family, despite everything I know and feel about the city, I am an outsider. Although my mother has spoken Venetian to me since I was born, when I open my mouth to speak *Venexiane*, I expose myself as a foreigner. My words are correct, but my intonation lacks the melody. I can hear, but not reproduce, the local rhythm. Likewise, although I look stereotypically Venetian with my red hair, long face, and heavy-lidded eyes, the way I dress and move (hesitantly, unobtrusively) is Canadian.

At home and not at home.

Another year, we rented a *cappana*, a hut on the Lido beach. At first, the Venetian families, who had rented their *cappane* for three generations, ignored us, branding us tourists. But after a visit from a cousin, our position changed. "So, you're related to Michele," one mother said, taking us up and in. The Venetians offered food, advice, and conviviality. They also observed and criticized. We were expected to dress with a certain taste, to perform ritual courtesies, including shaking hands on arrival and departure each day, to eat three-course lunches on proper dishes, not sandwiches cupped in napkins, to rest quietly for two hours after lunch: in general, to follow all the unwritten rules. "*Signora*," a voice would intrude. "Haven't your daughters been in the sea for too long?" Or, "Shouldn't the girls change out of those wet bathing suits?"

At home and not at home.

Home Is Where We Start From

The Venetian lagoon was first settled in the fifth century by Roman citizens of nearby towns seeking refuge from Attila and his Huns. With each new barbarian invasion, more refugees fled to this delta of three rivers, this swamp of shifting sands. Searching for the safest, most protected spot, the settlers moved from island to island. Heraclea, Mazzorbo, and Torcello took their turns as the major centre. In 810, when Pepin and his army invaded the lagoon, the inhabitants retreated to Rivalto, or Rialto, the core of the present city. And for a thousand years, until Napoleon, Venice was unconquerable. A thousand years of a great Republic. The series of sights the tourists come to see exists because the city was never assailed. Venice needed no thick walls, no fortifications; she could flaunt her splendours.

Venice remains a contradiction: a city built on water, stone that floats in air. Ambiguous, Venice has long inspired its visitors to fantasize, rhapsodize, and create bloated metaphors. Centuries pass, yet both the Romantic poet and the latest tourist off the *vaporetto* call Venice a ship, a haven, a museum, a backdrop, a raft, and a bride of the sea. Venice is compared to a seraglio, a freak, a fairy tale, and a mausoleum. Since Venice's decline in the eighteenth century, the city has been a symbol of decadence, death, and dissolution. *Dust and ashes, dead and done with*, Napoleon said as he handed the city to the Austrians: *Venice spent what Venice earned.*

It is the strangeness, the sheer otherness, of this slippery city that causes it to be classified as a place of reversal, of transgressions. I played with the notion in my first novel. The wicked carnival city, where nothing and no one is what it seems. But with age and experience I am more skeptical of received ideas and literary conceits. Visiting Venice is such a sensual delight that I wonder if her reputation for wickedness sprang from an Anglo or Nordic puritanism. A place so dedicated to pleasure must be evil.

If Venice is sinking, her doom is recent and comes from ignoring ecological, rather than moral, truths. Her survival is threatened by a loss of the delicate balance between sea and city, by the pollution and the tourists, and by her transformation into not the city of the dead, but the city of the near dead, the old. The younger generation is exiled to *terra firma* or solid land. "Very few of my old classmates live in the city anymore," says Tony, a younger cousin who has managed to stay by buying a tiny wreck of a place and, doing all the work himself, rebuilding from the foundation up. "None of the boys I played basketball with at the parish hall. All gone." They cannot afford the price of apartments in the city, driven up by the international rich, who can pay an exorbitant sum for a second home. Venice has been reduced to a holiday resort, the majority of houses (especially in the better neighbour-hoods) uninhabited for most of the year.

I bemoan the trend, loudly and sincerely. But if I had the chance – say I won the lottery – I would buy an apartment in a minute. On the last visit, we contacted a real estate agent and toured various renovated flats. All four of us found ourselves fantasizing yearly visits, then a home. Having breakfast on the terrace, setting a computer up in front of that window. *Isn't that all it takes? Cash? You buy a home and it is yours.*

You wish. Home is not simply the place where you live. Home is a feeling, a haven, a cage, a heaven, a trap, a direction, an end, and the generator of more metaphors than Venice. If I claim that I am both not at home and at home in Venice, it is longing that keeps the contradictory states from can-celling each other out.

On Via Garibaldi where we went to buy sweet peaches and melons, arugula and tomatoes from an open stall, and yogurt, mineral water, and toilet paper from what was called the supermarket but was not much more than a hole in the wall, goods piled to the ceiling, aisles where you had to turn side-ways to pass; on Via Garibaldi, the widest and some said the ugliest street in Venice, though the buildings were deep red, sand and buff and geraniums bloomed at the window; on Via Garibaldi, where we sat out in the early evening and sipped *aperitifs* and watched the parade of young and old; on Via Garibaldi where each time I passed the last house, the one that faced out to the lagoon, I paused and read the plaque: *In this house lived Giovanni Caboto, explorer and discoverer of Newfoundland.* Almost superstitiously, I paused and felt the glimmer of that other place, where I lived and which I should have called home.

Edmonton in Venice and Venice in Edmonton: in each place, I feel the presence of the other. (Nostalgia is always double, double presence and double absence.)

Who belongs? And where?

When I was growing up in Alberta, going to twelve schools in seven years, when I was at university, I felt different, out of place. I thought I would never belong. Like the dream, I would never arrive. With the years, my attitude has changed, partly because most of the people in my life do not have a specific place they call home. They are hybrids – different in complicated and interesting ways.

My husband grew up in California and though he feels an affection for the climate, the dry, fierce heat, and for the fecundity of that inner valley land, he insists he never felt American. Or rather, he never felt only American. It is entirely appropriate, he thinks, that he has three nationalities (Italian, American, and Canadian). My adopted sister was born in Yugoslavia, spent her childhood in a refugee camp in Genova, her adolescence in Calgary, her working girl years in New York city, and the last twenty-five years in Puerto Rico, married to an ex-Cuban, who also spent his early years journeying from country to country. These are the lives we lead now – in transit and flux.

Home Is Where They Have To Take You In

Since the beginning, for century after century, Venice was a haven for refugees: Byzantine Greeks, Sephardic Jews, Armenians, and Slavs. They were not given citizenship; they had their own neighbourhoods and churches or synagogues; but the culture they brought influenced and altered Venice. The aesthetic principles seem more eastern than western – gold mosaics and onion domes.

To arrive was to be safe.

In the last few years, the new migrants have come looking for refuge. In the Mercerie, between Piazza San Marco and the Rialto, the Somalis and Sengalese alight on vacant squares of pavement and spread out their wares:

fake designer bags and sunglasses. The newspaper complains of the Albanians squatting in an empty palace while I notice more beggars planted at the foot of bridges. A gypsy woman stretches her hand out to me. "Need," I think she says. "The war." Others have their cardboard signs, "BOSNIAN REFUGEE" written in pencil. They look – wretched, hungry, desperate. Yet there is a system of refugee aid, with offices in the neighbourhood police stations, jobs and housing provided by the city council. *Extra communitari*, the Italians call them, those from outside the community, and despite Venice's traditional role, now the citizens debate their responsibility. Many of the Venetians complain: what about us, what about the homeless family camping in the middle of Campo Santa Margherita, what about our sons and daughters who are forced to move away.

Venice for the Venetians.

(*France for the French. Germany for the Germans. Serbia for the Serbians.* And so it goes.)

Home: Where They Have To Take You In

My grandfather, Renato Pagan, was born in a house on the Calle delle Rasse, a narrow street that runs behind St. Mark's Basilica. According to family lore, the Pagans, like the rest of the Venetian upper class, had lost their fortune years before to the gaming tables.

Renato went to sea to win a new fortune, or at least, a more comfortable living. He found land and a wife in Dalmatia, for centuries a part of the Venetian empire. And he prospered, a pretty house and eight healthy children, he prospered until the First World War. Although Dalmatia was a part of the Austro-Hungarian empire, he could not imagine himself fighting on the side of the Austrians. He was a Venetian and an Italian. Like many men in the towns of Dalmatia, he joined the Italian navy, sailing under the command of Nazario Sauro.

But the family and the historical stories divide when explaining how he died. My mother claimed that he drowned in a submarine; one cousin insisted he died of hunger, of want – "That's our history," he says. Meanwhile, the history book states that Sauro did command a submarine that ran aground. The patriots were captured by the Austrians and tried for treason. Your ethnic background makes no difference, they were told. You live under our empire. *You owe your allegiance to us.* They were executed.

My grandmother, Caterina Letich (a Croatian), and her children were forced out of their house. Soldiers confiscated their belongings, transported them to Fiume, and loaded them onto cattle cars. (With other wives and other children of Sauro's troops.) *Go back to where you came from.* Though she and all the children were born in Veli Losinj. Still, they were not sorry to be going to Italy. They thought in Venice, with grandfather's family, they would be safe. Instead, when the train reached the Italian border, the Italians declared them foreigners. The doors of the cattle cars were closed. And they were shunted from place to place. In the dark, without food and with little water. They were all ill; one aunt, Antonietta, nine years old, died. They were locked in with their body wastes and her corpse. And when finally the door were opened, when they were let out, my grandmother and her children found themselves in a camp in Sicily, a camp for *enemy aliens.* I know little of their experience there. My aunt Maricci, who was the oldest, told me that they were given nothing to eat. Since my grandmother spoke Italian with an accent, it was she, Maricci, who had to beg the guards to be allowed to take potato peels from the garbage.

Who belongs? (And where?)

At the end of the war, they were allowed to settle in Venice. Twenty-five years later, my grandmother was dead; the seven siblings had dispersed to jobs in the greater Veneto area. One aunt had married a fisherman and lived in Chioggia, a fishing village on the southwest end of the lagoon. By 1944, the Veneto had become one of the focal points of the war. A German soldier warned my aunt: *Take your children to Venice. They'll be safe there.* And she did, leaving just before part of her street was destroyed.

My mother, working for a bakery in Padova, was in a bomb shelter when it was hit. Since she was claustrophobic, she found the crowded shelter almost unbearable. She stayed by the entrance, and her position saved her. In the centre, everyone was killed. Body parts, she told me, shattered flesh. Nothing else, she said. My mother moved back to Venice. She knew neither side would ever bomb that city. It meant too much to both sides, beloved as it was of Goethe and Wagner, of Byron and Ruskin. In fact, Venice was not touched.

A safe haven.

My father was a Royal Engineer in the British army. My parents met in Venice, when my father's company requisitioned the house where my mother and two aunts were living. (Which is why I am Welsh/English/Italian and Croatian.)

Who belongs? And where?

My sister, the Yugoslavian/Italian/Canadian/Puerto Rican, visited Venice as a child. Thirty years later, arriving again at St. Mark's Square, she burst into tears. "I felt like I had come home," she said. "Though it didn't make sense." She reminds me that my longing for the city is commonplace, rather than unique. The city is both strange and familiar to all its visitors. For its image is everywhere. As James said: "It is the easiest city to visit without going there." The world claims Venice as its own, and as its home, calling it, in the words of a UNESCO document, "a vital comment asset." An international movement argues the city is too precious for the Italians to continue to mismanage. Venice can be saved, the group argues, only if it does not remain a part of Italy but is made a world city. *It belongs to the world.*

This spring a group calling itself Armata Veneta Serenissima and calling for the separation of the Veneto from Italy unloaded a tank on St. Mark's Square and seized the campanile. In a survey conducted by the city's newspaper, a majority of Venetians named these separatists not terrorists but patriots. *Venice for the Venetians.*

Extra communitaria: one who is outside the community, yet comfortable, at home. When I wrote my first novel, I thought I would be able to exorcise my dream of Venice. But the dream repeats itself. I find myself writing this essay.

Venice again.

In explaining the origin of the name Venezia, Ruskin quotes Sansorvino, who claimed that Venezia come from the Latin *venietiam*, come again, for he said, no matter how often you come, you will always see new things, new beauties.

Return.

Hiromi Goto

Not Your Ethnic Body

There is always her body.

She has been here after all, just that no one really saw her. (Actually, they pretended not to notice in the din of remarking on their own.) She has always known she has a body and that her body is not like theirs. They, in their clamour, glance possessively through the swell of their words. They had not wanted to know her for as long as they could. But she can no longer be ignored. Nor can they make her feel like their body is superior to hers. She feels their gaze through the thickness of jeans and flannel. The prickle of razor-thin superiority. She shrugs. She knows her body is beautiful and that they wish it theirs.

How remarkable, my body, she smiles. That she can gaze upon herself with eyes undistorted. How remarkable. This me, this self, this utterable.

She brings fingers to her lips like she is kissing, not to blow them to whoever is watching, but to actually kiss herself. She likes herself, she likes her body. She hasn't always liked her body, and there are small white scars, ridged and gleaming, the parts she had hated most. People suggested that her body wasn't pleasing. She was young once. She believed them. She is glad that she didn't tear out her tongue.

She leaves the computer hum and sinks on to her futon.

Ahhhhh, they sigh, yes.

Shhhhhhh, she'll hear us!

She smirks one corner of her lip and ignores them. Stretches enormously, arms above her head and toes reaching for the edges of blanket. She closes her eyes and they wait, breath burning inside their lungs.

And the computer hum.

The tak tak tak of keyboard letters wording text on a glowing screen, a sign, look, a sign, they gasp pointing their fingers. They stare mouthing words they think will somehow save them.

Her Tongue.

Glad she didn't tear it out, in the supermarket the tongues of cattle rolled under itself, wrapped in cellophane, but not every day. No one could eat tongue daily. Good for licking, easy to burn, she liked rolling her tongue into a straw to suck up spilled milk, never cried over it, saved by her tongue.

There was a boy named Ben a year older who could touch the tip of his nose with his tongue, her older sister went steady with him and when she asked her sister if they kissed and her sister said yes, she shuddered, that her sister would kiss a boy whose tongue could lick his nose, cow-like, swiping clean any mucous with the mouthly organ.

If you cut out tongues from people of different races, would you notice the difference, she thought, smirked at the Benetton potential.

She would never pierce her tongue, still wonders how the clack clack of metal ball would feel against teeth and the roof of the mouth. Her mother could roll her tongue but not her father. But he could flip his over with a twist, underside facing upwards.

Hssssssssss, see, we told you, the words are the same as any other, who can tell? It's pointless to differentiate. Writing is writing. All that matters is if it's good.

She rolls over on to her belly, knees bent and kicking barely back and forth. They turn their gaze towards her, maybe she would be more exciting, she's lying on a bed after all. But she drops her legs to the flat of the futon. Just brings her fingers to her lips once more.

Hsssss. Wait. They turn together to watch the words that tak tak across the screen.

Her Lips.

The girl was told she had her mother's mother's lips. The old umeboishi baba, her father spat. Mari covered her smallish mouth with her slender hand. She quite liked umeboishi, especially with hot rice with green tea poured over top, but her father made it hard to enjoy. She spent a lot of time in the bathroom, staring at her inherited lips. They didn't look like a salted sour plum. She licked them and they tasted pretty normal. What was it her father saw? She puckered and kissed the cold pane of glass until her lips were numb.

What are you doing in there! her father shouted.

She didn't say. And she didn't open the door.

The doorknob clattered. Don't you ignore me, open this door right now or you'll be sorry! The knob clattered some more, panel of wood shaking, then it was silent.

She kissed her lips icy and breathed moist circles on the surface of mirror.

Door swung open, bang! against the wall, Mari almost toppled off the counter where she was perched, her father triumphant with a slender bamboo chopstick he used to jiggle the lock open. He smacked the top of her head with the ohashi and tears filled her eyes.

Don't you be practising that sort of thing, you hear? If I ever catch you being bad in that way, you'll wish you were never born!

Yes. That's better, they nod. And implied reference to a distant homeland. Markers of ethnicity. Foreign words, chopstick, exotic food. Follows a narrative. A traditional patriarchal father figure. Yes, we like that. It tells us what things are like for people on the periphery. Things we don't know but actually do, this is perfect.

She sighs. They don't even bother to look at her now. The way she rolls her body on to her side, so she can watch them watching the magic of the text. The way the blue glow of her computer shines upon her skin.

Her Skin.

It was just like he had imagined. How he had dreamt all his adolescent life. Her skin was gleaming like polished cedar and her long silky black hair hung in a mysterious curtain around her face and shoulders. He reached out with trembling fingers to uncover her face.

She was so lovely he almost wept. Her gently upward-tilted eyes, almost looking like she was smiling even when she wasn't. And her smooth, smooth skin. She smelled rich and ancient like incense in a temple. I will love you, he thought, I will love you as you deserve to be loved.

George-san, she whispered. George-san, and a single tear pearled down the exotic plane of her face.

Oh, Su Zu Ko! George shuddered. That I'm finally here, in Japan! This island of temples and incense and haiku gestures. Oh my little Suzie.

George-san. You have made a name for me?

Yes, oh yes! he held her to his chest, her tawny skin making his the more white. I am finally here and I can finally make my dream come true. I will write the novel I always knew I had in me. It will be called, I Wanked Off In Japan And Now I Wrote This Book.

Giggling bursts from the futon and they angrily flick their gaze upon her. She is convulsing, wiping tears from her eyes with a corner of the blanket.

Hssssssst! They are not amused.

What is this! What kind of mockery. We are serious in our intent. We are only trying to understand. We will not be deliberately antagonized. We will talk of ethnicities, not race and certainly inappropriate to talk about racism.

She raises her eyebrows. They make a big show of turning their backs toward her. Willing the text on the computer to say what they need.

Her Skin (Revisited)

Her skin was a code that covered her entire body. Her skin, her hair, the shape of her eyes.

Junko took one last look into the mirror and fell in, swirling, billowing, snaking like strands of snow across the highway, she fell, fell, faces whisking past her, Michelle, dear Michelle, Junko reached out a hand to grasp, but gone, just the after-image of her lover's pale blue eyes, her eyes, what did she see through those eyes, was she lovely, was she special, was she somehow spinning, whirling, black hair streaming behind her, she opened her mouth to shout but the cold almost froze more, and more. The snow, the ice, history books snapped like crocodile jaws, to take bites out of her skin, she cringed, winced back, the tornado roar, kicked the monstrous books away, her mother, her father, spinning close then whirling away, sisters, brothers, they spun too, arms outstretched to try to hold her, but just as vulnerable, just as frightened, the television sets, reporters, actors, high-school teachers, all took photos, asked her questions then answered them themselves, she shook her head, no, no, listen, the blasting roar, the razor cold, the ceaseless barrage of white-out, white-out, white-out...

They are at quite a loss. The text they read is saying things they rather it didn't. Obviously, what the screen offers isn't what they are looking for. They turn, slightly embarrassed, to the woman on the futon, thinking of ways they can thank her and let her know, at the same time, that they think her body is just fine, but it's not the kind of body they are interested in.

She is naked.

Some turn away, shocked, others stare boldly, but she just stands there, naked, central to her own body.

You see me, but you don't. She utters. You would like to know me, but you won't. You call me ethnic and you seek to possess me like you have possessed the term ethnic for yourselves and everyone else based upon your own definitions.

She steps toward the humming computer and they jostle aside, in the face of her troubling nakedness.

She turns to them once more with a tiny smile on her lips.

You think you can imagine me in my place, but really, she winks, really, do you think so? She grins. Imagine this! and steps into her computer screen, her body smoothes into the light, narrowing, shrinking into a dot and the screen goes out. The sudden silence in the room leaves an echo of a hum in their ears. They punch on the keys, the switches, pull the plug out then back in. But she is gone.

Joseph Pivato

My Father's Escapes

The film *Seven Beauties* opens with two Italian soldiers running through the woods in central Europe to escape pursuing German soldiers. One of the Italian soldiers, played by Giancarlo Giannini, is caught after stealing some food and survives a labour camp to return home to his family in Italy. The scene of soldiers escaping into the woods is vivid in my mind because it recreates an incident in my father's life. As a young man he was drafted into the Italian army to fight in Mussolini's wars in Greece, Albania, and southern France. My father was in the Alpini artillery and survived these fronts: enduring night bombardments, guiding mules along narrow ledges, climbing cliffs, fighting artillery battles from mountain ridges, sleeping in rain and mud. One month his regiment received orders to go to the Russian Front and were issued winter gear, only to have the order changed as they were boarding the train. Many of the Alpini from his region never returned from Russia. The whole of the Julia division disappeared. My father was lucky to escape that fate.

When Italy surrendered to the Allies on the 8th of September, 1943, Italian soldiers in German-occupied northern Italy became German prisoners. My father's regiment of Alpini was stationed in southern France near Grenoble. They woke up one morning to find themselves surrounded by German soldiers. My father and his companions were taken to Modane, on the French-Italian border, and used by their German captors to do dangerous bomb disposal work. One day during a detonation of a bomb, my father and two other soldiers ran into the woods and never looked back. Much like the characters in *Seven Beauties*, they ran blindly through those wet October woods. Later they climbed across narrow mountain passes, crawled, and hid to avoid being captured. Their alpine training in Albania and Greece was useful. From Bardonecchia they walked all day and all night to get to Susa. There was more hiding and walking to reach Rocciamelone, then north to Biella, then around to Cattinara and then Novara. They had to avoid the cities of Torino and Milano, where there were concentrations of German soldiers. Any Italian soldiers found there were taken into Germany to work in labour camps. From Novara my father travelled alone across northern Italy to reach his village of Tezze sul Brenta, east of Vicenza and west of Treviso. The distance he travelled was about 420 km. That he escaped and managed to avoid German patrols is a feat he often told us about. He would list the place names of his journey as if they were stations of the cross: Modane, Bardonecchia, Biella, and Cattinara. He had help from several people along the way: one women hid him and gave him potatoes to eat. Later in his journey another gave him a change of clothes, and he was able to get a ride on a train. He managed somehow to send word home and his younger sister, Bianca, was able to come to get him at Fontaniva, a few kilometres from their farm. He got home half-starved and so full of fleas that they had to burn the clothes he wore.

After he got home he had to remain hidden for weeks. German soldiers were active in the area, as were partisans. In the nearby town of Bassano del Grappa the Germans hung twenty-one men one Sunday morning as a retribution for the killing of one German soldier by the local partisans. Then the Germans retreated north across the border. And for a time there were bands of outlaws roaming the countryside. Slowly my father recovered his health. He used a local remedy, *ovo col vino*, a tonic of raw eggs mixed with sugar and red wine. As children we were often given this tonic.

To my father, even after fifty years, these memories were so vivid that he could tell these stories in minute detail. He recalled the smell of the stable he slept in one night, the feel of the hay on wet clothes, the taste of those boiled potatoes, the cold water from a mountain spring in Piemonte. At other times he seemed reluctant to recall these sad events, as if the suffering and death of companions and neighbours were too painful to relive, even in Canada. He never had much use for the depiction of heroics in war movies. We must remember that for many Italians the war did not begin in 1939, but years before in 1926 when Mussolini invaded parts of North Africa to meet Italy's colonial ambitions. By the 1930s young Italian men started coming home in wooden boxes. My aunt showed me my mother's class picture from grade school and pointed out the nine boys who had died in the war, some having disappeared on the Russian Front.

My father, from the generation of 1917, was lucky to be alive at the end of the war. He was alive and in love. He enjoyed telling us the story of how he met my mother in a dentist office in Citadella. They then conducted a courtship between Tezze sul Brenta in Veneto and Nogaredo del Corno (her village) in Friuli, a distance of 100 kilometres. In that part of Italy there were no trains running in the last months of the war, and my future parents had to travel back and forth by bicycle and by rowboat across rivers where all the bridges had been blown up either by aerial bombs or the retreating Germans. When we drove the distance years later it was hard to believe that they were able to bicycle back and forth. Besides the bad roads and wide rivers there were soldiers, partisans, and outlaw bands.

This region was a battle front in the First World War. Towns were devastated. It is the area romanticized in Hemingway's novel *A Farewell to Arms*. My family does not share this romantic view of these years. My grandfather, my mother's father, fought in this first war. He returned from Canada, where he was working as a stone mason, to defend his home territory. He was in the retreat at Caporetto and saw first-hand friends and neighbours die. My father had uncles who died in the white trenches and limestone caves of Monte Grappa. And twenty years later my parents were tracing the steps of dead soldiers across this dangerous landscape of granite war memorials and military graveyards.

In 1991, a few kilometres from these war memorials, Europeans were killing each other in the wars of ethnic cleansing of the former Yugoslavia. When I visited Friuli in 1992 I met Slovenian and Croatian refugees. Did these people escape into wet October woods to save their lives and their families?

Just after the second war my parents got married in a poverty so severe that there are no pictures to record the wedding. To escape the poverty my father went to work in a coal mine in Belgium for a while. He did not stay because of the danger of the work. He would ask, "Did I survive the war and escape the Germans to die in a coal mine?"

Then in 1951 he emigrated to Canada. My mother, my sister, and I followed him a year later. I grew up in Canada. I learned the language and the culture of North America. We forgot the Italy we left and my father put the war far behind. And Italy too forgot about us as it neglected millions of other emigrants. When I read the English history books in school there was little mention of Italy, Italian soldiers, or Italian immigrants. Yes, we would read about the great men of the Renaissance, but this seemed far removed from the simple immigrant culture we lived day-to-day. Was I aware that there was something missing?

Like many Italian immigrants my father worked in construction. In the 1950s there were few safety measures in place for construction workers. In March of 1960 five Italian workers were killed in a tunnel cave-in at Hogg's Hollow in Toronto. At another location my father was also buried in a deep trench cave-in and survived. And even in the 1960s, after safety measures came into force, the work was still dangerous. In one high building a man working on my father's floor fell to his death. On another site my father was crushed when a tall scaffolding tipped over on him. He was pinned for some time in this trap, and was only saved from mutilation and death by the chance occurrence that the falling scaffolding came to rest on some building materials behind him. He shrugged off this narrow escape like many others in his life. It was just fate.

We grew up in Canada. We became Canadian, but somewhere I was also aware that my family was different. The Veneto dialect that my parents spoke, the Italian regional dishes that we ate, and the Italian people we socialized with reminded us that there was another aspect to our identity. For us the backyard garden was an extension of our kitchen. Every vegetable and fruit had a meaning and a link back to Italy. One Christmas my father came to stay with us in Edmonton and brought some cuttings from a fruit tree in the backyard. It was a fig tree that Italians had developed to survive the Canadian winter. In Edmonton we planted it in a big flowerpot inside our sun room and it has flourished ever since and produced figs. Italians have always transplanted their culture. We were not conscious of it at the time, but my father's stories, my stone mason grandfather's migrations, and other family tales were part of this identity.

When I began to read the stories by other Italian-Canadian writers I became conscious of these family stories of escapes and migrations. There was often a dead grandfather in the background; an almost forgotten mother or an old uncle who had survived to retell some old family story. These younger writers, the sons and daughters of immigrants, were trying to reconcile their lives in Canada with their roots in Italy, migrations to Argentina or Australia or New York. Beyond the summer trips to Italy, the search for lost family recipes, the home-made pasta, and the home-made wine, we wonder if there is an Italian culture outside of Italy? Can we capture it in a poem or song?

My father lived for eighty years, and he was always physically active. Two days after I said goodbye to him in front of our old family house in Toronto he died in his garden. It was a cool morning on the 23rd of October, the anniversary of his escape from Modane, and he was getting his garden ready for winter. He made one last escape. He quietly slipped away before anybody could notice. And he is probably still hurrying through those cool October woods with the other Alpini.

Nigel Darbasie

Bridge Boys

On weekends my father would invite the bridge boys over.
They'd talk their strange talk: "Five spades."
"Three hearts." They'd drink *Old Oak* and *Vat 19* rum,
Johnny Walker and *Bells Scotch* whiskey.
They smoked cigarettes. I'd collect the stubs,
take them to my hiding place under the back stairs,
roll the unburnt tobacco into copybook paper.
I was always disappointed, lighting up,
that I'd never had an ecstatic rush,
just bitter choking and bleary eyes.
I sneaked out their rum and whiskey too,
liking the effervescent tingle of the chaser.
Perilous experiments, troubling like a scorpion sting
to think of what would happen if I got caught.

The bridge boys were Negro, and Indian men;
huge, towering, most of them. Funny,
teasing, with their deep voices.
"Well, look this youngster!" they'd say.
My head in a span of thick fingers
when I didn't want to be held. When all I wanted
was just to watch, from behind corners
or through the crack in the door of my room,
these men with skin from black to brown;

hair, kinky to straight; lips, full to thin;
noses, flat to sharp. Affirmations of markings
I had learned from classmates at school.
Yet, nigger, coolie, and dougla
didn't fit the bridge boys
in whose camaraderie and worldliness
notions of tribe lay obliterated.

The sessions would last through the night,
in the living room. The windows open
to a chorus of cicadas and frogs,
a buzz and croak timed like clockwork.
Before going to bed I'd look in
on my father and his friends,
heads bowed before their cards.
A pall of smoke at the ceiling light
where moths flew in frenzied circles.

Western Carnival

Downtown on a flatbed truck, jammin' calypso
for a Caribbean carnival parade.
Our exultant rhythms rebuffed,
echoing cold off high-rise buildings,
alien to these clean, broad streets,
these refractory onlookers
who won't even tap their feet
or shake a little waist self.
Our celebratory jump-up,
a laborious trundle.
Sombre demeanours,
resplendent costumes.
Masqueraders transplanted
like immortelles to a boreal forest.

Noah's Offspring

Geneticists say that racial divisions
by skin and geography are as mythic as Aryans,
as delusional as the flatness of the earth.
We could at least be scientific,
dividing ourselves by the possession
of anti-malarial genes; or the enzyme lactase
which would allow claims of racial superiority
by ancient lines of milk-drinkers:
Europeans, Arabs, India's northerners,
Africans like the Fulani.
The rest of us constituting a lower caste
of lactase-negative throwbacks.

As for purity, science shows
we've long been roving packs of mongrels,
true to our God-given nature. At least until
the coming man-made perfect man.
His predecessor's looks, the colour of his skin,
hair, eyes, seared into memory.

Tololwa M. Mollel

The Olive Tree

Within months grandfather had doubled the number of coffee trees in the farm, ferreting out with infinite patience the smallest bare patches of ground and into each striking one, two, three coffee trees. Besides coffee he had as well, years ago, planted wood in the farm. According to the old man, the farm was to provide for firewood and timber for the next three generations. Following the example of the big white settlers, he had also turned the farm into an orchard, planting every imaginable type of fruit, including one olive tree.

After several rains everything was flourishing wildly, and the farm looked like a small jungle. Venturing into it was like trespassing into a shrine. And if you climbed atop one of the tall eucalyptus trees, the spread below looked like an impregnable unkempt grove. But there was nothing unkempt about the farm, you discovered on entering it. The old man kept it nicely dug up and cleaned out at all times of the year, with the leaves and twigs from the pruned coffee collected around the coffee trees. Within the farm, the atmosphere was nice and cool, a good refuge from the severe heat of February. The sun never penetrated to the soil below, and during the cold season from June to July, it was not the place you would choose to be.

At night the place was simply forbidding. It was taken over by nightmarish demons driven off the compound by grandfather's lengthy evening prayers. On moonlit nights they lived in the long shadows of the sky-high eucalyptus and among the sprawling ones of the coffee trees, ready to spring on your neck at an unguarded moment. On dark nights when there were no shadows, the demons could not leap out at you within sight of your terrified eyes. But this, far from reducing your anguish by masking the presence of the demons, actually held out far more killing terrors. You did not see the demons about to spring at you: you felt them, you heard them, in the pounding in your head, in the hammering of your heart, in your breathing. They pressed in on your imagination with their prickly presences.

The olive tree marked the farthest point in the farm, which was called *olmukuna*. No one knew how the old man had come by such a rare fruit tree, or how it was that there was only one of its kind in the entire farm. Neither could anyone remember the tree ever bearing fruit. But the tree served the old man well. He used it to punish boys who showed cowardice during a night errand. Somewhat late at night, for example, grandfather might remember that he had to borrow an important tool for a task that, for some mysterious reason, he just had to do at dawn. (Grandfather was famous for his early morning tasks.) To save the situation, someone would be sent out to ask for the tool at the neighbouring compound.

Whenever you were on such an errand, you walked tall, seemingly unafraid, however deep the night happened to be. And there was no fooling grandfather. He could always tell whether you had run terrified or walked calmly as a man should who has nothing to fear except the old man's god on high. Yes, he could always tell. A thumping chest, the inexplicable terror in your eye, would not be lost to him. And it would be off to *olmukuna* with you, through the demon-infested foliage in the coffee farm, and you were not to come back without a leaf from the precious tree to show that you had made it through the demons; either that or the cutting edge of grandfather's strap that was rumoured to have been fashioned out of the hide of a hippopotamus.

To grandfather, cowards were the worst scourge on earth. He hated them with an intensity that he reserved only for liars and pilferers. An ardent Christian, the old man said he wanted his grandsons to grow into confident men, afraid of no one but God. Cowardice was a sin, according to him. "Man is a house of God," he said time and again. "Let not cowardice live in it!"

Over the years, it was said, many a boy had been sent to the olive tree and they had come back more dead than alive. With the leaf. Except for a few who had preferred grandfather's hippopotamus whip.

Nyangusi, due to his survivor's cunning, had so far been lucky. Like the rest of the boys in the compound, fear of the night always lent him wings. But he had always been smart enough, before facing the sharp eye of the old man, to obliterate all signs that he had been running. He stilled his heart and put himself under manly control that invariably met grandfather's taciturn approval. Until the night his luck ran out.

It was a night of the deepest black and Nyangusi had been on errand for grandmother. On leaving the compound, he had started running, his eyes closed, preferring the darkness of his eyelids to that of the night. He knew the path well, knew that there were no obstacles the whole way to Njaapaya's compound where the errand was taking him. And, well, the darkness was such that it made no difference anyway whether or not he had his eyes open. Even as he ran the pounding of his feet and the racing of his heart turned into a hundred *nenauner*, a half-human, half-rock creature in grandmother's night stories. They swarmed after him, their stone legs shaking the earth and their banana fibre wrappings rustling in the dark. Stories related to him floated into his terrified imagination, of people who actually had had a face-to-face encounter with *nenauner*. They were never the same, it was whispered. They had gone insane, mumbling things no one could understand.

In this terror, little did Nyangusi think of the possibility that the old man might choose tonight to make one of his occasional nocturnal tours of the farm. This the old man did whenever he grew impatient waiting for his supper to come from grandmother's kitchen. He was the only person, to anyone's knowledge, who could plow into the unearthly stillness of the farm at night, as stolidly as if it were broad daylight. Still less did Nyangusi think of the possibility that his path of flight might just bear him into a collision course with the old man. But this was exactly what happened. There was a crash and he was sent flying into a hedge. He could not see in the darkness but could tell that the thing he had knocked into was clearly a living creature. The old man stood there, seemingly rooted into the night. Nyangusi's screams flashed across the night, wave after wave after wave. They came so involuntarily they seemed to be from someone else. Before he knew it a crowd of neighbours, with someone bearing a lamp, had gathered around him. Nyangusi looked up.

A face was bending down on him. With unutterable shock, he finally realized who he had knocked into.

"Boy, are you hurt?" grandfather asked, calmly watching the pitiful bundle painfully straightening itself up.

Nyangusi mumbled, in a voice he could hardly recognize as his own.

Back home, Nyangusi waited anxiously. But to his surprise, he was not sent to the olive tree. In fact, nothing much was said of the incident. The only reference made to it was when grandfather asked grandmother for some hot water to assuage his foot, remarking, "Your grandson almost killed me. I've strained my ankle."

Two weeks later the incident had been forgotten or almost forgotten. The live tree was the farthest thing from Nyangusi's mind as he sat in grandmother's kitchen reflecting.

In a month or two this time, he was thinking, he would cease to be a boy and become a man. The thought had been occupying him for some time, but the more he thought about it the more it hardly seemed real. It had always been other boys, and it had seemed an impossibility that a time would come when he, too, would face the circumcisor's knife. Would he cry? What if he did? He shivered involuntarily at the thought of the circumcisor's fingers on his genitals and the terrible thing their touch might make him do. The thought that he might actually cry out with pain hung over him like a nightmare. He looked unseeing at the younger children sitting apart from him, laughing and playing around a furiously boiling pot, ignoring grandmother's helpless reproaching noises.

Grandmother's hut was a round affair built of mud, with a thatch of dried banana fibres. Here slept grandmother with the younger children, her grandchildren all. A cow with its calf was tethered firmly out of reach in one part of the hut. Nyangusi, approaching manhood, slept in grandfather's *olmuchalo*, but during the cold spells he availed himself of the warmth of grandmother's fireplace. This was a rather questionable thing to do, for a boy his age. But he thought he could afford to throw his pride to the winds, because even grandfather could not resist the pleasant sensation that grandmother's hut gave to body and soul in the deadly months of cold following the heavy rains. The smell of cow dung and cow urine hung heavy in the air, but this only added to the warm sense of belonging in the hut.

Grandfather's voice cut through the night. "Nyangusi!"

A hush fell over the fireplace as Nyangusi howled, "Oe!" jumping to his feet. Grandfather did not like to have to call twice. Sometimes even when it was hard to tell whether he had called or merely sneezed, it was wise to respond.

Unlike grandmother's hut, grandfather's *olmuchalo* had a corrugated iron roof and was divided into two bedrooms and a sitting room. One of the bedrooms was occupied by Nyangusi, except when there was a guest. Then he had to go and sweat out the night in grandmother's crowded hut. Nyangusi took great pleasure in living in grandfather's *olmuchalo*. What he particularly liked about it was the smell of grandfather's pipe smoking which marked out the house as some kind of men-only territory. Once or twice Nyangusi had had a couple of stolen puffs from the pipe, although he knew grandfather would skin him alive if he ever caught him at it.

Nyangusi knocked timidly on grandfather's door and entered when he heard the old man's grunt. The old man was lying on his bed, tired from the day's work but still fully dressed in his work clothes. A small *koroboi* lamp, with a thin blade ending in a fine trail of smoke, dimly lit the room, leaving in the shadows the corners of the room and the old man's face. The shadows and the heavy tobacco smell always created for Nyangusi the atmosphere of the biblical anecdotes that the old man, in his talkative moods, related to him.

But this was not one of his talkative moods.

Nyangusi waited for the old man to say something, and he tried to see into the shadows and grandfather's face. But the old man said nothing, and the silence built up until the old man's thoughtful knocking on the wall above his bed and the distant barking of the dogs seemed to be all that was left of the world.

Finally, without raising his voice or seeming to look at him, the old man spoke. "I want you to go to *olmukuna*," he said, and Nyangusi thought perhaps he had heard right, but in the same tone of voice, his grandfather continued, "yes, go to *olmukuna*, and bring me a leaf from the olive tree. Go."

The moon stood out full and clear, its light covering things in a silvery solitude. Somewhere a eucalyptus tree creaked mournfully as a breath of wind passed, deepening the chill of the night. But Nyangusi seemed oblivious of all this. His heart beat wildly, not from fear but from a budding rash anger that was rapidly bringing him to a resolution. He would show the old man! He would go to *olmukuna*, he thought, and he would bring back not one, but five, ten, twenty leaves, just to see what the old tyrant would say. In a month or two he would become a man. He must show that he was deserving of the honour. As for his grandfather, someone had to show him that there was at least one other man besides himself who could face the night without defecating all over himself. He would punish the old man, Nyangusi decided, by denying him the satisfaction of his fear.

As he plunged deeper into the night, the moon was swallowed up by the dense growth. He stopped abruptly, and stood still. He listened to the night and the sound of his breathing. Suddenly his resolution seemed foolish. He wavered. How could he hope to punish the old man? He imagined him silently reclined on his bed, his arms folded across his chest, his eyes closed, his body tensing up for his supper, the knocking on the wall getting more and more impatient, and he, Nyangusi, all forgotten. He shook his head of these reflections. The old man had to be punished.

But he had not gone five steps when from behind came a hooting of an owl. The owl was an omen of death and ill fortune. Nyangusi leapt and the last thing he remembered was a terrific bang on the head. Long after he had regained consciousness, he would maintain, to howls of laughter from other boys, that it had been *nenauner* who had scared him so, because not only had he recognized its voice but had actually seen it!

Nyangusi was lying on a bed in grandfather's *olmuchalo* when he came to. His head was on fire. The room was packed with people, talking in far-away voices. Nyangusi felt his head. There was a bump as big as a mountain. The murmuring in the room stopped. There was a mixture of relief, concern, and mild amusement in the pairs of eyes that looked down at him. Nyangusi recognized many of the neighbours. Then someone remarked on the bump on his head. Several more people patted the bump and remarked about it. Nyangusi searched the faces in the room.

He did not see grandfather.

Just then, a hand touched his head, the bump. Nyangusi turned. Grandfather sat on a chair by the head of his bed. Grandmother came in with a dish of warm water and a piece of cloth. Grandfather soaked the piece of cloth and massaged the bump on Nyangusi's head. As he slowly rubbed the painful spot, he leaned forward until his lips were inches away from Nyangusi's ear. And in a voice so low that no one else caught the words, he murmured, "Get well soon. You still owe me the olive leaf!"

Nyangusi stared incredulously at him. The *koroboi* dimly lit the room, and he couldn't quite make out the expression on grandfather's face. But from the tone of the old man's voice, there wasn't the slightest chance that he was teasing.

Nyangusi wished he wouldn't get well for a long, long time.

David Albahari
English translation by Ellen Elias Bursac

By the Light of the Silvery Moon

My name is Adam and I don't know why I'm here.

Here: in a city standing indecisively between the Rocky Mountains and the Great Prairie, not really part of the snowy peaks or the grassy plain, always at the cusp of the divide, on the cutting edge of difference.

In a certain way, all this began as a joke, or at least now I see that it was a joke I was playing on myself, though then, when it began, it was coloured with a grave sense of decision. When we distance ourselves enough from watershed moments each of us demonstrates an awe-inspiring capacity for altering the past and falsifying history. I remember how miserable this made me feel a few years back, when our propaganda machine began to chug full steam, manufacturing various chronicles of honour and dishonour. Then it hit me that I was doing precisely the same thing, regardless of the fact that in question were more innocent matters: a present which has no objective vantage point – for, in fact, no such vantage point exist – can hardly produce an objective past; instead the past is composed of the same number of small, smooth surfaces, a little darkened, perhaps, like an old mirror, that comprise the multiple face of the present.

Of course I did not come up with this straight away. Days, weeks, months went by, there were villages that vanished from the face of the earth, there were cities reduced to heaps of rubble, people again became numbers on lists, cows wandered around the devastated regions and gazed at the pale moon. Life turned into a department store where all manner of versions of the past were on display. Some were attractively packaged, others were crude and coarse, but everyone was supposed to buy one. Anyone, like me, who opted for passing through the store and going out the other side with no purchases in hand ended up, slowly but surely, alone. Men separated from him, women showed him no kindness, children looked straight through him as if he did not exist.

And indeed he did not exist: I did not exist. And that is why, perhaps, from here everything starts seeming joke-like. Here, where every sense of self merges into the overabundance of space, this convulsive attachment to something which, as they said on serious television shows, "defines identity," had to look pretty silly. In vain friends and acquaintances knocked on my door, called me on the phone, ran into me in the street.

"Life exists," they said, "only when you see it in historical continuity, the present is no magic carpet propelling you through time and space, the only person who will have a future is the one who in it sees the re-shaping of the past."

I kept quiet and retreated into my loneliness. Mine was no noble solitude which man chooses of his own volition, but rather a plagued apartness imposed by others. In short, no matter where I turned I was met by a void: people moved aside as I walked by, and sidestepped my destination. The only things remaining behind me were dead.

And so it was that one day I got onto a city bus, went to the Canadian Embassy, and took my place in line. I filled out the first form, returned home, waited, received new forms, filled them out, waited again, went for a doctor's examination, got all the necessary documents, went for the interview, shook hands, signed the reception of an émigré visa, bought an airline ticket. All those verbs, the string of independent clauses, all of that was accompanied at the time by gravity and decisiveness, even a feeling of the inevitability of destiny. Only later, here, I began to see that all that time I did believe it really was some kind of a joke, that I was waiting in lines, going for interviews, and holding my breath at the x-ray only so that I could mock someone, that I could show that, aside from the present, nothing else existed, least of all the past, especially a past we choose ourselves.

Now I wonder: what have I chosen? I cannot find the right answer. Everything I come to, regardless of whether I am standing in front of a window or walking along endless streets or staring into a mirror, is: silence.

At first, while I hurried from office to office, filled out forms, and was assigned an array of numbers instead of my name (and my former life, of course) in powerful computer systems, I had the feeling that something was opening. I didn't know what. I thought in simple images, like: life is a corridor lined with doors, or: life is a stage, or: eyes are the mirror of the soul, the heart is a machine, the stomach is a sack, a dream is a postcard from a journey, I am someone else.

Then I felt how I was falling: I sank, and over me, with a slam, lids and shutters clanged shut. When the first snow fell, the whiteness blinded me. When ice covered the river I went out on a bridge, took off my cap and gloves, and let the frost bite me. The sun neared the far-off mountains and day became night.

This didn't worry me, I thought. In a certain sense, it is easier to walk in darkness than in daylight. You needn't worry about anything. You can be naked, the way you really are.

All of this was, of course, pure denial, vain efforts to find comfort, and I talk about it all now when words have long since lost their meaning and when every word, when it is said aloud, sounds foreign and I have to look it up in dictionaries.

In fact, the decisiveness and firmness drained out of me while I was still in the airplane. As I flew I thought I was getting further and further from that seething abyss which was caving in on itself, but, though I didn't know it, I was getting closer and closer to another abyss, one hidden inside of me, every bit as seething and empty, every bit as subject to doubts and uncertainties. When I stepped off the plane, straight into a freezing north wind, I swayed in my clothing like a scarecrow of straw. Only my heavy shoes kept me, with their weight, on the ground; everything else no longer existed.

I rented an apartment in the northern part of town, on the edge of the artistic quarter. The apartment was small: a bedroom, living room, kitchen, and bathroom. The walls were bare, the floors covered with worn carpeting, the windows had no curtains. Next to the refrigerator there was an outdated promotional calendar. Beyond the sliding glass doors, on the terrace, two plastic chairs were collecting dust.

There is always one easy way to see whether some place can truly become a home, my mother used to say. You buy a plant in a flower pot, and you try keeping it alive. If you succeed, you can get a cat. If you do not, there is no furniture or hearth which will warm your soul. But watch out, she said, each person has his own plant, each person has to raise his own flower.

OK, I thought, my plant, my flower. I found a florist shop and went in. From the dozens of flower pots, flower arrangements, bouquets, and wreaths of dried flowers spread a close, oily smell. Cactuses, exotic blossoms, vines, violets, fica plants, nettles, never before in such bounty, I was fearful that I would not find myself. Then my eyes lit on a cyclamen. I knew nothing about cyclamens, or rather I knew nothing about any of the flowers, and the sales-girl, when I asked her, only smiled and shrugged her shoulders. "Everything is written on the sign," she said. It said on the sign: "Keep out of direct sun-light; do not water excessively; do not keep in the dark."

I could not imagine why anyone would want to keep a cyclamen, or any other plant for that matter, in the dark, but those three commandments became the foundation of my entire being. Everything was subjected to them: my first activity in the morning, my last gaze in the evening, my movements during the day, my search for work, hamburgers and pizza in stand-up joints, in shopping centres, beer when I came home, staring at the muted television set which I turned around, just in case, so that I might reduce the influence of its ghostly radiation. I bought a watering can, a little bottle with mineral nutrient additives, a miniature set of gardening tools – a little spade, hoe, and rake – for working the soil: the only thing I couldn't find was a handbook on cultivating cyclamen plants. I would enter the apartment, after a brief or longer absence, take off my shoes and rush over to the flower pot sitting on a shelf by the window.

Light, water, minerals, dark. Soon everything became that simple rhythm. I would open my eyes, drink a glass of water, eat corn flakes and french fries, sink into sleep. The cyclamen did not budge. At first it looked as if I might be succeeding, although I felt that, for true success, I ought to start speaking in the first person plural, that the cyclamen should become a part of me only if I became a part of it.

One night, when I couldn't fall asleep because of the strong light of the full, silvery moon, I sat in the other chair, next to the cyclamen, and stared out into the empty street for a long time. Once, as a boy, I had believed that

things will happen if you believe in them long enough. I tried to tell this to
the cyclamen. I did not tell it that now I know how things happen in spite of
our will, attending to the will of others, perhaps, but not to our own. We are
mere witnesses to our own lives.

I fell asleep on the chair with my head against the sill. When I woke, I saw
two wilted leaves. I raked the soil, added a few droplets of the liquid with the
minerals, poured water into the little dish under the flower pot. At noon I had
to go out to a meeting with my adviser from the government employment
agency. The agency was on the other side of town, and while I was still quite
far from home, in one of the buses, I felt a momentary lapse, as if my heart
had stopped for an instant or as if it bent over to peer into a newly formed
void. I got off the bus and began to run.

No matter how I ran I couldn't change reality. Superman may be able to
turn the course of events back and spin the world in the opposite direction,
but as far as all the rest of us are concerned we can only go along in the
general direction and follow the inevitable sequence of day and night, waking
and sleeping. When I entered the apartment – the place – the cyclamen was
already dead, though it took a few more days before all the leaves and flowers
had dropped over the edges of the flower pot.

Then the snow began to fall. It fell all night and all the next day and again
all that night, and in the morning when I got up it was showing no likelihood
of stopping. I opened the window and the large flakes began to float into the
room. One fell on the wilted cyclamen, I felt another on my face, three nestled
into the yellowed carpeting.

I sat on the chair, crossed my legs, hugged my arms, closed my eyes.
Under my closed eyes I saw myself striding over whiteness: I was walking
away leaving no trail behind. I put out my hand, without opening my eyes,
and tried to find the edge of the chair across from me. I couldn't find it. I
stretched out the other hand, again without success, and I sat there, like a
blindman, while the voice from the whiteness shouted out words in various
languages, none of which was mine.

Robert Hilles

A Gradual Ruin

I

The only doctor in town was Tailgate Smith. He walked four miles through deep snow to deliver my Aunt Shirley, who was a blue baby. Had he not turned his head against a gust of wind at the last minute, he would have missed the kerosene lamp my grandfather had left flickering in the kitchen window and would've arrived too late to save Shirley from the breach position. It took some work, but Tailgate turned her around, delivered her, and held her up to the light. My grandmother screamed at Shirley's colour – the other eight babies had been born without the least bit of trouble – but Tailgate put his mouth to Shirley's lips a few times and she slowly turned pink. While he rocked her, everyone watched, as if he could suck the devil out of any one of them and breathe something good in his place.

From then on, whenever someone in the family needed a doctor grandfather yelled for one of his kids to get the *Devil Doctor*. To everyone else, he was still Tailgate Smith, the boy left by his unwed mother on the tailgate of his father's truck.

Shirley was a cranky baby who kept everyone up with her crying. Even when she was older, she seldom sat still for very long, as if what Tailgate blew into her left her jumpy and anxious. When she was fifteen, she ran off with a boy from Dryden who had bad teeth and breath to match. Every day for several weeks he'd drive up to her school in his old Ford half-ton, shirt sleeves nearly to his shoulder in a tight roll. Shirley would look for his dull red truck as she stood with several friends smoking cigarettes and talking about boys. She was in no hurry to get home even though she knew she'd catch hell. She was used to catching hell.

"Hey Shirl," he'd say, then lean out the window to smile at her.

"Don't he look *good*," she'd say to my mother, or whoever was standing there, not really expecting an answer.

Shirley liked it that he didn't yell obscene things like the other men from the mill who drove by. He'd just rev his engine a few times to show off, then drive away slowly as if he was in no hurry to leave her behind.

The night before she left for good, she didn't come home at all. Her parents had no phone, so her father mumbled to himself for several hours, finally taking out his Bible to read long passages aloud, each word uttered through tense lips.

Late that night, he woke my mother with a sudden outburst "The devil's got her. I knew he would. He's got her."

He said it so loudly my mother covered her ears, and as she turned to the window facing her bed she caught the moon spying on their lives as if it too knew this would happen all along.

Shirley showed up with Danny about noon the next day acting as if nothing out of the ordinary had happened. She slipped a cigarette from her mouth and said as loud as can be, *This here is Danny, we're getting married*, as if anybody had a right to make such a statement. Grandfather didn't say anything at first, just looked through her as if she wasn't there. Shirley took a drag on her cigarette, and for a moment it looked as if she would blow the smoke in her father's face. Instead, she held the smoke inside, daring him to do something, if not for her benefit, then for Danny's. Grandfather walked slowly up to her and hit her full in the face with such a hard blow from his closed fist that my mother heard the crack of bone, though she wasn't certain whose. Everyone froze as Shirley dropped to the floor. When her head hit the linoleum her cigarette went flying from her hand and she let out a dull moan, then kicked at her father's legs. He looked down at her as if she were dying and he could put her out of misery with one quick kick to the stomach. Before he could move, Danny caught him full on the jaw with a right hook and knocked him back against the kitchen counter. Dishes flew as he thrashed to catch his balance.

When he righted himself, Grandfather held a large frying pan in his right hand. Danny grabbed his arm, twisted the weapon free, and forced him to his knees. He was about to kick him in the chest when Shirley, still lying on floor, caught his leg and held him back. Everything went quiet then.

Danny stepped back from Grandfather, and Shirley got to her feet. The left side of her face was red from the blow, the skin beneath her eye already swollen. She wobbled a little on her feet, and Danny helped steady her. They both looked at her father crouched on the floor, then slowly backed toward the door, not taking their eyes off him. When they got inside the truck they both sat breathing heavy, as if they'd just come up a steep hill. Grandfather came out of the house empty-handed. He went to Shirley's side of the truck and stared inside.

She spit at him, and saliva spread across the closed window then slid in sad streaks down the glass. Shirley laughed at his cold stiff face, and Danny stepped hard on the gas. The truck spun gravel all the way to the main road and the trail of dust that drifted back covered grandfather with a grey film. He didn't move for a long time, just dug in his pocket and wiped the dust from his face with a handkerchief. My mother was still in the house, not daring to look out. Her mother straightened the kitchen, picked up dishes scattered all over the floor. Some were shattered into pieces, and as she lifted each shard, careful not to get nicked, the glass caught reflections from the window and gave hard shapes to the afternoon light.

2

My mother kissed God. Not on the cheek like Judas, but a lover's kiss full on the mouth. That was before she took sick and started to talk to herself and had to be sent to the mental hospital in Port Arthur, 300 miles east of Kenora. Before I was born, even before she met my father.

"Just because you can't see heaven when you look into the sky doesn't mean it's not there," she'd say and then smile as if nothing she said could be disputed. That's how she talked after she took sick. Everyone in my family, except my father, referred to her madness as *after your mother took sick*, as if she'd suddenly been laid up with some grand illness worthy of everyone's pity. To my father, though, her strange behaviour was just "your mother's way." His words carried no shame.

My mother claimed that she'd flown to heaven several times in an airplane to visit God. Not on a scheduled flight, but on one available only to those who believed. When I asked her when, she said, "before you were born," as if on the day of my birth the world stopped being miraculous.

Whenever I asked her what God looked like she answered with the authority of first-hand experience. He had broad shoulders, much broader than my father's, and an intelligent smile. But he looked tired from keeping long hours. His eyes were wide apart and set deep in his head. He had soft fingers and his hair was cut short and always neat. His eyes were blue and they lit up after she kissed him. He smiled at her as if surprised. I asked her how God could be surprised, didn't he know everything before it happened.

"He didn't know that I was going to kiss him because I didn't know until that second. I just leaned over and kissed him and then he smiled. Never said a thing. Just smiled and then walked away. We kissed for a long time and I didn't want it to ever stop. His breath was so sweet. Nothing else happened, but after that kiss I knew I was going to like living in heaven."

As far as I knew no one else had ever kissed God or even tried. I thought my mother was bold and special because she'd kissed God right on the lips and hadn't been turned to stone or condemned to hell fire.

I imagined my mother and me flying to heaven and landing on its wide runway. When I was older and no longer believed many of my mother's stories, I still held on to the hope that somewhere beyond the sky, heaven waited balanced on God's broad shoulders.

Jesus knew all along that Judas would betray him, but God never suspected that my mother would lean over and kiss him. But she did, and then she took sick. Perhaps her madness was the only way God could get his power back.

At least that's what I believed when I was growing up. God turned my mother mad to punish her. I didn't learn the truth until I was twenty and then only by accident. Perhaps some things are meant to be hidden forever and if uncovered they turn the world askew. But that comes later. For now her story begins with a blue baby and a bitter snow storm just outside Dryden. The year is 1931 and my mother is two years old.

3

Shirley never married Danny, just lived with him for a while in a small apartment over the Fonda Café in Dryden. They didn't have much furniture, and no one from her family dared to visit. Only Alice came by once, after work. The two giggled while Shirley served tea, as if still playing house. They half expected their father to poke his head inside the door and tell them to get back to their chores, but this was different; even if they felt awkward with each other for the first time, at least what lay ahead had to be better than what they had left behind.

Shirley was never without a cigarette, then, and she slipped one from her mouth to lean into the round grey Formica table. "I don't miss him. Just mom and you, sis." She looked sadly at my mother as if she wanted to save her, as if she should be able to but didn't know how.

"What does he say about me?"

"He doesn't. Most of the time he pretends you don't exist, though I can tell he's hurting bad."

Shirley smiled at that, and her eyes lit up. "I'm glad he's hurting."

"The other day he was talking about the day you were born and how much it snowed that day, as if that was what was important. Then he went quiet for a moment, then he said, 'She shouldn't have lived, all blue like that. She was born dead as sure as anything. God meant for her to be dead, that's what blue means. That damn *Devil Doctor* had no business bringing her back to life like that, no wonder she has the devil in her, that's what he blew inside her, or else he put her soul back in wrong. She's never been right. Not since that day.'"

"He's the one that's not right. Babies are born blue all the time, any doctor could tell him that. Just means I wasn't getting enough oxygen, that's all. He thinks he can do or say anything. He ain't my father anymore. He's the one who's the devil, not me. You tell him that." Shirley took a drag on her cigarette and inhaled deeply.

Alice sipped some tea and nodded at her sister. "You got it better here, away from all his crazy thinking."

"He should let a person be. Even the Bible says that, if he read it closely, or looked at something besides the *Book of Revelations*. He just wants to see the world burn up in a sea of fire, that's what'll make him happy. He needs to control everything and have the last word, as if between God and him no one else should get a word in."

Both sisters laughed and sipped more tea, holding their warm cups as if all that was good in their lives was right there in their trembling hands.

Danny came in from work and headed to the fridge for a beer. His hands were covered with scars from work at the mill. He sat at the kitchen table and in between sips of beer he asked Shirley what was for supper.

"Soup," she said, and laughed.

"Fuck we always have soup." He took another swig, then stood. "I'm going to the Café." He was out the door before either woman could say good-bye.

Alice stayed a while longer, until she noticed the time. "Jesus, I better go before Dad starts to wonder where I am."

"You're not still letting him tell you what to do, are you?"

"Jesus no, I just don't want him ranting all night or taking it out on mother."

Shirley stood at the door just staring at Alice. "I'm so glad you came."

They kissed quickly on the cheek, their perfumed faces nudged cheek to cheek just briefly before parting, their eyes held tightly closed.

Danny turned cruel when he drank, and one night he came home drunk with a waitress from the Fonda Café. The woman looked at Shirley and turned to leave, but Danny pulled her to him and only nodded at Shirley.

"You can either join in or leave," he said, his eyes red and narrowed.

"Fuck you, asshole!" Shirley pushed him against the living-room wall. He lifted a hand to strike her but she was already out the door, slamming it so hard she heard something smash to the floor. She drove off in Danny's truck, circled the few streets of Dryden until the gas ran low, then she parked in his stall at the paper mill and slept.

In the morning, Danny was still asleep, but the waitress was gone. Shirley watched Danny as she packed.

Several times he opened his eyes, and once he said, "What the hell are you doing? You can't leave me. You've got nowhere to go."

"Anywhere is better than here. Besides you're a shit. I've had enough shit in my life. I'm not taking any more."

Danny motioned to get up, but he grabbed his head in pain and lay back down.

"Don't bother looking for me, either. We're through. Get it. Through. There aren't any second chances with me."

She looked around the bedroom once to remember where she had started from and left. She didn't slam the door this time but eased it shut. Danny didn't hear a thing.

Greg Hollingshead

Daughter of God

It was the sound of frightened cattle that woke him. He sat up. The sound had come from below. There was no light. The rain was not so heavy but it had not stopped being rain. On the heels of his hands and feet, crablike, a rubber crab, he moved down out of the sumac, closer to the edge. He was still moving when something astonishing happened. A few hundred yards below, and it was no more, a ball of light travelled fifty feet across a surface of moving water. Upstream in the flash of it he glimpsed a barn, downstream a narrow clapboard farmhouse, water all around. In the next illumination – the light travelling the same path – he could see, on the far side of the barn, close to it, a tree down on a hydro pole, or on the wire strung on that pole, weighing the pole obliquely, practically into the water.

The fireballs were travelling the wire.

Now he saw from inside or possibly from behind the barn a flickering light. He saw the beam of a flashlight sweep across an upstairs window and inside wall of the farmhouse. Another travelling ball of electricity, and this time he saw the light of it reflected in both front windows of the house. In the darkness then he could see the flickering from the barn reflected there too. Not clapboard, the narrow house wasn't clapboard but sheathed in battered aluminum siding. Battered and peeling. Sections missing to expose tar paper, itself peeling. He could see that the water was no more than halfway to the floor of the front porch. There was a car in the yard, an old Plymouth or Dodge. Water to the hubcaps. As for the barn, it had been built on an elevation possibly four feet higher than the ground the house stood on. People with their

monkey heritage, sprightly climbers, had given advantage to those low phleg-
matic grazers their cattle. The water had not reached the foundations of the
barn. Suddenly the beam of the flashlight appeared on the farmhouse porch.
A bolt travelled the wire, and he saw that the flashlight was in the hand of a
tall woman in a white nightgown, and she could have been her. She wasn't
but she could have been. The flashlight switched off and the next bolt from
the wire showed her standing on the porch looking across at the barn and at
the maybe thirty yards of two-foot-deep water. In the next flash she was turning away from this sight and in the next there was no one on the porch.

He could only think that the river had overflowed its banks this far up
because, as he had surmised, some nest of flood debris had created a dam
farther down, at a narrowing of the ravine. A blockage of flow he had passed
unknowing in the night. He looked to the farmhouse and to the barn. The
bolt might have been a Tourists Welcome sign, randomly flashing. Welcome
to what? A floodplain-terrace subsistence farm nobody poor enough to be
willing to work could afford to buy. Did not even own a truck.

These would be renters.

The fireballs along the wire had ended. Only darkness but for that light
from the barn. The rain still coming down. And then the front door of the
house opened and the flashlight came straight out. Straight down the porch
steps and across the water, the beam slashed heavily by rain. He could see
that the nightgown had been replaced by a man's shirt and she was wading
hard against the current towards the slope to the barn, which slope she
climbed to throw open the doors, causing a great white cloud of smoke to
issue forth and the glow inside to brighten, and he understood that the flickering from inside was not a lantern or emergency lighting: the downed pole
had started a fire. He saw her pull the shirt to her face against the smoke, and
he saw that with the shirt she wore only underpants, underpants and high-
top sneakers, and then he saw her go in.

He waited for a long time. Three minutes, anyway. She came out leading
a cow by a rope. She led it down the slope and into the water. It didn't want
to go, it was pulling back against the rope, but she was strong and went with
it through the water all the way to the porch steps. The cow was reluctant to

climb the steps, but she tugged and shouted at it in a loud, mannish voice, and eventually she got it into the house. Now in the light from the barn, the barn doors standing open, he could see that there were eight or nine cows outside, crowded before the slope, mooing and bellowing. She came back for another, and this time four others followed of their own accord, single file. All this time the water rising. He could see this from the way the cows stumbled sooner now against the porch steps, there being more of those steps concealed by water. The third and last time she came back there were two cows and one yearling calf remaining on the slope. The cattle inside the barn were screaming. She pushed past the three on the slope and tried to go into the barn, but the smoke overpowered her and she came out with her hands on her knees, choking. The two cows meanwhile, sorrowful and disgruntled at her neglect, had gone into the water, but once in they did not know where to go and wandered to the right (probably the direction they always went in, along the river), but the water was deeper there, and the current picked them up and swept them, slowly only at first, around and past the house, and he could hear them mooing as they sped away upon the flood.

Now she was leading the calf toward the house, and he could see the arduousness of her task. The water was above her waist, and the calf was floating and swung round past her, and though she kept a grip, the current seemed likely to snatch it as it had the others and pull her with it. But she held on and after great exertion she got the calf to the porch, now level with the water. A cow was standing with its head out the door of the farmhouse, bellowing encouragement. Another was standing on the porch silently watching. And then as she pulled the calf stumbling up the steps, the cow half out the door still bellowing, the one on the porch, stepping backwards, fell through in a sudden eruption of boards, its rear legs jammed astride struts. Piteously it cried out, its front hooves scrabbling. The woman pushed the other cow inside and got the calf in too. She closed the door on them both, and with the rope she had used for the calf she tried to haul the foundering cow out of the hole in the porch and could not. After much effort, nothing changing, he saw her kneel at the edge of the hole and examine the cow's rear legs. Even from this distance it appeared the left was broken. The question then was, Did she have a gun? It seemed that she did not, though this surprised him. A twenty-gauge surely, at least. But right away she turned from the cow back to the barn, and as she did so he became aware once more of the screams of the cattle still inside. A soundtrack of agony to this starlit scene.

The barn was glowing now like some great wooden lantern, every slat and rive and knothole a perfect delineation of light. The flames tonguing up over the tin eaves. The woman was halfway to it, the water mid-chest, her forearm across her eyes, slowed in her progress not only by the current but by the heat, when the structure exploded into pure flame, the wall nearest him erupting in a solid sheet of yellow, and vividly he saw her stagger back in the water, and even he on his prospect could feel the heat. The flames were so bright he looked down at himself, at the shadows of his rubber knees against the illumination of his rubber chest. He looked around and saw the range and extent of the sumac grove behind him. He looked below to the water and saw some of the cargo of the flood: tree branches, a surface and corner of some small outbuilding or shed, a drowned fawn, an oil drum, all eddying briefly before sweeping on. In the gravelly turf where he sat, the brightness made a ragged thin shadow of a seam that ran on either side of him and passed behind, and he moved back up beyond it and into the sumacs once more. The flames of the burning barn reflected off steam that now rose from the water all about it. They lit the rain and they lit the flood, which had reached the lower branches of trees that grew on the far slope of the ravine. They also lit the trees that had been torn from the earth or from shallow balance on rock and now churned revolving upon that roiling, fast-sliding surface.

For a long time he sat and gazed at the house and the burning barn. After an hour he could see that the water had reached the sills of the first-floor windows. He could see the force of it as it reared back foaming against itself and eddied wide at the corners. He was watching the Plymouth, the water now past the tops of the wheel wells, when slowly, as if someone had climbed into the driver's seat, the old car backed up, swung round, and entered the current. Accelerated past the house and was gone. And then, in the light of the burning barn, he saw a further remarkable sight. A wave of water perhaps two feet high, more like a low wall or step than a wave, its own flotsam-charged height behind it, came down the ravine. He saw it before it reached the farm-house. The barn foundations deflected the force of it, but as it came through, the flood rose three-quarters up the front door of the farmhouse, halfway up the windows on the ground floor. He had not had time to wonder at this before the seam in the sod at his feet opened and everything the other side of it fell away with a great soft sigh of gravel parting from itself, a languid splash. In the light of the barn he saw a mighty wave with a solitary travelling peak of yellowish foam run temporary crosswise interference to the main surge of the flood and splash up almost to the eaves of the farmhouse.

"Lordy me," he whispered.

On heels of hands and feet he shifted higher still into the sumacs. There he imagined a weight of uprooted timber and other flood litter gathered upstream against the bridge at the power-line road, making a dam. He could not remember what kind of bridge it was up there, but he knew it was no culvert, and he imagined it giving way and a great dark wave of water and debris sweeping down the ravine taking everything not rooted fast in the shallow sediment.

He marvelled that the house had continued to hold. Surely at any moment the frame would shift and tip off its foundations and be borne away upon the flood.

She was wearing the nightgown again. She opened an upper window and also the other window on that side of the farmhouse that he could see. As she was opening the second window a cow stuck its head out the first and uttered a great moo into the night.

All this in the light, like day, of the burning barn. The sheets of the tin roof curling and crumpling and melting. The flaming walls beginning to buckle and cave.

He wondered if she had dragged that cow up the stairs or if it had climbed of its own accord. He wondered how many cows she had managed to drag or coax up and how many had been left swimming on the ground floor, bumping into floating furniture, into each other, the water rising, their muzzles lifted in the firelit darkness to rattle the brass-and-cut-glass chandelier. How well he knew these country interiors, though not so well when half filled with river water and cows. He wondered if in such a circumstance a cow would bite. If she would think, My sister offers necessary purchase, why should she be wanting to climb on me? He supposed that she would, that anything would.

After that the level of the flood as measurable against the side of the house receded slightly. To him it seemed that having withstood this much the wretched structure would survive, the narrowness of the front of it combined with the deflective upstream elevation of the barn a double advantage perhaps. Not without some disappointment he moved farther up into the sumacs, where as he slept all he had witnessed became previous fantastic dreams of brightness and dark, or memories of a faerie spectacle too outlandish for human eyes.

What woke him was the complete cessation of rain, but it was dark yet, the stone enclosure of the barn glowing ruby and beige in domes of rain-dimpled ash, like catalytic heaters just cooling, and he slept again. When he woke next it was early morning, an hour, he judged, to dawn. The sky was heavy, but nothing was falling out of it. He looked below and saw the river already shrunk to merely brimming its banks. That downstream obstruction too must have given way. He considered the scene. The barn's foundations held smoking ashes, now grey. Along the far wall among twisted sheets of tin he could see the carcasses of cows melted blue-black like slag. Smoking too, a darker smoke. He could see the unmarked small tract where, among muddy bent-looking pieces of farm machinery, the Plymouth must have been parked. He could see the house, its siding peeled back in narrow strips of metal that flapped a little in the breezes. The mud line halfway to the first-storey lintels.

It was a pleasure to be moving once more in daylight. He found a way around the newly sheer embankment and slid down to the smoothness of the ravine floor. Plodding through that sticky, puddled yellow silt he saw beer cans and pieces of plastic packaging and clumps of grass and other trash caught on bushes a short distance above his head. To his satisfaction – signs and portents everywhere it seemed – a spruce had come to rest across the raging channel a short distance downstream from the house. Carefully, stepping through mud-caked branches, he crossed the racing flood.

From the house, as he approached, no sound. From the barn the upwind stink of wet smoke, charred offal. The cow that had gone through the porch had drowned there, its carcass impossibly twisted in a drift of silt against the front wall of the house, the broken leg still caught. The screen door mud-plastered wide open against the wall. The front window smashed either by the animal in its thrashing whether living or dead or by something else. The front door stood open, the downstairs a sorry mess. It was a snapped-off fir that had come through that window, just short enough, once inside, to clear the sill. Three cows stood in the stinking muck, crowded by its branches into one half of the space. Flanks scored. Gazing bleakly. Two at him, one out the silted window on the river side. Two more lay drowned in a lacerated heap on a collapsed chesterfield against the downriver wall.

He climbed the stairs. A hognose snake had wrapped itself around the muddy banister. He poked at it with the gun but it just looked at him. She was not in her bed. The calf was down the narrow hall, eating wallpaper. When it saw Troyer it bowed its head to the floor and picked up something in its mouth. As if it were a pup and wanted him to play. Troyer stepped forward to take the thing. A small stuffed bear, of calf-chewed fur, losing straw. Black glass eyes. He pushed the calf aside and looked into the small room there. A low bed, no child. He slipped the bear into the pocket of his jacket.

In the first room, where the bed had been lain in, were two cows, one sitting, one standing. Both animals seemed to appraise him. He found her hunched in the nightgown, inside the closet. He lifted her chin with the tip of the barrel. She wasn't beautiful. She wasn't young either, particularly. Red-nosed. Complexion poor. A certain congenital weakness about the bones of the face. A thickness or heaviness through the eyes. The kind of woman's face that bore too strongly upon it the print of her father's, him being the kind of man you would not, if you could help it, have anything to do with at all.

Overcome by a shaking, her eyes flat with terror, lips silently going.

"Come out of there," Troyer said. "It's no occasion for prayer. There's no Devil, you know, just people, and if that's any consolation, we need to have a talk."

Suzette Mayr

Toot Sweet Matricia

The legend goes like this:

A lazy horny fisherman, classy as a goat and smelling as good, finds what he thinks is a seal skin. This fisherman is not very clever – no one on land would ever marry him.

The selkie sunbathes naked on the rocks; her skin tucked away in what she thinks is a good hiding place. The fisherman hides the seal skin from her, and the selkie is forced to be his wife.

These are the rules.

The selkie makes a wistful but loyal wife and no one in the neighbourhood asks questions. She dutifully suckles her babies, her husband, but her eye is always on the sea, or the lake, or the plastic swimming pool, or the goldfish bowl where Darth Vader the 75-cent feeder goldfish blows "I love you" over and over.

Her two-year-old's fingerprinted glass of lemonade makes her so homesick she wants to puke. All her children and her children's children have webbed fingers and toes.

But the day comes when the selkie decides to give all the clothes in the attic to the Salvation Army, or sweep up the mouse turds in the basement once and for all, or clean out the ancient dirt in the upstairs closet, and then she finds the trunk, or the canvas sack, or the plastic Safeway bag and inside, where her husband's hidden it, her selkie's skin. Suddenly she's gone out to her yoga lesson and strangely enough forgotten her yoga mat.

The horror is she never looks back.

Crueler men burn the skins. These wives are doomed. Prozac, scotch on the rocks, varicose vein strippings, house renovations, feigned and real illnesses can't stop the mourning, the inner burning. These are the kinds of wives who one day set their houses on fire with themselves inside, or in a matter of hours turn into lesbians, or slash themselves with their husband's razors just so they feel something.

I feel something.

Putting on the skin when it's not really yours is like putting both arms into a bog and drawing up pieces of corpse. Ring fingers still wearing rings, arms, palms and hands (these are harder to identify), legs severed at calf and mid-thigh. I have found no heads yet, not yet felt the horror of hair twine around my fingers, then yawn of a mouth, a thick flopping tongue. Body bits perfectly preserved.

I look in the mirror at the skin around my shoulders, draped over my head. I look like my grandmother.

Matricia said that with the chemical straightener, my hair felt like the stings on the bow of her violin. The afro roots of my hair winding and colliding from my scalp, the straightened ends down my shoulders, dry and crisp as winter twigs. She fingered and stroked my hair, buried her hands in its coils while I kissed her breasts. I tugged at her nipples with my teeth through the layers of her sweater, her blouse, her bra. Her armpits seaweed-fragrant.

Her body smells like perfume and sweat. Matricia is a very black woman, much blacker than me, her hair scraped back from her face and into an elaborate coil, and I picture the excruciating smoothness of her inner thighs. I dragged her up piece by piece from the bogs of memory and horror. The smell of her. The smell of her hair and my skin.

I try to lose myself to the river by filling my pockets with stones from my mother's rock garden.

You'll only rip the seams of the pockets, my sister says. It'll never work.

Detergent foam, empty pop cans, floating cigarette butts swirl my ankles. The denim of my jeans sucks at my thighs.

Don't think you're getting out of washing the dishes! my sister calls.

I smell tears; they smell the same as water-fear. That horrifying lurch when my head is pulled under and a long fluid gasp fills my lungs. My mother drags my sputtering body through unnaturally bright pool water, and when she lets go I sink and inhale the water like rose petals. For years we did this every Sunday, she teaching me how to swim, me foundering, flailing, my hair afroed from my head in all directions, dry even under water and strung-out from chlorine, my eyes bitter-red and bulging.

I have watched too many television documentaries about the Titanic. This is why I hate the water. The documentaries never show the body remains; pieces of bodies just outside the picture, inedible chunks of skull, the flat, silver eyes of fish ogling the newly sunk banquet, the flat, silver lips shredding and tearing away at the sad skin under the soaked fabric, the taut necks, the soft flesh of human bellies. The camera focusses instead on a well-preserved shoe. A barnacled chandelier. A brooch filled with hair in the shape of flowers.

The tv camera never shows the people who live where the Titanic sank. The ones who stare up through the water's surface with the faces of the drowned, the ones who crunch through bones like sharks.

I look into a cup of tea and see my eyes flat, silvered with salt-water cataracts. Submersion, immersion, mouth an open, wavering cavity. There is even danger in dish-water. Drowned angry children hissing through the drains sing me to sleep.

The water licks and licks at my sister's boots. Every step she takes swirls whirlpools. My body floats face-down in the river, stopped by the branches of trees caught on my clothes. The stones in my pockets don't hold me down.

You can stop faking it, my sister says.

She watches my blue lips sputter awake when the paramedic with prematurely grey hairs in his nose gives me mouth-to-mouth.

He's gay, you dummy, she says. He's gayer than Paree.

A year later I marry the paramedic. On our wedding night at the Royal Wayne Hotel he pushes it away and says, Phew! That reeks!

I get up from the bed and pretend to steal another motel soap. When you have webs between fingers, you can't cry.

And what if you are the kind of woman who slips from world to world, slides through sewers and between the walls, propelled by will alone? This is not just a metaphor for a black woman with a white father, a lesbian who likes a little cock now and then, a vegetarian who craves Alberta beef. This is a question of heredity.

If you are the kind of woman who slips from world to world, slides through sewers and between the walls, propelled by will alone, the more you travel the in-betweens, the more you play an either/or tourist, the more you realize home was never really home.

When Matricia reached the shore, pulled her blubbered body up onto the jagged rocks, she peeled off her skin. Not like a banana because you can't peel banana skin back on. More like the ripping of a membrane, a hymen; a hymen can be unripped. Her skin tears from her body, the grey silver black speckles of her slick skin rip away like so much sausage pelt and there she stands. Her black skin, not black like coal or chocolate or velvet, her black skin, black.

Matricia pulls on her pants-suit and Italian shoes. Tucks her skin in her bag. My blackness in the middle of the white prairie makes me an easy target. My marriage, job are water-soaked; panic flush, slip of fingers, suck of whirlpool. Vulnerable desire.

Matricia paints her nails algae green.

$\boxed{\text{B}}$ut then there are the other women in my family.

Never before in the history of this family, says my grandmother, have the women had to fake orgasms.

My grandmother strokes the scaly patch of skin on her wrist. The scales glitter like seed-pearls, scratch like sand-paper against our faces. She also has scales behind her ears, in the small of her back.

Eczema, says my mother. She will not believe anything not in the science books.

Selkie blood, says my grandmother, and she lights another cigarette, her mouth pursed fish-like against the paper tube.

Of course mother won't believe this either. There's no ocean where she comes from. She was born in Saskatchewan. Grandmother's skin the colour of the old teak coffee table.

The scaly patches prove love, my grandmother says.

What they never talk about in that selkie story, says my grandmother, is the bed. How important the bed is. If the man's nonexistent in bed, then why would you stay?

According to the rules, if my grandmother, being a selkie, ever retrieved the skin she would leave immediately. But she's the one who left the water, saw the liquid muscles of her future lover's forearms, the silver bubbles trapped among the hairs. Watched her fisherman up through the waves and fell in love with the vibrations in his throat, the cracked skin on his fisher-man's hands. And he stared back at her in water, couldn't believe his eyes.

Mixed marriages never work people say, but my grandmother stumbled up into air, her addiction to cigarettes and wearing men's trousers more a problem than the fact that she enjoyed her fish still gasping. Scales, gut, and open fish mouth pulled down her throat.

Toot sweet, she says and smacks her lips.

She kept her skin like a wedding gown wrapped in muslin, stored in cedar to keep away the bugs. Kept the key on a chain around her throat and as far as we could tell, never opened the chest again for as long as she lived.

I, on the other hand, open her chest again. And again. And again.

❧

Matricia slides in and around and among the neighbourhoods like a crocodile in a sewer looking for me. Too much time in the world and she looks at her watch.

Matricia comes for me. She smells exactly like the ocean.

We were the only two black kids in the junior high school, Matricia and I, and then her father kidnapped her and I was the only one. Or so the legend went.

The legend goes like this: We are the only two black girls in the school. Matricia wants to be my friend, but this is against the rules. I ignore her. She disappears. Her father stole her, everyone says. My horror mouth open because I didn't save her. I remember the dandruff flecks in her hair, the green tinge on her fingernails, the seaweed smell of her skin.

❧

I will eventually be kidnapped by water for good. This is how all women in my family die. When the water finds me, when it inflates my lungs, it will be crammed with the faces of drowned relatives. Women in our family avoid river banks, cliffs, wave pools, backyard fish ponds, sinks too full of water, they move to the centre of islands, high on mountains, buy dishwashers, but water always finds us.

I am not safe anywhere.

I kick my rubber boots hard against the polished floor of the museum, the security guards run, their basset-hound jowls and full bellies bouncing, navy-blue security jackets streaming past glass cases, marbles of naked women, paintings of ornate gardens, and they try to grab me by the collar of my shirt, my sleeves and legs, try to pull me from the canvas-painted oily storm. I will hang in the water for hours before they can retrieve my body. My pockets filled with priceless, deformed pearls.

I die for love. Matricia, body sleek in waves. I die for love.

Her skin is the same. Her skin is the same as mine. She is my ghost. Digging for treasure, I found mismatched pieces, assembled and resuscitated her. She tastes like licorice. Water beings always have the faint aftertaste of licorice. I have tasted licorice myself on their lips when they come up from between my thighs to kiss me.

I wanted to steal her skin. Force her to marry me.

When Matricia left, I got up from my bed and pretended to steal another motel soap.

They say fish never blink; selkies don't cry. I wait for the diamonds to come trickling from my eyes. I have not been a maid since I was sixteen and she stole my maidenhead.

In love with the ocean through my rubber boots.

Asthma returns with a splash on the cheek. I am allergic to hairy animals. This is how I know she is for real.

And now girls can say No Thanks from the safety of their mermaids' tails or selkie skins. Dust sifts through the air. A desire for the parts of other women. Skin brown even in the womb, eyes grey until they ripen into Caribbean brown. An appetite for other women. I pull her up piece by piece from the muck and memory. Assemble her into the ex-lover who gave the clothes to the Salvation Army, swept up the mouse turds, cleaned out the closet, who left with my heart in the trunk. Of her car. She comes to life in the prairies, in the murky river that drowns prize begonias.

Toot sweet Matricia. I stretch my lips and blow.

Ken McGoogan

Chasing Safiya

You talk as if Africa were uniform," I said. "As if Ghana and Malawi and Tanzania were interchangeable." It was late afternoon, sweltering hot, and we sat under a colourful umbrella, Safiya, Daniel, and I, on the patio at the New Africa Hotel. We'd been in Dar es Salaam three weeks and I'd grown accustomed to playing Ahriman's advocate in discussing the so-called Otherness of Africa.

"I take your point." Safiya sipped orange squash, which to me always tasted like soda gone flat. "Yet even so, most African countries share attributes or characteristics that they don't share with Canada. Characteristics which, to a Canadian, at least, make them alien, exotic – primordially Other."

"Africa hot, Canada cold," Daniel said. "Africa black, Canada white. Africa outdoors, Canada indoors."

"Africa poor, Canada rich," I said. "Who cares?"

But this was their favourite game and they wouldn't quit.

"Africa is congregating at night to dance and beat drums," Daniel said. "Canada is screaming yourself hoarse at a hockey game."

"We know they're stereotypes, Raff," Safiya said. "Yet Tanzania reminds me that I come from a cold country full of rich white people. Wouldn't Nigeria do the same? Or Ghana?"

"But why focus on differences?" I said. "What about universalities? Those things that as humans we share?"

"Not nearly as much fun," she said. "Though I can see where a visitor accustomed even to the semi-tropics – an American from Florida, say, or

Louisiana – would probably find Africa's palm trees and giant snails less exotic than we do."

"And a Caucasian American from just about anywhere," Daniel said, "would probably have more experience as a visible minority than his Canadian counterpart. And so feel less threatened to discover himself the only white person, for example, in a crowd at the bank or the post office."

"Torontonians excepted," Safiya said. "But nobody who grew up in Canada – black, pink, red, or yellow – would ever feel at home in Africa."

"Surely you knew that before you got here?"

"Yes, but I didn't know that Otherness would teach me so much about myself. That it would throw the recent past into such stark relief."

In Africa, Safiya finally found the courage to confront Taggart Oates – though also he'd returned to Sri Lanka to complete his residency, and no doubt the distance helped.

But I've left too many blanks.

Back in New Delhi, I'd wangled a visa for Tanzania, no problem: I put one hundred American dollars on the right countertop and picked up my visa next day. Daniel, accustomed to African red tape, bribe or no bribe, couldn't get over it: "It's magic."

Again Safiya told him: "Get used to it."

As a citizen of a British Commonwealth country, she didn't require a visa to enter Tanzania. And Daniel already had a residency permit. We flew into Dar es Salaam shortly after midnight. When we stepped out of the plane onto the tarmac, whomp! the humidity hit like mid-day in Delhi. "Dar's at sea level," Daniel said, chuckling at my reaction. "And directly below the equator."

The tiny airport, run-down and over-crowded, looked like an American bus depot except for the uniformed guards carrying rifles and pistols. Six or eight of them strutted around with machine guns.

At customs, an American businessman argued with an official and a guard led him away protesting: "You can't do this to me! I'm American!" I feared a similar welcome, but when I showed my passport and visa, the customs officer grinned and stamped them: "Welcome to Tanzania. Karibu."

We collected our bags, piled into a battered taxi, and made for town, swerving back and forth to avoid the worst potholes. The moon hung huge and white in the sky. Palm trees lined the highway. As we rolled into the city, rattling and bouncing past tin-roof shacks, I caught a whiff of tar and curry. But mainly I was struck by the number of people rambling the streets, and Daniel explained that the sweltering heat had turned Dar into a city of night owls. Safiya was moving in with Daniel at the International School, so they dropped me downtown at the New Africa Hotel.

My first morning in Dar, I made my way to Kariakoo market and purchased a bracelet. Back in my room, I emptied my fabulous green bag, a bag in which once I'd carried expensive Tommy Hilfiger shirts and Reebok runners, and counted fire-worthy souvenirs: Mesa Verde, New York, Las Palmas, Barcelona, Genoa, Rome, Al-Mayadin, Athens, Meteora, Colombo, Galle, Kandy, New Delhi, Udaipur, Jaipur, Agra, Dar es Salaam. Seventeen. And magical places? Mesa Verde, Rome, Meteora, Agra, Udaipur, Kand, and now Dar es Salaam, the legendary Haven of Peace. That made seven.

I was ready. Likewise, Safiya. And Daniel? He'd long since gathered enough mementos, but he was still suffering over Victor. And, as he reminded us one evening at the Palm Beach Hotel: "The time's got to be right. Also the people, the place. Some things you can't force."

"Daniel, I've got a daughter lying in a coma."

We were sitting out front on the patio, drinking beer out of big brown bottles. Safiya said: "Give him time, Raff. If you'd lost a best –"

As she spoke, a large African man stormed out of the hotel carrying a single suitcase, waving his free arm, and yelling at a desk clerk who'd trotted after him: "The Chinvat did this. The signs are everywhere. Didn't I tell you to keep special watch?"

Somebody had ransacked the big man's room, taken clothing, stereo system, pots and pans, the works. Lugging his remaining possessions, and vowing that all of Dar would hear of this carelessness, the furious man huffed over to the adjacent taxi stand, jumped into a cab, and disappeared forever.

Safiya and I looked at each other. If I were going to remain in Dar for more than a couple of weeks, I'd have to move out of the over-priced New Africa

Hotel. Why didn't I move here to the Palm Beach, which was more of a residential hotel, and also just a five-minute walk from the International School? Obviously, I would have to keep a close eye on my souvenirs. But maybe the Golden Flame, and not the Chinvat, had seen to getting me a living space.

At the front desk, the clerk said the angry man had vacated a small suite, but went grim and silent when Safiya said innocently: "Who did he blame? The Chinvat?"

Reluctantly, after Daniel said something ominous in Swahili, the man showed us around the two-room suite. He pointed out the worn furniture, the peeling paint, the stained carpet. I noted the excellence of the location, far from the noisy bar at the front of the hotel, and checked that the air-conditioning worked. Then I slapped down one month's rent and threw in an extra twenty dollars.

In Dar es Salaam, most Westerners live in housing supplied by companies or institutions. To find decent accommodation outside this infrastructure is considered impossible. Daniel slapped his forehead: "A two-room suite at the Palm Beach Hotel? I don't believe it."

Safiya laughed at his astonishment. Me, I began to worry: if this twist constituted a Shamanesque miracle, how long might I end up residing at the Palm Beach Hotel? My anxiety increased next day, when Safiya acquired a temporary job. Daniel arrived home from the International School with news that a French teacher had resigned. A Dutch woman in her mid-forties, she'd returned home for a visit and called to say she wouldn't be coming back. The school could keep its bonus.

That afternoon, Safiya visited the headmaster. She couldn't claim qualifications as a teacher but neither could half a dozen other "Europeans" the school had hired locally, most of them spouses of visiting engineers or university professors. Certainly, Safiya spoke French well enough to teach elementary and junior-high students. Besides, she needed the money.

That evening, when she told me about the job, I responded badly: "What? We've got a quest to complete."

"Yes, but we can't set forth without Daniel. And he feels the time's not right."

"The time's right, damn it. Something's wrong with Daniel."

Safiya sighed, shrugged, and showed me her palms: what could we do?

End result? I did a lot of solitary, restless rambling in the downtown streets of Dar es Salaam, where instead of highrises you find a riot of first-floor shops in low-lying buildings, most of them owned by hard-working "Asians" – Patel's Canned Foods, Chandwani's Shoes, Dipti's Fine Fabrics – and carrying goods imported from China or India, colourful saris and silks and knickknacks. I remember chasing the whine of a muezzin around street corners and down back alleys to discover an ancient mosque I would never manage to find again.

But the people who thronged those streets, I remember: women carrying babies on their backs or jugs and baskets and bundles of firewood on their heads, most of them wearing wrap-around khangas, brightly coloured and boldly patterned, while others, despite the heat, wore black. The men wore white caftans and rimless cloth caps, Muslims; or else leisure suits with short sleeves, the secular middle class; and still others sported western clothes, cuffed trousers and frayed white shirts rolled up at the sleeve, the ubiquitous working poor. I remember these men standing beneath palm trees in groups of eight or ten, waiting for buses, while the lucky few zoomed around on "fix" bicycles they'd created from spare parts.

At the sprawling Kariakoo Market, a chaotic city block of narrow walkways and makeshift stalls, men in khaki shorts and torn T-shirts sat cross-legged on mats and tried to interest shoppers in buying stalks of sugar cane or newspaper cones full of peanuts, and the air hung heavy with spices and smoke that rose from charcoal burners over which half a dozen men held sticks strung with fresh meat, and from a distant corner you'd hear the squawking of chickens, or the voice of a man crying out prices in Swahili, dropping them slowly, reluctantly, incredulous and finally angry, unable to comprehend how a prospective buyer could pass up such a bargain: "Tatu! Tatu shilingi!!"

I remember sitting under a shade umbrella on the terrace of the New Africa Hotel, drinking orange squash while reading *The Daily News* from beginning to end. Daniel had drawn my attention to People's Forum, a letters page stranger than any I'd yet encountered, and also to Action Line, a column that supposedly "solves problems, gives answers, cuts red tape, and stands up for your rights," but always ended up reiterating the government line.

For an American, reading *The Daily News* was like looking into a funhouse mirror. You'd encounter these bizarre reflections and distorted images of yourself. A wire-service article treated an economic summit held in Europe. The story said nothing untoward, but an illustration done locally depicted the leaders of the G7, the American president prominent among them. Above this, in seventy-two point, boldface type, the headline blared: "Club of the Rich."

The Otherness of Africa. It surfaced in *The Daily News*, but also I remember food shortages – traipsing from shop to shop in the heat, hunting a loaf of bread and admitting finally that today none existed in Dar. I remember the "mwizis" or thieves and the penny-pinching Danish engineer who, believing his house secure, rejected offers from three different askaris to guard it. He returned home after two days on safari to find the place cleaned out.

I remember the humidity, the stuffiness of the library in the late afternoon, where I'd gone to hunt references to the Golden Flame but found none, and sweat rolling down my back in rivulets until the sky cracked open and down would come the rain, falling so hard I couldn't hear myself think. The pounding rain would turn streets and back alleys into seaways and suddenly stop. The clouds would disperse and the sun come out. Rain and hot sun, rain and hot sun.

How did Daniel put it? To live in Dar was to live in a greenhouse. The climate created a nether-world of frangipani trees and cactus gardens, of palm trees and baobabs and bougainvilleas, of flat-topped acacias, papaya trees, lemon trees, and a tree whose bean-filled pods Daniel turned into noisy maracas. Too, I remember the fruit: how you could buy a fresh papaya, halve it and fill it with chunks of mango, banana, orange, grapefruit, tangerine or passion fruit. You could squeeze a lemon over this concoction and call it lunch.

But tropicality has a downside. To the heat and humidity, other life forms have adapted better than humans. Slugs and snails grow as big as your fist and snakes as big around as your arm. Shiny, black beetles reach golf-ball size, and no matter how I scrubbed the kitchen counter, every morning I'd find columns of ants marching back and forth between cupboard and window.

Some of the mosquitoes carried malaria. I'd spray my bedroom before I retired, trying not to think of what I was doing to my lungs. For the rest I'd rely on the geckos, those finger-sized lizards that cling to the ceilings and walls. Never mind that sometimes I'd awake in the middle of the night to a flurry of activity on my bare arm or a skittering across my cheek. I loved the geckos because they decimated my real enemies: the ants, the flies, the ticks, and those lethal mosquitoes.

That left only the sundry spiders, most horribly those grey-brown tarantulas with fist-sized bodies and eight sturdy legs twinkling with hair. Think dazzling mobility. Think all-star broken-field runners. I saw this for myself one evening – an evening I'd been dreading – when, attracted by the light, a tarantula skittered under the front door into Daniel's ground-floor apartment. It scuttled across the tile floor into the centre of the living room and stopped dead, antennae twitching, suddenly aware of our presence.

First impulse: get your feet off the floor. Second impulse? Daniel cried: "The broom!"

As he dashed into the kitchen, Safiya said: "Poor thing."

The tarantula scooted halfway up a wall and waited, pulsating. Daniel returned with the broom, swung and missed: whack! I've mentioned the spider's speed and mobility? Whoosh! It raced down the wall and disappeared under the sofa.

No way we could leave it there, because what would it not do in the night? From the kitchen, with noticeable reluctance, Safiya fetched a bottle of insect spray. She handed it to Daniel and sadly took the broom: "Do we have to do this?"

He sighed loudly. She stationed herself at one end of the couch and nodded her unhappy readiness. From the other end, Daniel began spraying. And now I picked up on the tarantula's baleful intelligence. The creature understood that these humans meant to kill it. From beneath the couch, enraged by the relentless spraying, the spider exuded waves of malevolence. I couldn't believe how much spraying it withstood, never mind how much it hated us. I yearned to jump up and cry, "Wait!"

But I remembered how, in my waking vision, that's precisely what I'd done: jumped to my feet and cried out. This whole scene had evolved differently. Where now, for example, was Daniel's friend Nathan? Yet I didn't dare act.

The tarantula remained the central event and I restrained myself. Perhaps, by not rescuing the spider, I would change the future just enough that Safiya wouldn't disappear while sailing? I didn't like my chances, but neither did I enjoy many options. The tarantula made a break for it, came skittering across the floor, zigging and zagging – but with far less energy than before. Whap! Whap! Safiya nailed it on her third slam: WHAP!

She called it "murder" and felt guilty for days. Every time we sat drinking cold beer, she'd say: "Did we really have to kill that tarantula, do you think? Couldn't we have just driven it out the door?"

The Otherness of Africa, then: omnipresent, impossible to ignore. Physical, certainly, but also psychological – and, yes, spiritual. And if, for Safiya, this Otherness cast the past few weeks into relief, it did the same for me. Evenings, when they weren't taking Swahili classes, Daniel and Safiya would stroll over to the Palm Beach Hotel and together we'd drink beer on the patio. Sometimes, looking over at Safiya, I could hardly bear the proximity: so near and yet so far. Daily, she grew more lovely. I began to wonder whether her distant nearness didn't constitute part of the quest, which I'd come to regard as a torture test – a particularly pitiless finale.

Behroze offered a clarification: "Love is the fire, and sighs the smoke."

The poet Robert Southwell. At least Behroze hadn't abandoned me completely. But, oh, I was burning, all right. Obsessively, and in the temporary absence of Taggart, I analyzed the bond between Safiya and Daniel Lafontaine. One evening, when a normal person would have been too far away, I heard her whisper: "You can't imagine how good it feels, Dan, to be back with you, just the two of us."

"Is it me?" he'd responded. "Or is it just being shut of Taggart?"

"Don't be silly," Safiya said.

Even so, my heart began pounding. If Daniel was right, I could still hope. Later that evening, in the washroom, I said to him: "It's amazing how quickly you two have got back together."

He eyed me strangely and said: "We have a task to accomplish."

"Approach the Shaman, you mean."

He nodded, gauging my reaction. Obviously, only one of us could finally approach with Safiya. Playfully, I punched his shoulder and said: "No doubt you're meant to set forth, anyway."

We both laughed, more friends than enemies, and I said: "Why do you think, metaphysically speaking, Taggart got involved?"

"We didn't know enough. He was brought in to teach us. I wouldn't worry about Taggart."

"I think you underestimate him."

"Joka la mdimu linalinda watanudo." Daniel smiled grimly, then translated: "The dragon of the lime tree guards against those who pluck the fruits."

"Meaning the Shaman will take care of Taggart? I wonder."

But these proverbs, I realized, formed part of an unconscious strategy. Daniel had been more hurt than he knew by Safiya's refusal to come with him to Africa. And her subsequent departure with Taggart? He wasn't ready to explore that pain.

In dealing intimately with Taggart, then, Safiya remained alone. She recognized that her relationship with him was a self-indulgent soap opera. Yet even now she couldn't find a way permanently to free herself. After the debacle in Agra, that horrific drunken scene in the Indian restaurant when I'd punched him out, Safiya might have cried, "Enough!"

Instead, when Taggart sobered up and took responsibility, contritely begging forgiveness, Safiya gave it to him. Worse, before leaving India, the man worked one final bit of voodoo. He accepted that Safiya would now travel directly to Tanzania but implored her not to abandon him: "That would destroy me."

Taggart would return to Sri Lanka and fulfill his professional commitment. But when he visited Tanzania, he wanted to take Safiya travelling – his treat. While they waited for the right moment to invoke The Shaman, they'd visit Ngoronogo Crater, explore Olduvai Gorge, see Mount Kilimanjaro. This would only be fair. After all, in Sri Lanka, he'd allowed Daniel to show her round.

Finally, to shut him up, Safiya had said, "I'll think about it."

Big mistake. Taggart interpreted this as a binding commitment.

So Safiya confided in Dar. The insanity of it filled me with foreboding, but also guarded optimism: Safiya really did need me. With Daniel, she could no longer discuss Taggart. He'd heard enough. Me, I made it my business to find out more than Safiya realized. From Sri Lanka, Taggart wrote letters, as many as two a day. The early ones remained bright and newsy. He missed Safiya but he'd visited Kandy, he'd found a Hindu temple in Colombo, he'd travelled south and bought a carved mask.

Taggart's letters didn't turn dark until Safiya revealed, belatedly, that she'd taken a job and couldn't go travelling. He replied that he'd fallen into a depression. He'd started a new novel but now he felt sick. He'd had periods like this before. Did she remember her Windigo dream? Last night, he'd seen that insatiable ice skeleton. He'd written a suicide note and sealed it into an envelope. His adult self had felt contemptuous, disgusted, but his child self wanted to lie down on a sandy beach and let the demon have its way.

Taggart had complained bitterly, during the freighter cruise, that Safiya had already left for Africa. Now, in Tanzania, she lived partly in Sri Lanka – though with dread, not anticipation. Where before she'd savoured a dream, now she endured a nightmare.

Hers was a different trial by fire than my own, though recognizably of the same genre. She opened Taggart's letters with psychic trembling and trepidation. Always they left her shaken: depressed and angry or both. Yet she couldn't wait to read them. At recess she'd collect them from her mail slot, return to her classroom, and close the door. If she'd drawn duty, she'd head out into the school yard and read by the swings, end up standing mired in Taggart's misery while around her uniformed children chased each other in a game of tag, laughing and shrieking, a blue-and-white whirl of happiness.

Taggart speculated that his shaky mental condition arose out of the darkness of the raw material he'd begun exploring in his latest novel, all those skeletons clicking bones in his head. Sometimes he'd write with tears pouring down his face. He guessed he'd been having a nervous breakdown. Brainstorms shook him like a tree in a tempest. He didn't understand the Windigo side of his personality, which proved as destructive towards him as towards other people. He had to keep writing to control it at all.

Taggart wrote (blatantly lying) that he'd never wanted to destroy Safiya's relationship with Daniel. But he didn't want their relationship, his and hers, destroyed either. He remained committed to Safiya. Did she know what that meant? Together, he and Safiya had a great task to perform. Surely she could understand that to ask him to come to Dar es Salaam and NOT spend time alone with her would be asking him to endure an unbearable agony? If Daniel hadn't enjoyed that stretch in Sri Lanka, sleeping with Safiya, being intimate with her, then Taggart might not feel so badly. But he'd expected the same kind of break in Tanzania.

It had never occurred to him that Safiya wouldn't want to make love, given the strength of their bond. He considered himself married to Safiya. They didn't need a ceremony. Maybe Raff was right and a three-way marriage couldn't work. If not, they needed to find another way. Could Safiya do what she demanded of him? He needed her – and not just to approach The Shaman. He yearned to be with her. It couldn't be all the time and he understood that – but it had to be part of the time.

He didn't blame Safiya for his depression. Yet he felt that, by accepting a teaching job, and so precluding a travel holiday, an African safari, she'd abandoned him. Betrayed the original agreement. Never mind. He'd come to Tanzania no matter what the emotional toll: he needed to see Safiya and that was that.

In responding to this self-indulgent avalanche, Safiya explained that she'd ruled out sex because she simply could not survive another bout of now-it's-this-one, now-it's-that-one. It made her schizophrenic. When Taggart wrote "time alone" and meant sex, he invited her to immolate herself. Look what had happened in India. Ultimately, he'd found three-way sharing intolerable and went ballistic, incidentally nullifying any "original agreements." She didn't blame him. They'd had no business expecting the extraordinary of themselves. They all three possessed artistic talent, but so what? The rest stood revealed as run-of-the-mill human frailty.

Taggart responded that his mental state was deteriorating. This morning, he'd seen hell in a plate of fried eggs. Safiya remained his only friend in this hemisphere. As such, she bore a responsibility. He was sorry Daniel had gone over to Rafferty, especially after he'd enjoyed that vacation in Sri Lanka. Even so, Safiya couldn't change the rules now. This particular game, the original three wandering amidst alien corn, had long since passed the midpoint.

On and on he went, ten pages, fifteen, twenty. In refusing to see his point of view, Safiya showed a cruel streak. Daniel had made love with her in Sri Lanka and Taggart felt entitled to equal time. He felt embarrassed to keep begging. She should send him a telegram, yes or no. Besides, with whom did she think she could approach The Shaman? Daniel hadn't recovered from the death of Victor. Rafferty was a know-nothing poseur who couldn't hang on to his keepsakes and mementos. Did she propose to invoke the Sacred Fire with one of those two? All he could say was, "Good luck."

Taggart had a quest to complete. He would come to Dar es Salaam no matter what forces opposed him. And if, for two or three weeks, or even a month, Safiya had to shuffle back and forth between Daniel and him, so be it. She owed him that much. They both did.

At this point, Safiya visited me at the Palm Beach Hotel. We sat drinking orange squash on the patio. She began catching me up and I said: "Safiya, I've been keeping tabs."

She looked startled, then shrugged: "Raff, I don't know what to do."

"I think you do."

"You mean break it off? I'm afraid Taggart might…do something to himself."

"That's not all you fear."

"You're right. Taggart's famous for his occult thrillers, but he also wrote a particularly vicious roman à clef. The woman he savaged committed suicide."

"You don't look the type."

"You're right," Safiya said. "That's not reason enough, is it?"

"Anyway, you could write him into the ground."

"What about The Shaman's Fire?"

"You, me, and Daniel can set forth. We don't need Taggart."

"Yes, but Dan's not ready. He seems…reluctant."

I summoned a confidence I didn't feel: "He'll heal sooner than you think."

That evening, Safiya wrote telling Taggart that she felt as if he were holding a gun to her head. Thanks, but no thanks. No more agonizing, no more argument. She couldn't do it. She felt he was trying to manipulate her. Or maybe, as he'd suggested, he'd succumbed to forces he couldn't control. She did understand his point of view. But he wasn't begging, he was choosing. And she couldn't do what he asked.

Maybe Taggart shouldn't come to Dar es Salaam at all, not feeling the way he did. There, she'd said it. He'd spelled out his terms and she couldn't accept them. She couldn't take it anymore. She still hoped he'd change his mind, his state of mind. But if he couldn't, then she agreed with him: he couldn't very well come to Dar. Certainly, given this new situation, they couldn't hope to approach The Shaman together.

Taggart responded with a four-page telegram. He'd come to Dar no matter what she said – and he'd bring a surprise. He wanted her to send him the address of the British High Commission. He'd come to Dar, not because Safiya was there, but because it was the best place from which to set forth. Besides, he had to get out of Sri Lanka, where people were getting blown up in the streets.

Maybe Rafferty would put him up for a few nights? If not, he'd find his own hotel. If Safiya wasn't going to make love with him, then probably he wouldn't see her. He'd come to Dar and so straight to a hotel. Maybe he'd see her and maybe he wouldn't. If Safiya wanted to see him, she should book him a double room at the Hotel Kilimanjaro...

Of the many letters Safiya sent Taggart from Dar es Salaam, she drafted only one of them twice:

Taggart Oates:

This is an official de-invitation.

If you ever loved me, do not come to Dar es Salaam.

If you love me now, or if you love me still, do not come to Dar es Salaam.

If you come to Dar, I will understand it to mean that you never loved me – that you love only yourself and images of yourself, and I will treat you accordingly.

Taggart Oates, read these words and understand.

I will not meet any airplanes. I will not book any hotels. Can I make it any clearer? I DO NOT WANT TO SEE YOU HERE.

This is my last communication until you write and tell me that you are not coming to Dar es Salaam.

DO NOT COME TO DAR.

Myrna Kostash

Unmasking the Polish Dissident

In Warsaw that spring of 1987, I knew immediately we would not be lovers. From where I stood in the baggage retrieval area of the airport I could see K behind the plywood and glass partition holding a cellophane-wrapped bouquet. Even from that distance he seemed shrunken, his blue corduroy suit ballooning around him, his body curved forward from the shoulders as though to fend off blows to his heart. Up close I saw that his hair and beard were greyer than a year ago and that the flesh of his face seemed to have slid off its underpinnings. I could see that he had no cheekbones. He was frail, not virile, distraught, not self-possessed, and even though he would bend over my hand to kiss it with a soft nibble of his lips and repeat that nothing of his feelings had changed, it was clear he was neither going to seduce me nor be seduced.

The present did not belong to us, it belonged to the dying B. K's caring spirit was saturated with B's dismal need. Her life force was dwindling, yet there was between her and K a *nuptial* faithfulness that I accepted. With K I had only the rapture of the past, on the shores of a Slovenian lake, or perhaps the rapture of the future in the Polish woods, a blanket, and a bottle of wine, miles away from B's grave.

Under the skies solid with whitish grey cloud Warsaw lay sombre and featureless. This was Poland in the Spring of the Generals. Solidarity had vowed that, though the Generals would have the Winter (especially that first deadly December of the coup in 1981), they, Solidarity, and the "people," would have the Spring. This was it, then: citizens stood forever at bus stops, hugging themselves against the chill wind.

K took me to lunch in the cellar of a summer palace of the Radziwills. After the meal we walked slowly, arm in arm, through the green sweep of the palace gardens and the cultivated stands of lindens along a small arm of the Vistula. There was a chilly breeze and we pulled our coats closer to our chests. "This is not my country anymore!" K blurted out of the blue. He described Poland as a nation of two hostile camps, the State and underground Solidarity, with himself as a sad, lone man walking a thin line between them.

I did not understand K's feelings about Solidarity. On the one hand he berated the movement for having "given up" without a fight. This was not, of course, strictly true; there had been resistance to Martial Law in the early 1980s, but the movement had then split into factions. Of course, he continued, it is in the Polish tradition to fight against all odds but even this hopeless romantic wreckage would be preferred to the mediocre politicking of mere survival. The politics of resistance, he seemed to suggest, had been recast as compromise, bickering, and self-justification.

I wanted to argue with him (as with myself, but didn't): who was he, in his safe sinecure at an officially approved editorial office, to berate Solidarity for a lapse in revolutionary bravado? Whatever shabby deals the *realpolitik* of Martial Law had forced the veterans in the shipyards to make with the authorities, nothing could diminish the importance of their courage in 1980 in leading almost the entirety of the Polish working class into strikes against (what one can only think of as) their history since the Second World War. Some had gone to jail, some were underground, others were in permanent exile, refused permission to re-enter their own country, many were dead. K would say he was "with" them, but had grown bitter and sad because Solidarity *was supposed to have made a difference.*

Just who was K "with"? At least one of Solidarity's advisers, he told me, as if divulging classified information, was a millionaire (from overseas royalties). The leaders all lusted after western television sets and refrigerators. They went to church. They were not Communists: what could one expect?

They circulated slander against K in one of their underground journals, claiming he had called for the exclusion of all pro-Solidarity writers from the Writers' Union. I looked closely at K to see how deep that particular barb had landed, but he was merely gloomy-eyed, and stroked my fingers clean of the crumbs of coffee cake with which he had treated me.

Unforgivably, Solidarity had accused his friend Z of being in the pay of the police as an informer. Z who had been chairman of the writers' association in Lwow (L'viv) at the time of the Soviet occupation in 1939, and who continued to show up at his office, right up to his arrest by the NKVD (Soviet secret police), keeping to his post while his fellow members had rushed off to join the Communist-sponsored union.

It was when he told me this kind of story, which he did not do often, and told it softly (with strain pulling at the crinkled skin around his eyes) as though he didn't even want an audience, that I remembered how I had fallen in with K in the first place. *Listening* to him, suspending all judgement, hoping for the miracle of fellow feeling.

Nevertheless I struggled to keep my erotic energy focussed on K and away from the young men in denim, fists curled inside their pockets, grease slicking their boots, a gold crucifix at their throat, who sat in jails and swore revenge. Their buddies would remember this incarceration for them, as K had remembered for Z the many days of his lonely and absurd vigil in the vacant rooms of a deserted writers' association.

At another lunch in a restaurant in the former smithy of the Wilanow estate, we ate blini with smoked salmon and drank Bulgarian wine. "The situation is hopeless here," he said. "There can be no change. Technology and industry are crude and underdeveloped, we have nothing to sell, people are desperate to make ends meet. The Soviets will never loosen their grip and the Germans could come again." As for his own situation, he saw that, once there was no more taking care of his journal and his women, he would kill himself.

The trees were in full leaf near the Vistula but it seemed as though all of creation lay bleached beneath the sky. We shivered. I thought: If I want a Polish lover, I will have to dream him up.

Out Among the Rumours

I find myself in little scenes among Warsaw's chattering classes, sitting in small rooms on small hard chairs, breathing in the fumes of schnapps and

Polish tobacco mixed with the dust shaken off the piles of curling papers in the corners of bookshelves behind my back. I am trying to be a good guest. I do not wait to be fussed over. I ask questions. I have brought flowers. I am also of course trying to put two and two together.

I meet M at supper, at the home of a visiting scholar from England. M is short, bearded, and rather jolly, obviously in good spirits as he prepares for a move to North America where he has been invited to teach American literature. You can sense his relief, as though his relaxed body were already expanding to fit the comfortable dimensions of the American casual.

Now, here at supper, he can afford to be unhappy about his Polish university. It has suffered disproportionately from cutbacks because its rector has been "too tolerant of unofficial activities," for example of the unofficial student group selling underground literature right under the noses of the authorities. M seems unsympathetic with the students' situation. Because of them, he claims, the university has been forced to suspend its publication program and has budget enough only to send one professor to one international conference a year. M makes more money tutoring and translating in a week than he makes in a month's salary. "My salary is for cigarettes and one meal a month in a restaurant," he informs me with a wave of his cigarette as if this were already a curiosity of Polish life with which he will entertain his hosts in America.

I am interested in M because a friend has told me, "M has no use for K."

"No use at all," is the way she put it, adding that M these days "is close to Bujak." This would be Zbigniew Bujak, hero of the Solidarity underground, who has lived on the run, scattering a paper trail of theses, programs, and manifestos. I look more keenly at M, trying to discern the outlines of the intellectual in whom a hunted man would have confidence, but all I see is the jolliness.

Perhaps M is simply a professor with an active fantasy life about the underground. I pursue the story with two young anarchists: the story does not excite them in the least. "You hear all sorts of things," they say, pointing out that you cannot trust in rumours and gossip because you simply have no idea where their source is. Sometimes the source is the police themselves. The police will raid an illegal meeting and arrest all but one person – well, you can imagine the gossip that circulates about the hapless survivor! I accept this as an instruction to me – picking up stories at cocktail parties, for heaven's sake.

I think again about K and his susceptibility to gossip and rumours, and my own to his. Is this a surrogate life for the one lived by heroes in a web of conspiracy and danger, of which he and I are unworthy?

I huddle under his arm in his car where we wait by the river for the winds to blow warm, and imagine myself under the blankets on the mattress in my lover's hideout, a stone's throw from the Ursus factory where we met, knowing that it was just a matter of time before we realized our street was being watched, and he would wash the dishes, kiss my hands and throat, and slip away.

In an extraordinary "roundtable" some years after the lifting of Martial Law, former Solidarity activists reviewed their experience as antigovernment militants. Their conversations were collected in a book, *Konspira*, which I picked up for a song on a sale table in Edmonton.

The guys (they are all guys) are remarkably unsentimental about themselves, but then everything had turned out all right in the end and they were spared the more normal outcome of Polish drama: martyrdom. It is shocking to learn that the historic Lenin Shipyard of Gdansk, motherlode of the movement and its strikes, was taken by two tanks. And that it had simply "never even occurred" to Zbigniew Bujak, so savvy and stalwart, that the army could impose a military dictatorship. Activists were "shouting and swaggering... shooting off at the mouth" while outside the shipyard gates the army was getting ready to shoot for real.

Underground, they learned that the crush of the public's expectations – Do something! Something spectacular! – cost several hundreds of thousands of zlotys for "actions" that lasted only a few hours, like the giant speaker installed in a cemetery that broadcast Solidarity propaganda briefly and then fell silent. Bujak described a tedious operation in which a group of people spent days and nights writing out information in tiny script on sheets of onionskin paper which they then rolled up into tight cylinders and hid in the washrooms of trains travelling west. Not a single cylinder, however, reached its addressee: no one at the other end had bothered to pick them up.

They could also be brilliant. At the peak of the nationwide strikes in 1981 when telephone lines had been cut in strikers' towns, Solidarity "published" their most important news by scrawling messages on the sides of intercity trains.

On reflection, Bujak was to call the underground a "myth of superficial heroism," a projection of the fear of losing face, perhaps, to the imperturbable General in sunglasses who had won. There were those who tried to put an "ethical" face on it. They refused, they said, to live in fear of a "piece of government paper," but even self-respect is a kind of performance. And the spiteful dream of outliving the colonels is pure braggadocio: "The Winter may belong to them but the Spring belongs to us!"

As they talk, another kind of self-understanding emerges: underground man as sexual lone ranger. One hundred and fifty-eight pages into *Konspira* here they are, talking about loneliness. Since partings are "burdensome," says one ex-activist, the trick is not to form any attachments, and to survey the women on the street not for their beauty but for the possibility that this one is a snoop for the Security Service, that one an underground courier. Beware the temptation to buy booze and pick up Solidarity groupies with the union's money just because you are "making sacrifices" for millions and they "owe" you.

Some did fall in love with a fellow conspirator and portioned out their loneliness or went into hiding at an old girlfriend's place – the wife's is under surveillance – where the woman's sacrifice of her own security and the respect, not to say awe, in which she held her heroic lover were a kind of company, the only "warmth" on offer.

On January 22 and 23, 1969, student agitator Adam Michnik (future dissident and political prisoner), almost a year after sustained student protests had shaken up Party and government, had his day in court. I imagine him still slender but with a sensual suggestion of fleshiness around his shoulders and thighs. Probably he doesn't bang the dock rail or glower melodramatically at his accusers. If anything he is a little pedantic. But he is ardent with heresies, and he recites them all for the court, from eleven-year-old red-neckerchiefed Communist scout to high-school member of the Contradiction Seekers Club to twenty-three-year-old member of the university-based *komandosi*, who have seized the torch from the faltering Reds of October 1956.

"We believed," he addressed the court, "that the duty of a Communist is to combat every evil, every instance of lawlessness, every wrong and injustice he encounters in his country." In a nice turnaround he became judge, and acquitted himself of all wrong-doing. After all, in that courtroom he was the only believer.

They say The Komando Kid, ex-jailbird, ex-Solidarity adviser, is now fat, and chummy with a retired general who once threw him in jail. But in 1986, on the cover of his book, *Letters From Prison*, the Kid is an angel. The shadows of the bars of his cell door criss-crossing his soft face fall around his brooding right eye and his plump lips like stigmata. Here, then, is the doomed lover from my own generation.

I did not mourn for him in his prison cell. It was precisely where he expected, even desired, to be in the wintertime of the generals' coup against Solidarity, just as he had calmly entered prison in 1968. There was no question either of his loneliness or sexual solitude. He was an outlaw. I might press against the bars from the other side, sliding the tips of my fingers across his mouth or blow kisses into the shadow where he slept, but for him there was no taking. The man who sat defiantly immured within the jail of the generals was not one to dream of creeping into a lover's bed to get away from the cold. Besides, he was an angel.

I have drifted far away from K here, to rejoin my own "Sixties" people. Born twenty years after K, the students of 1968 arrived with fresh outrage into political struggle while the men and women of Polish October had already made their "adjustments." The Kid viewed them with "affection" and "respect," but saw how they were folded back into the bureaucracies, orthodoxies, and surveillance that had bred them. The Kid had wanted them to press on – "Show us the source of that evil" – but they had lost their nerve.

Another twenty years further on I meet K whose "October" was so ghostly it did not even cast a shadow as we danced.

There is a postscript to this, long after I have lost K. "A base for Polish democracy is being created today," Adam Michnik had written in his prison cell. "It lies in the moral sphere." More than a decade later, Poland has its democracy. Now a highly respected journalist and newspaper editor, a rare voice of intelligence in a sometimes poisonous political atmosphere, this inscribing angel is seen arriving at a costume party dressed wittily in the uniform of the KGB with "nymphets" on his arm.

I have a photograph from my last visit to Poland in 1988 taken in the courtyard of Warsaw University. My subject is a bulletin board behind glass. Something has caught my eye. Behind the glare of the pane and the smudge of the photocopier's ink is the black and white face of Che Guevara – waves of dark hair flying from under his beret, black parenthetical moustache over his lip. CHE SI has been stamped over his eyes so his expression is inscrutable but we all know that what he is looking at is the shining path that leads to the heaven on earth of *campesino* freedom.

I wonder if the Polish students see that too, or whether they see the soldiers waiting in the gloom of the little church's portico in the Bolivian village near Santa Cruz who will come out to kill him. Well, maybe Che sees them too, on the path. They will make him an angel.

Peter Oliva

A Day in the Life
of Yevgeny Yevtushenko

7:57 pm

A tall man (six feet, three inches) wearing a purple, single-breasted dinner jacket is coming toward us, waving the back of his hand as if to brush us all away from Gate Two. As he gets closer to us I notice that his jacket is actually neon-spattered with webs of pink. A total of seven gold-coin buttons are plugged into this web. Five gold buttons run down the man's stomach to match the single coins on the ends of his sleeves. The other two can be glimpsed on the middle his side pockets, only if I shake my head – in disbelief – from side to side. His lapels are so wide that he could well fit into a 1930s gangster film, provided the twentieth-century colourization experts were shot and killed, face-mashed into their damaged control panels during the movie's opening scenes.

Some barren life I lead: it strikes me that I've never actually seen a tie-dyed suit before this moment.

"Must be the flight from Las Vegas," says Patrick. "One day too long inside Caesar's Palace and that's what a man can turn into."

"Salt Lake City," I say, "and that's our man."

I am still holding up the book I'm using in lieu of a name card, when legendary poet Yevgeny Yevtushenko sees us and waves at my prop like a tired, old friend.

"Yes, yes, is my book," he says. "I wrote that."

Patrick says nothing. The both of us are still standing outside the wooden, makeshift corral that Calgary International Airport resurrects before every Stampede season. Patrick's face is leaning over the edge of the corral, staring at Yevtushenko's pink pants – his nylon pink jogging pants – the kind that wrap up into a little ball and never see the outside world except on ski slopes or aerobic mats.

Yevgeny Yevtushenko, Russia's "voice of the thaw," published his first poem in 1949 at age sixteen, his first book three years later. He was the first Russian writer to speak out against Stalinism and by 1957 he was expelled from the Young Communist League because of his "individualism." In 1961, his epic poem "Baba Yar" inspired Shostakovich to write a symphony using Yevtushenko's words. Another known fact: his public readings in Russia have been known to fill stadiums.

His new novel, *Don't Die Before You're Dead*, is billed as "a contemporary epic that merges autobiography with fiction," but Yevtushenko calls his book "a Russian borscht" of a novel that includes elements from every part of contemporary society.

"My nickname is Genya," he says, with a thick, pleasing Russian accent. He drags his mouth over the "Ge" of his name as if to speak French, and begin the phrase "je m'appelle…" To my ears this sounds vaguely like "Je-Enya" – two words that might sound better stretched, then mashed together with benefit of a mouthful of Port. But after we get over these awkward, foreign introductions, he gives us the first of many plans: "Let us get out of this airport. I need something to eat."

8:45 pm

We stop by the side of the road, at Calgary's "Lover's Leap" to see the view of the downtown skyscrapers. The wind is cold; it shivers across the Bow River and climbs up the cliff toward us. Patrick explains the absence of submarine races in Alberta and Yevtushenko – Genya – seems genuinely interested in this dialogue. He's turned away from the wind, focussing his eyes on Patrick's mouth, watching the words come out, one at a time, until I notice Patrick has stopped speaking.

9:30 pm

"I want to try your Canadian wine," he says. "Usually I prefer the Italian wines, but you cannot buy Italian wine outside of Italy. You cannot even believe the labels that they glue to the outside of their Italian bottles. Listen to me: this is true. I have many Italian friends. I can tell you. The Italian wine that you buy outside of Italy is from Albania."

We settle on a bottle of Okanagan red.

When the bottle arrives, Yevtushenko waits for the moment itself to settle, when all eyes are on him, then judges the quality of this Canadian wine, rolling the juice in his mouth.

Another moment passes.

Finally: "Is good wine," and we smile together.

Yevtushenko reaches for the book I'm still holding, a copy of his novel. We've done the requisite book exchange and despite holding his glass of wine, firmly in one hand, he's suddenly flipping wildly through my book, looking for something, he says, "that is Siberian custom between writers."

"We must discover our destiny," he says. "I will go first."

Still with the glass of wine in hand, he flips through the book and looks up at the ceiling. Our eyes follow his until we realize he is searching for a thought, not a sign from God.

"Page 107," he says finally, "line 7."

He counts down the page. "Yes," he says, "yes, yes, is good destiny I think. Listen. This man. Celli, who is this man?"

"A miner."

"A miner. Good. A working man. I too am a working man. A man of the people. From Celli's breath comes these words. I ride on the breath of the ordinary man. Is good destiny."

Smiling broadly, Yevtushenko breaks the book's back with one hand, and pours wine across the inside of the book. The edges of the pages bleed wine over the table, then he moves the book to the side and sprays a stripe of wine on the floor as if rinsing a paint brush.

"Is very good destiny," he says.

Our waiter doesn't notice the remains of our destinies dripping from the tablecloth, so I am inclined to agree.

By the time we leave the restaurant we are fast friends, I think. Italian food and cheap wine splashed over several books will make friends out of any group of people, and Genya grasps the two of us as we walk toward his hotel.

"I know you like my twenty-one fingers," he says. "Is old Siberian expression."

It's the kind of moment I've heard about from other writers, during other Yevtushenko visits to Canada: John Metcalf has just spoken a few words of Russian to welcome Yevtushenko to the table, and Genya is so pleased to hear the words, the courtesy shown, that he jumps up from the table, in the crowded room, to hug a grown man. The room grows quiet. Nobody puts down a fork. No one touches a glass. And that is when Yevtushenko suddenly notices the silence, and the crowd's stares.

"We are not queers!" his voice booms, gripping his new friend more securely, "we are Slavs!"

11:30 pm

Patrick and I leave him in the lobby after giving him a copy of tomorrow's itinerary.

"Four interviews tomorrow? Is too much. We must call this woman directly, this publicist, what is her name? Give me her number, I will call her myself immediately. Is impossible for one man."

Next day, 9:00 am

Gzowski, CBC Radio interview, speaking on the fall of Communism and the division of the USSR:

Y: "Nothing unites people more than a common enemy and nothing divides people more than a common victory."

G: "Have you written too much?"

Y: "Is too late to discuss about this. I published 135,000 lines of poetry. Seventy percent of this is – I'm trying to find polite word – is rubbish. But sincere rubbish."

10:00 am
Fax Transmission to Colonel R_____, Base Commander
Number of pages including this page: 1.
Dear Colonel R_____,
Having spoken to your secretary yesterday afternoon, I am writing you to request some military equipment – a camouflage jeep or (hopefully) a small armoured vehicle for the literary event of the year... There is enough space for a jeep or tank to sit out front, and I could arrange for chairs to be placed in front of the vehicle, with Yevtushenko standing on the tank as a symbolic podium for democracy...

Still no word from the military. My fax, I believe, will never be answered by written correspondence, other than getting me on a list somewhere. For the record: Yevgeny Yevtushenko is the only man who I would consider getting a tank for, and I am not particularly interested in asking for a tank ever again. Certainly not a large tank. Nothing so garish. I only wanted a small one to sit out front of the shop, something to commemorate Yevtushenko's efforts in freeing Mikhail Gorbachev from the 1991 attempted coup.

If the rain lets up, I do have the phone number for a friend of a mechanic's cousin who has a couple of tanks I can borrow (amazing what people have sitting in their backyards).

But going through so many middle-men somehow makes me nervous. Such offers are suddenly appearing every way I turn: a Russian businessman calls to offer me his old service uniform, a rifle, and his daughter (strictly for translation purposes), should I have use for these things.

The catch: "It would be very pleasurable evening to meet Mister Yevtushenko," he says, "for private dinner with very few people."

At this moment, only the weather seems capable of confirmation – not the tank, not the mechanic, not the dinner – only the dark clouds that seem bent on raining-out this military exercise. I look up at the sky for the twentieth time today and finally decide on an indoor reading.

11:00 am

CBC Television Interview, Alberta News Hour, taped in the bookstore, to be aired nationally the next day:

Yevtushenko: "When you choose between your conscience and fear, what do you choose, conscience or fear? I choose conscience. When I protest against our tanks in Czechoslovakia I remember I was ready to be arrested. I overcame my fear. A little bit I underestimated my popularity because they just couldn't arrest me."

The interviewer pushes him further along on the subject of fear, and toward the attempted coup in August 1991. He was there, she says, on the balcony of the Russian parliament building, using his poetry to defend freedom.

Cut to film coverage (day shot) showing a wet crowd standing with umbrellas beside a tank and a row of flowers, placed next to the road. Camera pans up. Cut to night shot of tanks, lit from underneath as if on fire. Soldiers walk calmly beside the tanks down a narrow Moscow street. Cut to gloomy day shot. A white flag is tied to a tank's radio antenna, six people climb over the tank, as if searching for a vantage point to see something out of camera range.

Cut to parliament building, day. A mass of Russian fur hats, incomprehensible Russian signs and tri-coloured flags move as if in slow motion. Pan upward, to balcony shot: there's Yevtushenko in a dark blue overcoat, a red scarf tucked into his collar. He leans into the microphone and his jaw disappears just as the translator's words cover Yevtushenko's voice: "We are all for freedom, but not for the freedom of murderers."

Yevtushenko looks up.

The poem ends:

> ...the Russian Parliament
> like a wounded marble swan of freedom
> defended by our people
> swims into eternity.

Camera cuts to the crowd below.

One hundred thousand hands rise up, a sea of open palms.

Cut back to CBC interview, bookstore.

Yevtushenko admits: "I was scared. Even my wife was screaming. She was calling me stupid. She was screaming something like that: Look! If they'll kill you do not come back to our house! You know she said this, she became crazy because she was worried about me."

12:00 pm

Genya returns to the bookshop with Marilyn Wood, publicist, riding shotgun. His energy is on the upswing, despite the fact she has changed the day's itinerary and actually added an extra interview. She fit him into three separate interviews by keeping him in the CBC building and having the hosts move around him. Coast-To-Coast Newsworld, the Homestretch, a quick plug for CBC Sunday Arts program, then back to the television studio, then back to Kensington to meet for lunch.

Yevtushenko smiles broadly.

Across the street at an Italian restaurant that shall remain nameless (I have since been banned from this place for life), Genya arranges himself at the table, while Marilyn, two Russian professors, and myself make the introductions.

We decide on an Italian wine. "Is enough to try the Canadian grapes yesterday," he says. "Now we must extend our experiences to another country."

A soup arrives and seems to scald his mouth with the first sip.

"Pepper!"

"Pepper?" I ask.

"Pepper, pepper, PEPPER! Is full of pepper! I've been to Italy many times," he says. "And pepper is always on the table, not in the recipes."

Genya sends the failed offering back to the kitchen, then two more soups come and go, then three entrees, a bowl of tortellini, and finally a plate of spaghetti marinara. Rocco the chef, an imposing girth of a man, comes out of the kitchen with Yevtushenko's plate in his hand. The plate is tilted in Rocco's hand so the food seems ready to slide off the side or smash into the side Yevtushenko's smiling face.

"Pepper," he says.

"I don't put any pepper in my food. I don't know what your problem is."

It strikes me strange both men are speaking a foreign language, English, yet both would probably be happier to discuss this matter in Italian.

"No pepper in the pasta?"

"No pepper in the pasta."

"No pepper in the vegetables?"

"Not in the vegetables."

"What about the sauce?"

"I make the sauce myself. There is no pepper in the sauce."

"The tomato sauce?"

"It is from a can."

"Ah," says Yevtushenko, nodding his head to the rest of us, "the tomato sauce."

Rocco fumes silently for a second, slightly derailed, then recovers admirably with the firm statement: "I don't put any pepper in this food!"

People are watching.

Yevtushenko pauses for effect, then announces to all: "I have tried all of these dishes you have on your menu. I can tell you, the only thing I have found here without the taste of pepper is the wine!"

Rocco seems to totter slightly to the left of our table while Yevtushenko raises his hand to the side of his head and waves his open fingers to shrug off this sudden comprehension.

"The canned tomato sauce," he says.

With a moment of triumph safely secured, Genya shakes his head and graciously admits: "Maybe it is just me. Maybe I am crazy."

"I think you are crazy," says Rocco, stepping closer to the table. There is a moment when I think this could well turn into an international incident. The headlines flash in front of my eyes: Russian Poet Brained In Restaurant, Victim Forced To Eat Weapon.

The spaghetti slides a little further to the side of Rocco's plate while Yevtushenko looks at Rocco, a confident smile seems to wrinkle the edges of his blue, Siberian eyes. He is, I think, genuinely "bemused."

Rocco takes another step toward us.

"You are absolutely crazy," he says.

Enough, I say: "basta." I raise hand, but I'm too far away from Rocco to stop his approach. I want to rise to my feet and say something like, "This man is my guest," but the moment quickly disappears when he notices his wife leaning into his field of vision. All Rocco's Italian sensibilities seem to kick into gear, and with a mutter I can't understand our "gentle host" shrugs, retreats back to his kitchen.

A white plate appears seconds later, with a pan-fried chicken breast upon it. No garnish, just a slightly brown chicken breast which Yevtushenko gobbles down his throat before he leaves the table with Marilyn, the both of them already ten minutes late for their next set of radio interviews.

7:00 pm

The Russians are coming. More Russians than I ever knew existed in southern Alberta. Some of them pound on the window. When I open the door I am hit with a dozen questions all at once.

"Yevtushenko. He's coming here? Here? To this place? You're sure?"

"Yes," I say, "I'm sure."

"Where is he now? Where is he staying? Have you seen him yet?"

More Russians are coming. They are arriving early, standing outside in the rain while we stack chairs on the main floor and the second floor. There's a problem with the main microphone, but the cordless one is working fine.

7:10 pm

The shop is chock-full of Russian speakers and the sound of English is fading quickly. Over 300 people wedged into a 1,800 square-foot bookshop. Over 100 chairs are bought, rented, or borrowed from neighbouring bars. The rest of the people are standing, already shifting themselves into some kind of ebb and flow. They seem to take turns breathing, so they don't bulge the walls out any more than necessary. One small, cannonball of a woman knocks me over by the stairs, muttering to herself on the way up. Two steps later, she looks back at my wincing face, and answers the question I was too afraid to ask:

"You think there are no more seats left upstairs for me? ME? I am small and I am Russian, you are not Russian, I am Russian. And I know Yevtushenko better than you and I am going upstairs."

When I put up my hand on the rail, grasping for some transitory sense of balance, she takes the gesture as license to move up the stairs and disappear into the crowd.

7:15 pm
Still no Yevtushenko.

7:20 pm
No Genya.

7:29 pm
An old man stops me as I'm going to the back door to check yet again for Yevtushenko. "There are too many people here," he says. "You should have had this event in a different place. You should have reserved seating. Tickets. This is a terrible event."

"Wait," I beg him. "Wait until you've seen him. He'll be here."

He seems leery of this suggestion.

"Talk to me after the event," I say, "I want to know. Talk to me after."

7:30 pm
If there is an after. Still no Genya.

7:40 pm
Genya enters through the back door with a growl.

"Is there some place quiet we can go – I need to be alone."

I nod quickly and take him downstairs before any one can see him.

"Is probably no one here for this reading," he says, "just a couple of babushkas in audience. No one."

To make this moment worse, he adds: "You cannot believe the day I've had. Very bad news from my American publisher. I am not feeling well."

In a feeble attempt to change the subject, I say that his suit looks quite good. It is alive, I tell him, festive.

"This?" he asks, the Russian equivalent to *this old thing*. "I make myself," he says. "One day I was wondering how to make a suit, what is like to make a suit. So I try. Two weeks it took me."

Yevtushenko smiles and I imagine this impossibly tall Siberian man crouching over a black machine, fashioning a neon outfit for a trip to Las Vegas he may never take.

8:00 pm

The reading. We trade off, reading sections of his poems, four stanzas at a time, English first, then thick, glorious, incomprehensible Russian, drooling down his mouth, the words swinging like Tarzan over the podium. There is no way I can match his movements, the hand flourishes of this man. Even in my thankfully brief moments on stage, Yevtushenko's presence is too commanding not to watch. I can just glimpse him in the corner of my reading space, bouncing from side to side, a tennis player getting ready to jump on the tape as soon as the ball is served.

I watch this man grow large, loom in front of his audience to cinematic proportions, feeding off their enthusiasm with every poem he gives them. A natural actor, he performs his poems, line by line, picking one woman in the audience after another, each woman a virtual balcony he hopes to climb with his outstretched, open hands to the next balcony. The passion of this opera grows and Stenka Razin is on the verge of coming through the door and the room seems to pulse with KGB suggestion, blackmail, and sweet, Soviet nostalgia, and suddenly Yevtushenko (the great Romantic) seems to reach the highest balcony in the room and he ends a stanza by kissing a woman's hand. The next poem it is an arm, then a shoulder, a cheek, Patrick's stomach, a young woman's open palm, and in one case: the lips. A babushka faints, falling into her chair, and I finally understand the Beatles' frenzy.

Genya moves on. We eventually descend the stairs, to visit the main floor because, he says, "this is Democracy. We cannot favour one group over another," and the crowd parts for him to pass.

I turn to follow him and someone grabs my sleeve. It's the old man. Tears fill his eyes. The moment hangs – neither of us speak – then he smiles and pushes my arm away, prodding me down the stairs to follow Yevtushenko's poems.

9:00 pm

Between these poems, there is commentary on all things Russian and literary:

"The social stage appeared in 1953, some slim, fragile figures of some girls and boys – almost teen-agers – my generation, they began very uncertain how to talk about the necessity of freedom of speech, writing their words against anti-Semitism, chauvinism. That was role of my generation. We were at that time...there was not any kind of dissident movement, because all potential dissidents were already killed. So we were one. We were everything during those years. We were brought up under very hard censorship. And, you know, to live under this house censorship, it's like, oh, it's like breaks your bones or it fucks you forever.

"And probably, in a way – paradoxically – sometimes censorship is very helpful for metaphorical language of poetry. Yes, is true, but unfortunately our censors, they were learning quickly too. They are greatest readers in the world because they were reading between lines beautifully.

"And afterwards it was time of goodness mixed with hopes. Our allusions [illusions?], some of them were broken. It was a beginning of new era in Russia."

9:20 pm

"In Russian this (poem) rhymes. You know that is tragedy. Because in our poor Russian language we have exactly twenty-four times more possibilities for new, fresh rhymes than in English. It doesn't mean that I underestimate English; because I admire some English words. For instance: I was trying to translate one beautiful, irresistibly charming English expression, back-seat driver, but doesn't work in Russian."

9:45 pm

"I was always writing about love and politics. I understand if writers involve too much in politics it makes his style, his soul, drier. It is what happened with me once, I remember:

"For three years and half I was member of parliament. One general insulted me – another member of parliament. Let's have all members of parliament insult each other. Probably only Canada is the exception.

"So he insulted me and I was preparing my answer to him. And Gorbachev didn't give me a word. He could see I was furious. And fury is very bad adviser, always. It was the same the next day.

"'Tomorrow,' he said, 'you must wait for tomorrow.' And finally, after I hear this word tomorrow, again and again, I ask Gorbachev directly: 'When will be this tomorrow,' I ask him. 'When?'

"'Your tomorrow,' he said, 'will be tomorrow.'

"Probably it's symbolic.

"So I was working on this political speech, writing, shaping it, trying to be very polite and use poisonous, sarcastic remarks...and I heard some steps behind me.

"I ask: 'who is it?'

"'Your wife, Marsha.'

"'Do you have some new information?'

"She said, 'Genya, are you getting crazy? Yes, I do have some news. I have very important news for you. I just want to tell you how I love you before I go to sleep now.'

"She began to laugh and I began to laugh, because I understood that being involved in politics I just lost the sense of simple human feelings. All politicians they are fighters and when you fight, your skin could be transformed into a rhinoceros skin, a kind of shield. Of course, its shell saves you from daggers, but it doesn't give you possibility to feel just human touch. And this is politics.

"It is very dangerous for writers to concentrate on politics, but at the same time I could not respect writers who were completely indifferent to the politics. I am absolutely sure if they are indifferent to the politics they are indifferent to the people. Politics deal with the people. Politics destroy the people, humiliate people.

"It's the duty of the writers to protect their readers. And so sometimes I know those such [writers] who declare a beautiful indifference to poltics, snobbishness. They declare sometimes very high-flown style. This is nothing more than cowardice, hidden cowardice. They are just cowards in my opinion."

10:00 pm

A selection of personal quotations Yevtushenko writes into other people's books:

– Judy, you say my book exhausted you. I only wish I could exhaust you in some more delicate manner.

– I bless your destiny.

– Self portrait (drawn, showing a stick man on two spires, reaching for the sun).

– With my great faith in you.

– With my best feelings.

– To Mona. From her unsuccessful admirer.

– To Jill & Rob. From a couple who were engaged before they were born.

– I am sure that you will let down neither your friends, neither yourself.

– To Patrick Rengger, with my brotherhood forever.

– With my respect and belief into your great future.

– I would like if the wheel of the 21st century will be in the hands of young people like you.

– To Jennifer, with admiration & with a hope that we will be friends forever. Good luck with your first novel.

– For Yevtushenkologist Number 1

10:45 pm

Answers to selected questions:

"The French say that translations are like women. If they're beautiful, they are not faithful, and if they're faithful, they can't be beautiful. I think this is not true about women, but is sometimes true about poetry."

11:45 pm

Glancing at an attractive CBC reporter, then to me, sitting across the table at Razzbarry's Cafe & Bar:

"She is volcano, she is Canadian volcano."

Looks back to the woman.

"Are you active or passive?"

Genya's thick accent too fast for her, she looks to me for the translation.

"He wants to know if you are an active volcano or a passive volcano."

"Passive, I think," she says meekly.

A moment later he is up on his feet. "I must drink to your beauty the Russian way! Give me your shoe!"

Her face turns red and she crouches further into her chair. She tries to hide her breasts between the wings of her shoulders and make herself disappear from this sudden attention.

"No, I can't. Oh my god, no. I've been wearing these boots all day long."

I look down to the floor and her ankle-high boots move closer together, hiding underneath her seat.

"Give him the shoes," I say, "just give them to him."

More prodding from the others at our table and the woman finally takes off her shoe and hands it to Genya.

He calmly puts his glass of vodka in the heel of the shoe and the rim of the glass disappears within the ankle's holster. Yevtushenko stands up, silver hair ruffled [intrusive authorial insert], and announces to the whole bar: "This woman is Canadian volcano. I drink to her beauty."

No one outside of our table can see the glass hidden in the boot, and while I marvel at the man's ability to discover a woman's ankle boots in a dark bar at fifty paces, Genya knocks back his head and completely drains her shoe.

Time Unknown

Later that evening, there follows a postscript to this story, entirely hearsay and probably fiction. The details can be left out of this serious chronology of events because they are fuzzy (at best) and the source is questionable (at her best). The rumour: another bar, another bottle of champagne, another woman, perhaps. There is a spurned invitation to visit his hotel room. Perhaps. The words:

"You Canadian girls are spoiled. Just drop me off at the nearest cat house. Before you do...can I have your address?"

An address is given. A reciprocal address asked for.

"You ask a lot for a woman who is not a lover."

A counter-postscript, next day:

Yevtushenko emerges from the Palliser Hotel, late for his flight. A sly grin spreads across his face as he admits that he was up late last night. When Marilyn goes to check him out, she learns that an admirer – from last night's reading – has paid for his hotel room. Genya blushes, coyly: a difficult feat for a sixty-two-year-old Siberian man.

10:00 am

Genya has lost his plane ticket. Marilyn tries vainly to get him on the flight, then waits with him for the next flight to Vancouver to appear on the airport screen in the departure room outside Gate Two.

"I think I am the most difficult author you have ever worked with, am I right?" he asks.

She nods and Genya beams.

"I must tell you this, Marilyn Wood: I will start my next novel before the plane even leaves the ground, only so I can come back to look at your legs."

11:10 am

Flight 649 leaves the ground and Calgary, the entire city – in unison – breathes out, exhales as though a great weight has indeed lifted. And somewhere to the west, another Canadian city prepares itself – unknowingly – for another day in the life of Yevgeny Yevtushenko.

February 1996

Douglas Barbour

The Shoes of the Titanic

The shoes of the Titanic
are walking slowly away
from the ruins

split in two
the great ship lies

& the shoes   –   of women
children   men in great
coats
              their shoes
are walking away

some day   they
hope to make it back
home

in the dream Daphne

the walls were built of books   it seemed
an I reflects in panes the dayblood flowing deeper into dark below
what you told me   I forget   within that room so full of words
& my words too   you edit you   particular
knowledge   wisdom   my pencil shifts
in an agony of change you tell me what it is I should do
beneath the artificial lights now flattening the surfaces
of desks & manuscripts   I do not understand in that moment
between sleeping & waking   I think
I know you once again in   that your purpose
eyes open to the dark   is gone

utamaro's women

the frame of the mirror & the sash of her kimono mesh to
frame her face   the space between   & her face   facing
away   facing her own face in the mirror mirroring one
quick delicate act in what moment stolen

she fingers her hair in the mirror   her stare from the
mirror rests on her hair hidden by her head her fingers tease
a hair into place   she had placed herself before the mirror
the better to see her hair   misplaced so   she reaches to
tease it back   into place   this place allows her a mirror
where she can stare back & forth   at her misplaced hair
there it is in place now   what are the two pairs of eyes
staring at

Tom Thomson: 'The Jack Pine' 1916-1917

If no ones present presence presents a vertical
movement the absent i partakes of sky *spreading*
(thats *not* sprawl all gone into the world of light or
dark hills hiding the just folks he paddled away from
every chance he got reds deep blues seize the day / light
slowly its taken 70 years now fading over the water
the leaves colour theres that rock at the bottom of
everything were supposed to pay no attention &
away away the lone line leaps beyond the frame up
toward the sky he you i drowned in is that ice
ice or only a reflection the reception of that gone
time hand moving on the waters continues

The National Gallery, Ottawa

George Melnyk

An Exiled Trinity

1. Sad Friday
We are cutting
shadows, cedars,
white snow willows
slavic
for a muslim grave.

On a stony hill
river distant
time places
fleshless,
palestine.

2. Searching
Ash grey freight
disappeared faces
somewhere...
bone dreams returning
to name me history.

Glistening rails
awaiting prayer,
voices I understand
grow narrow, distant,
mountains.

3. The Fall
Moon sweeps
blossoms from
identities, dry leaves
in the street.

A cloud black, and thin
crosses like smoke
from a cuban cigar.

Something big, orange,
round and sweet,
is turning white,
a long sentence
written without paper.

Carol L. MacKay

Dusted on the Road to Madden

He buzzes her

shoos under powerlines, barely overhead,

rubber across the roof of the cab

She rattles over gravel, over leaving

downs her lights to a slow

Doris Day blink, sickly but

a song of faith nonetheless

the draft propels her, prayerless.

Gibbous on Tape

It is the brightest moon of the century, the weatherman says,
bushbrows reaching such heights she gets up to see. Her heel
hollows into the concrete of the 10 foot by 4 foot patio, strung with
waxy constellations and cups of citronella. she squints, unable to
see anything but the merest pinpricks in the sky. She fetches her
rims from the table inside. She walks alongside patio moonspikes
in her yellowed canvas clogs to the front. Halogen beams off the
stucco to the path. She removes her shoes for the second time
to go inside, re-emerging through the screendoor with an
hydraulic bang and a pocketcam. There, between the hatches, is
history.

A Place of Clear Meaning

I've thought about following

Bread Crumb Trail, tracking

silent, sporadic tokes to

your cedar canyon

but here there are flatlines

waves lengthened

Hertzian mountains stretched to

a morpheme.

Kristjana Gunnars

Zoo

The pandas were asleep when she got to the zoo. It was five thirty, dinner-time, and she was hungry, but the keepers said the pandas would not wake up till seven. At seven they would open their eyes, eat some bamboo, and go for a breather out into the fresh air. They were sleeping behind tinted glass. It was virtually impossible to take a photograph through that glass cage. She took several anyway, of a baby-faced panda lying on the floor, looking dead. Eyes closed. Black circles around the eyes, like spectacles. There were seven keepers around the two touring pandas. That was because the pandas represented an endangered species. Soon they might all be dead.

There was panda hype in the city of Winnipeg. Everywhere you looked, pandas were being advertised. Billboards, posters, t-shirts. Shopping malls made dedications to the two visiting pandas, Ming and Ching. Buses were painted all over with pandas. City council temporarily thought of renaming the town "Panda City." Then there was a counter-reaction. Teenagers, the ones who wore black, who drew comic strips, whose fashions were used clothes and candles and cigarettes, declared war on panda-hype with counter-posters of their own that said: *If I hear another word about pandas, I'll puke!*

Later, when she had arrived in Edmonton, she saw the sun was finally out. Scattered clouds tore across the sky, long and filmy. Here the horizon actually went up and down a bit, undulating restlessly, unlike the horizon in Winnipeg. Back there it was flat and straight. Here, looking west, it was known that not too far away were mountains. That knowledge changed a lot of things. It provided relief. The relief of an ending. She came to Edmonton in the afternoon and waited five days in an empty flat, while rain came down in flurries and storms brewed up and instantly settled down again. It was cold. Balloonists were disappointed because they could not put their balloons in the air on Labour Day weekend. One brave balloon flyer went up anyway. On Labour Day. His bright yellow and blue balloon rose slowly from the ground, tongues of flame flaring into the centre of the balloon.

She watched the balloonist from her top floor skyscraper flat. Thirty stories up put the balloon at a level with her. She waved at the pilot in the basket, who waved back. She did not have her camera for this, let alone a zoom lens. The movers had her equipment. All of it. And they were late. She lost five days of work because the driver of the truck was dawdling in Calgary. Her penthouse flat had a darkroom. She pretended that was why she took it. Not every apartment has a built-in darkroom. It was just a bonus that the view was so fine: the Saskatchewan River bending below, glistening in the sunset. The city lights at night. The helicopters below her window, hovering over the park. The balloons on Sundays: four, five of them, sailing by. Birds flying.

Now she had to get to know a new city. It was not her favourite thing, moving. Getting to know a city is like finding out where the nerves in your body are. Important business, especially if you go around taking pictures all the time. There was definitely something different about Edmonton. For example, one morning she woke up to discover that there was no view from the windows. The air was thick and white and she was in a cloud. Like when an airplane descends through the clouds. You know by the texture of the stuff out there that it is not fog. It is cloud. She hated airplanes because they represented a form of captivity. She disliked space stations for the same reason. Now it seemed she was fool enough to live in one.

The problem with captivity is that it tends to crash on you. For example, on the same day the man in the yellow and blue balloon took to the air despite the weather forecast, the Snowbirds crashed into Lake Ontario. Two of the planes struck each other during an air show, the wing of one hitting the tail of the other, and they both went down. One went down in flames. One pilot died while the other ejected and came down in a parachute, sailing from the grey sky into the grey water. It was a good photo opportunity. Some startling photos appeared in the papers the next day. On that same weekend, a Brazilian Boeing 747 got lost in the Amazon jungle and over a hundred and fifty people, as well as the airplane, were lost. And in Italy somewhere, a lone gunman went on a shooting spree in an international airport. Passengers waiting to board found themselves gunned down and dragged by airport personnel out the door and into ambulances. The gunman was wearing combat clothes. He died too, shot by police.

It was useless to wait for the pandas to wake up, so she wandered about the Winnipeg Zoo that day, snapping pictures of anything halfway interesting. A peacock kept crossing her path in a hurry. Wherever she turned, there was the blue peacock with its green decorative tail, snapping up anything it could find on the walkways. Bits of popcorn, crumbs, a peanut, a slither of foil paper. It was a furtive bird, looking up irritably and suspiciously between finds, scurrying past people as if to conceal its identity. Every time she raised her camera for a shot of the peacock, it ran off in a desperate hurry.

She sat down on a bench near "Aunt Martha's Farm," where domestic farm creatures were kept for children to crawl around with: pigs lying flat in the thick mud, rabbits by the dozen nervously scurrying about the rabbit pen, a pony with its rear end firmly planted facing the visitors, a goose constantly sticking its head out through planks in the fence. The late afternoon light was good for photographing. Everything deepens in colour and texture when the sun is low. She sat down on a bench and pulled out a copy of *The Free Press* to read while waiting for the pandas. In the Home section, someone was building himself a fallout shelter on his acreage. In the News, a young woman planted herself on some church steps in Montréal, pretending to be mentally and physically incapacitated. On the Books page, reviewers were assassinating the character of Canadian authors, especially local ones.

She looked more carefully at the peculiar news item from Montréal. The woman's name was Justine and she was really from Portland, Maine, but no one in Montréal could identify her. She had no memory. She was spastic and sitting in a wheelchair. Whenever a reporter or a doctor came near her, she began to jerk and twitch this way and that, swaying her head back and forth, rolling her tongue out of her mouth, and staring at ten different things at once. But she was pretty. Her limbs were apparently out of control, moving about on their own neural impulses. After many weeks it was discovered that Justine had done the same stunt in Boston and Miami and had been taken in by philanthropic medical people and social workers in all three cities. In reality she was quite normal. Her father claimed, in an interview, that when she needed attention, Justine resorted to this far-out mode of getting it.

She could swear the light was different in all three prairie provinces. The air was mellower in Manitoba, grainier in Saskatchewan, starker in Alberta. Alberta was the most photogenic province, probably in all of Canada if she did not include the Northwest Territories. Up north, the world is always displaying itself for a spectacular photograph. She began to take pleasure in following the progress of the light in her empty penthouse flat. The light would start cautiously, hazily grey, then a burst of brightness would explode onto the landscape between six and seven in the morning. It was like a theatre when a show starts. The curtain goes up, lights come on, activity begins. Little tiny cars meander about ribbons of highway. Minuscule bicyclists struggle forward, rolling their miniature legs.

Would a person go to all that trouble just to get attention? Apparently. When she was in Hamburg to photograph doorways, of all things, she stopped to visit an elderly man who had been her high-school principal. Harold was his name. Harold lived in a small brick house in the suburbs. Out front was a small garden and there was a view from the living-room window, but she could no longer remember what of. Harold's wife was called Ingrid. Five years before, Ingrid woke up and decided she had had enough, her five sons and one husband had finally driven her insane. Every day they belittled her, put her down, criticized her, miniaturized her. She snapped. From that day on she had no memory. She spoke like a child of five and if pressed, she might come out with a nursery rhyme. She sat demurely and childishly, smiling stupidly but very gently in the living room, while guests tried to act normal and carry on a conversation as if nothing were wrong. It was not a brain tumour. They had her brain X-rayed and no tumour showed up.

People work in mysterious ways. She was a nature photographer now, did animals mostly, but once in a while a people assignment came along. She was once asked to photograph the wreckage of a helicopter crash. A Canadian prisoner had apparently feigned illness and a medical helicopter was sent to take him south for treatment. On the way there, the prisoner seized control of the craft and demanded to be flown somewhere else. When the pilots refused, there was a scuffle and the next thing the helicopter crashed. There was blood all over the wreckage, but when she got there the bodies had been removed.

Later she told the agency that was not her favourite type of assignment and would they find other jobs for her. So she was sent to the Winnipeg Zoo to photograph rare pandas on display from China. This was right after the massacre of students and protesters for democracy in Tiananmen Square in Beijing. A lot of young people wanted something they thought would be more freedom. Suddenly over five hundred of them were turned into corpses by an army of bullets. It was all quite unexpected. Startling photos appeared in the international press next day. Faces screaming, bodies being dragged across the square to trucks waiting to take them away.

Below her flat in Edmonton, in fact right under her balcony, there was a landing pad for a helicopter. It was usually a yellow helicopter that came in and an ambulance or a van would be waiting nearby. When the copter landed, the van would pull up and various things would immediately be carried out of the aircraft and into the van. Occasionally there would be a body on a stretcher. Someone sick. Or possibly dead. She noticed this activity first on a Sunday. Right outside her darkroom was a loud grinding noise. When she looked out the window she saw the yellow helicopter, so near the building she could see the pilots at the controls. The copter hovered over a grassy area encasing the landing pad, and for several minutes it just hung there in mid-air, like a balloon. Then it landed. The doors opened and a stretcher was pulled out.

The Winnipeg Zoo was not crowded at that time of day. Most people were at home having dinner. It was a bizarre job, anyway, photography. Never anywhere to settle, nowhere to call home, no stopping for more than a few months in any place. How did one get into this? She barely remembered. Like her friend Alexander from Russia. They met in Copenhagen, photographing candidates for the ministerial elections. Alexander came from a Paris agency. They had to go out of town to chase one of their subjects through a deer park. It took all day. Afterwards Alexander wanted to go to a café. They found a small restaurant called Mocca, which turned out to have first-rate espresso.

Alexander was a brooding type. A café person. He lived for the hours he spent in a small, dark café, reading local papers, watching personalities come and go, running into strangers. In the Mocca, he talked in a tone midway between languid and enthusiastic.

"I was in your country once to photograph the economic summit in Toronto. I looked for a café, but found none. Toronto is a terrible city. I walked for miles and could not find a café anywhere!"

He left Russia on a passport to Israel. Applying for Israel, he said, was the only way to get out then. He went as far as Vienna, and then headed to Paris instead, where he had been since. Now with Glasnost, as it was just then, his mind was blown.

"I cannot believe it!" he almost shouted. "Now I want to go back. I want so much to go back."

She wandered about the Winnipeg Zoo for a while. Young parents were there with small children in strollers and on their backs. Elderly couples sauntered about with objects hanging around their necks. On the way to the zoo she had run into a German photographer, presumably also wanting to take pictures of pandas. She knew he was German by his accent, and a photographer by the equipment he was carrying. A confused young man, very thin, obviously new to Winnipeg. It was on Wellington Crescent, a good distance from the zoo if you were on foot. The young man stopped her on the walking path and said: "Excuse me but where is the zoo?" She pointed the way to go. It was the wrong direction and would lead the German to the Red River instead.

She had been looking into another airplane crash a month before. A Korean Airlines passenger flight, en route between Seoul and New York. Flight 007. The computer on the plane caused the craft to veer off course and head over Kamchatka, in USSR airspace. The Russian ground controllers were madly leafing through the regulations book to find what the rules were in a case like this. The book said: *if the intervening craft does not respond, missiles must be used.* They did. The airplane blew up and crashed in the ocean. All the passengers were lost. There were no photos of this. There was no photo opportunity, except at the airport back in Seoul, where people were photographed as they wept and screamed and threw themselves on the counters in desperation at the news. Some startling photos appeared in the international press next day of people showing their teeth and writhing.

She was planning a photo pastiche entitled *Captivity*. She would arrange snapshots of all forms of captivity, whatever struck her, and pastiche them together. The way David Hockney did in his photo collages. All the little pictures, nothing special in themselves, would reflect on each other and the effect of the whole would be, well, *revelatory*. It was something one could hope for, anyway. What interested her about the 007 crash was the captain of the Korean Airlines flight. He could have turned around much earlier, as soon as he saw his computer was a little off course. But that would have meant that in order to land, he would have to dump all the excess fuel he was carrying, for the plane was still too heavy to land. He was caught in his own pride. Fear of disgrace. Culture could be so costly.

The odd thing about her Edmonton situation, she was beginning to notice, was the perspective she had on the birds. She was used to seeing birds from below, peering upwards with her camera to get a picture of the underbelly of a bird in flight. But thirty storeys up she always got the birds from above. They sailed below gracefully, most of them white, and she got their backs and wings spread out. She could now take an omnipotent stance in her photography: be an omnipotent narrator, so to speak, and give up the partiality that comes with being two-legged and wingless. She also had the trees from above, just beginning to turn colour for the fall.

In the zoo, two grizzly bears paced the floor of their intricately structured cell, from end to end. Either irritably or anxiously, she could not tell which. They waddled in circles up and down the cement embankments. Sometimes they met when one turned around and walked back. Then they touched noses or kissed. Occasionally they fell into each other's embrace, either fighting or playing, she could not tell which. A single polar bear in another confine lay lifelessly in its dirty white coat after the heat of the day. Monkeys of all kinds threw themselves about in their cages, from limbs of artificial trees to the fence, where they put out their little hands for a peanut. A mama monkey sat motionless while her baby crawled over her, back and forth. She took pictures everywhere, trying to catch interesting moments in the lives of these captive animals.

Just after seven she returned to the pandas. When she entered the building, all the other visitors were gone. The guards were in the corner engaged in a silly conversation and giggling. It was quiet. The pandas were still asleep in exactly the same position she had last seen them. Two of them, one facing the glass, the other facing the back wall. One lay on its side, the other on its stomach. They were oblivious to the world. So very tired. It was supposedly because of the bamboo they ate. Bamboo has so little nourishment that the pandas lose energy very quickly and sleep a lot. She sat down on the floor in the opposite corner, next to the one facing the glass and lying on its side with all four legs stretched out. Between her and the animal was the tinted blue glass. She looked at the panda's face. So tranquil. They did not know they were at the end of the line. The last of the pandas.

She thought perhaps she ought not to take that picture. Possibly, for that very reason, that they were so rare, she should get up and go before the animals awoke, helpless and ignorant, blinking their masked eyes, looking around at the barren walls of their cage. So tranquil. So sleepy. She put her sunglasses on, even though she was inside a building. Through the shades the tinted glass appeared even darker.

Yes. That was it. She got up, dusted her jeans off with one hand, put the lens cap on her camera, and left. The sun was setting, splaying the horizon with orange. Exactly the view from her Edmonton penthouse. The deep red sunset splashed its colours onto the barren walls of her empty flat, suddenly illuminating the room with the hues of the night.

Monty Reid

Nisidoro
For Adam Melnyk

The urban
has come to the island
in the form of stone lanterns
that dream stubbornly
on the path to the trailer.

Who put them there?
Who dug the trench
for the wires that could carry
light to the lanterns?
Who knows.

Already the soft lips
of moss climb upon the lanterns
whispering the sweet lie
that they wish to go
no further

and the lichens dredge
across their surface
like a kiss, knowing
what a kiss always
knows, that it is not
the surface that kisses
back, but the deep
patient minerals, all
their open mouths.

Is it any wonder
the lanterns cling
to the wires with a passion
only disappointed stone
can understand.

They are waiting for you.
They still believe
in explanation, that
you will arrive and light them
with civilian fire.

Until then, a small bird
has built its almost invisible nest
in one of the lanterns
and has left there
three inexplicable eggs.

Stones near Stanley Point

For Taylor Roth

Yesterday I was down at Stanley Point
watching the stones disappear.

They have gathered in their harbour
to discuss the serious decrease in the world's
population of stones. There are no stones
left in the rivers, none in the quarries, none
at all even to commemorate
the rockpiles vanished from
prairie fields.

The untamed stones of the mountains
no longer come down to taunt the local
stones in the moonlight. Even the
cemetery stones are disappearing,
in spite of the vigilant eyes of the dead.
And yet the sea
continues with its hunger.

There isn't exactly an air of crisis
about them. Their deliberations
have left a thick coat of green
on their tongues. They have gathered
the kelp and wrack as if they would
build fires to hold back the tide.
They know any two of them
could be struck together to
make a flame. Still,
there are no fires, and every morning
there are fewer of them.

You know what it does to them.
It makes them long for some beautiful
and memorable gesture, before they are gone,
and so they signal, however they can,
to the beautiful tragic yachts, there
off the headland, with their spinnakers
pulling them out of a cold wind,
to stay off the rocks.

Or they prop up our little wharfs
of passion against one more storm.
It makes them forget what they are.
Then comes the disillusion,
and they walk together into the sea.

Yes there is still a captive population,
like the ones in the rock wall,
but who knows whether they
could be released back into the wild.
And there are a few in the Arctic bays,
stacked into shapes vaguely like us.
They're beyond saving.

So I'm going down
to Stanley Point again to watch
them follow each other into the water.
When they return none of us
will be able to recognize them.

Gossip Shoals
For Dylan Mardres

The sea is always talking. Perhaps it is only us prairie people
that believe it all the time.

Yes, it's ok to say that the sea is talking. There was the story about
the young woman who waited

and the one about the man who quit making payments
and the one about the pig war.

It's ok to listen. You can stand on your balcony and watch the white
waves undress upon the point

where the sea lions were and know how much it would sound
like the shoaling of blood in a dependable

heart. If any of us had one any more. If you could get
close enough to listen. It's ok

to admit it. I know the potatoes didn't turn out
that great and everyone drifted

out of the kitchen as if all those restless plates
that make up the coast had been reversed

and went quietly back into the incessant alphabets of water
with their compliments still

unspoken. It's ok to like this weather. It's predictable
that the kids will leave

and that they will phone you from the mainland and will never
imagine that Hope Bay burned down

and so has become inexplicably
necessary to replace. They could come home.

Even among your contentment there is a need for a place
to return to. And so we have stayed

across the ranges in the stable basin of our winters.
The views are familiar. Unrelieved but familiar.

We are the people who will believe whatever the cynical sea
claims is true.

Fred Wah

Railing

The words geese zone in above these deck railings I've just levelled, hover along the parallel absolute of the opposite shore.

The pilings come out of the lake bed at my blurry eyes older yet sure of the osprey, the nest.

Goodbye water says moving, even waves.

Honks.

Artknot Forty Nine

Stick to you as patience
Breaking foreign chases
Waiting for disaster
Attracting back the meaning
Facing all the numbers
Taking off your clothes
Sighing by the stove
Obeying all the stars
Rather let this murmuring
Return to disappearance

Stick to you like pasture
Broken foreign chances
Writing more disaster
A tract of surplus wordings
Opacity in marching
Faking naked truth
Breathing through your toes
Climbing up the stairs
Forever playing thoughtful
Repeating all the prayers

Music at the Heart of Thinking One Two Four

Say "Sheh!" to get up from the log to get lost and put into cadence the synchronous foreignicity of zone in order to track your own ladder of exhaust swim into the next story some starving elephant as the imperial slacking of alterity just such a gap in trans to collate the terra of potency except for being frightened by hunting this dispersal of planned punctuation will rob the arrow of its feather the dart of its you.

Some juncture of the moment that requires action, needs to be voiced, even though one might fear a shift from the quiet sitting position to the forces of navigation and their necessary paradigms of anticipation, estimation, and trial. The synchrony of estrangement, the unknown, and mapping could be as simple as willing to climb a ladder in order to learn how to swim. This is, of course, a privileged style of movement and the common can be seen as a gridlock that excludes the external, starves the senses. Wherever potential openings can be located intention is reminded of its uncertainty and at the same time gains new guidance systems.

Music at the Heart of Thinking One Two Seven

The shoulders of eating, the sack full of ginger, the Blakean beach, the other word at the end of the word, the curl from kulchur, the grade for the course, the genome in their home, the rap at the door, the spoon full of the rice, the chop for the lick, the tongue in a knot, the circuits of surplus, the milk in the way, the valley beyond the valley, the end of the world.

No mass is without something else, something added, other. The one and the many. Taste is a gradation of foreignicity: we come across some abandoned specific with the realization that it isn't represented in the sphere of culture surrounding us. These particles of recognition and desire, subalterns and alternatives, solids that could melt into air, are what we use to intervent and domesticate those homogeneous aggregates of institution and industry that surround us.

E.D. Blodgett

Summer

Where the gate stood open, the smell of flowers came. It seemed that we
had stood beside this fence before – before we knew that we were we,
before we were the children that we were – and all the flowers were
invisible beyond the gate, no more than rapid blurs of colour that
were summer going past, as if it was summer only moving
there, not us, the smell of flowers passing us. We alone
endure, another summer standing up in us, a summer of

hanging fences where the smell of flowers floats serenely on
the summer air, and in them children, children that we were as we
remember them are playing, rising undisturbed by age above
the flowers, gazing at us through the fence with undiscerning eyes,
the way that flowers look toward the sun, their one eternity
in us, a sun for them they cannot see, but flowers that assume
that we are where they are, their summer us, the light we shed

upon them knowledge of their standing near a fence, the twilight and
the sound of people going by, a town forgotten under trees
that are unknown. A universe could pass, and with it hope, desires
and whatever came to be along the roads and under skies,
but they float up inside us, and alive, the sun we are a light
that is enough to hold them, nothing that they are more moving in
us than the colours that they are, no nearer than the summer air.

O

Certain things are noticed first: the colour of the sky is of
a colour that has stopped beside the clouds that are unmoving on
a colour that resembles palest blue, the trees have opened to
the limits of their most inspired largesse, the light suffused
from somewhere that remains unbidden by the sun, and every house
is standing in the place of its original foundation full
of light, reflecting clouds, the unbelievable resemblance of
the sky. A clock has struck, the echo of its music hovers in

the air and takes upon itself a colour of the sky that is
incapable of being other than its first expanse of blue,
an echo, then, of blue that falls again upon our faces that
appear to be another music filling space until the end
of music high against the sky from where it falls again, a rain
of distance and of blue, and all there is to hear within the air
is o and o and o that fills the country of our childhoods
with inarticulate, precise refrain. Our faces are no more

than this, each a round and periphrastic turn of blue, and there,
inside, roses stand, one a mirror of the other, receding
toward the farthest sky of roses echoing with roses. We
are innocence that strays unknowing into its incapable
and barely speaking o – or mirrors of a light that is of no
departure, light that only is and in its lightness places us
alone in our self-reflection, compasses of our where
that measures our replies that in our eyes is but roses and their o.

Kabbala

Think of God playing with the little stones, the stones becoming
alphabets, and universes slowly coming into sight
as anagrams, the sun a language of its own, its light upon
your face, a murmur in the dark of flesh conversing, filled with what
the sun might say, being composed of stones that speak in tongues, fires
of the Pentecost falling at random everywhere on us
and on the farthest planets, little stones of fire speaking of

our origin, of you and I in our flesh, uncertain near
the trees and grass, but you and I whose simplest words are not of our
possession, words that are an echo of the stones that God within
his fire cast upon the air before the air was anywhere,
a you and I that cannot know our merest sense, no more than we
can know what planets mean, possessing only kinship with the stones
that lie about us on the ground, their silence us in memory.

Playing

When we were young, we used to play dead. It was a ritual,
dimly understood, where we would lie with eyes closed, a hand
upon the heart. The game had no relief, except to wake and see
the sun, somewhere lower in the sky, to feel the grass beside
our bodies, waiting for life to enter us again. Sometimes our deaths
came back to us, stalking through the places of our memories
with ceremony and repose. The trees are always grander, skies

transfigured, light untroubled by our flesh, but passing through, and we
became by turns translucent, sensing angels. Now it is enough
to touch each other passing by for knowledge of the endlessness
of rituals and childhood to pause within our eyes, unsure
of where to place their grave observances, our bodies now become
what we recall but made flesh, the sun aware of its horizons
there, and children, mouths in flower bursting open in our hands.

Bert Almon

Feeding the Power Grid

As we drove through the Battle River valley
he gave us a social history of the farms
on the east side of the road: who had died
childless; whose children moved to town
and sold the land to strangers; who is banned
from owning any cattle after the winter
twenty of them stood starving inside
a fancy electrified fence. Once in a while
the stories are racy: "That guy married a big woman
with hair on her face who could whip
a grizzly bear with a switch." He doesn't look once
to the west, where great mounds of fresh clay
have been tossed up by the drag lines. The strip mine
will pursue the coal a hundred metres down
to feed the power grids of Western Canada.
This was the farm where he and my wife grew up,
the place where their mother's ashes were scattered.
"Dust to dust," "the common clay" – fine phrases,
but the mine goes deeper than gossip or Genesis:
there was no oral history in the Cretaceous.
His past burns like filaments in a light bulb.

Hampstead Elegies

20 Wentworth Gardens
The contents were brought from Vienna:
now Berggasse 19 is furnished
only with photographs of objects
you'll find here, like the famous couch, topped
surprisingly with a colourful blanket,
and the green bucket chair. A house
riddled with atmosphere.
The antiquities on the wide desk
and in the cabinets are funeral objects.
I liked best the little Egyptian boat
with its mummy case and entrail-jar.
It has three kneeling attendants
whose oars are lost. Prow and stern
have figureheads that look like bland sea-serpents.
Once there was a chart to the land of the dead,
and set answers for those who challenge the soul.

On one display I saw the x-ray
of a jaw eaten by cancer. I looked again
at the frieze from the Roman sarcophagus,
two mended fragments, the seam visible.
It was not the usual scene of Endymion
sleeping in a field, visited by the Moon.
It showed the crowding shoulders
of the mourning Trojans bearing the outsized
and mangled body of Hector above them.

Wentworth House

> "— for axioms in philosophy are not axioms until they are proven
> on our pulses."

The two houses were made into one
by an actress who owned them long after.
Some of the letters are on display
in glass cases covered with blue brocade.
You can lift the cloth to read the browning ink.
Every reading fades them by a tiny increment
but you can't resist. But when you reach
the final words, "Good-bye Fanny! God bless you,"
they're too private, replace the cloth quickly
and leave them in a harmless dark.

Outside is the second plum tree,
planted to replace the original
he sat under writing about the nightingale.
The replanting raises the same question
as the poem, about individual and species.
I'm told the basic problem of philosophy
is the relation of universal and particular,
something he asked of the nightingale,
something he asked by underlining
"Poor Tom" in his copy of *King Lear*
when his brother was dead or dying.

Rudy Wiebe

Watch for Two Coyotes, Crossing

And Cain went out from Jahweh's presence and lived in the land of Wandering.

—Genesis 4:16

• 1. My name was Kane. Paul Kane, painter. The work of a painter is to lend his eyes out.

I was born in Mallow, County Cork, Ireland, on September 3, 1810, and died suddenly (as they say in newspapers) in Toronto, Ontario, on February 20, 1871. If anyone remembers me now one and a quarter centuries after my death it is because of a singular journey I made across North America. When I started it, I had already been wandering for nine years, living as I could by my painting in the United States, England and Europe, and even a bit of Palestine and Africa. But who can count the thousands of painters, many gifted beyond the imaginable grace of God, who have endlessly repeated for us the images of those lands, seen with much the same eye because the painters have already made us see them so often? No painter had ever looked at what I saw on my ultimate journey, I started all the seeing. Perhaps I should say, I could have.

Love enters at the eye and, like it, is a circle; but moving I think.

When I was almost nine my parents emigrated to Upper Canada, to York, the village at the head of the Toronto Portage which a few years before the Americans had attacked and largely burned. From our ship entering Toronto Bay that muddy little place was difficult to see among the prodigious oaks and maples. Even the steeple of the first St. James' Church, which had not been destroyed and was grand enough at the time (though nothing like what it was later), looked lost on the quarter of a million acres of forest the Empire bought from the Mississauga Indians in August, 1805, for ten English shillings – it still has to be cleared, you know – paid for in their own Indian tobacco, I heard them say, and largely smoked on the spot.

Money. Who knows about that so-called "Toronto Purchase" for ten shillings? Few if any of the millions now living there. Can a travesty be dignified by an honest word like "purchase"? My father, Michael Kane, who had somehow survived Napoleon and retired a corporal of the Royal Horse Artillery, tried for years to be a wine merchant on the corner of Yonge and Adelaide, and he always preached the practical English dictum, "A deal's a deal, it's only good or bad in the eye of the dealers." And his sole other legacy was like unto it: "Just remember, money makes the world go round."

And I do remember, still. He said it so often I have no choice. Even though my mother Frances never agreed with him; she was Irish and insisted the world went round on something else.

• 2. I left Toronto on May 9, 1846, and returned to it October 13, 1848. Two and a half years, over six thousand miles on foot or by boat, canoe, horse, snowshoe, dogsled – not a single step of road, nothing of railroad – through the lands of eighty different Indian nations, I could not have imagined such visual richness existed in the north of America; in Europe wilderness is mostly thought of as always one, and "wildly" picturesque. I returned massively long-bearded and gaunt, but with a pencil journal of 119 pages and 500 paintings and sketches: stories and images to overflow the twenty-three years that remained to me.

On November 18, 1847 I was forced to leave behind my smudged, water-stained sketches in a tin trunk among the frozen brush of the frozen Athabasca River because – ugh, dates, statistics! the muck of accounting, money, money, how can I – the following spring voyageurs brought them to me again in Edmonton. I re-made them into some one hundred large oil paintings, I lost count of exactly how many but I lived on the money they brought, yes I painted to sell them, and the journal eventually became a book illustrated by my paintings and published in London in 1859: *Wanderings of an Artist Among the Indians of North America from Canada to Vancouver's Island and*

Oregon through the Hudson's Bay Company Territory and Back Again. It also appeared in French, German, and Danish.

Why I mention in the title that company name, now the oldest continuous business enterprise in the world, should be obvious to anyone living in the advertising nightmare of the 1990s: to go on my journey I had to convince the most relentless money-maker in Canada that my wanderings would be profitable to him. Sir George Simpson himself who, when not being carried about his fathomless domain on the shoulders of French Canadian voyageurs, sat occasionally in his mansion overlooking the Lachine Rapids, Montreal, Lower Canada; with his much younger, beautiful but white invalid wife Frances Ramsay, Lady Simpson. Through his governorship of the Hudson's Bay Company he had long ago decided that he controlled, by money, a land three times the size of Europe, from York Factory on Hudson Bay to the arctic Beaufort Sea and the mouth of the Columbia River on the Pacific Ocean, to say nothing of the northern latitudes of what is now Quebec fronting the Atlantic. For him money decided everything, a true 20th-century man a century ahead of his time – but with an added dollop of 19th-century aspiration: nobility. Sir George, Governor-in-Chief of the Hudson's Bay Company, but better known as "The Little (for his short legs) Emperor."

Immense colonial wealth, untouchable colonial power: surely achievements of true nobility for the illegitimate son of the eldest son of a Scots Presbyterian minister.

• 3. I stared too much into the deadly light of the sun on snow during the two long winters of my journey. And yet it was a journey too brief, I often thought later, an entire lifetime of preparation and then so little time, a little more than a dozen years of eyesight really, to exploit it.

Exploit. A fine Simpson word that, so effectively ugly. Whatever I saw was overlaid with his voice always as it were at my shoulder: "What a magnificent landscape – it needs development." For without his permission and his expenditures, I would not have been there to see it.

During the journey itself I had no time to notice that the light had begun to destroy my vision: I was too busy moving, staying alive, absorbing what I could in the strange changing worlds that confronted me, that tried to transfix me into motionless parts of themselves. In those later years, the 1860s in Toronto, when my wife Harriet would let herself into my studio on King Street where I kept trying to re-see what my often hasty sketches – fur brigades move seventeen to twenty hours a day in the long northern light of summer – provoked like an illusion of spirits dancing beyond control in my memory, she often found me crucified on the floor, my burning eyes hidden under an arm, no brush or pencil in my hand. She had such heavy work of it caring for me and our four small children, but her hand then was delicate as prairie mist in the morning.

"Harriet…Harriet," the tips of my fingers see every tiny particularity of her face, though I know I will never again be able to draw it. "You could be Margaret Harriott, my Harriet."

She laughs; it is a game she has created for the sake of her participation in what she in loving kindness accepts as my to her inexpressible memories. "But that, Mr. Kane," she says, "is merely an accident of sounds – my name is Harriet Clench."

Frances Lady Simpson was no "accident of sounds," and so easily avoidable as a play of verbal memory. A secret that lived in my most solitary visual recesses, her hand and extraordinary skin almost exactly mine, a quarter of a century younger than her stumpy husband's. And my finest paint then dared a glance, to dream it.

But to continue the play with my loving wife, I always answer. "Your name was Harriet Clench," gathering myself again with a small laugh. "Marriage changes names."

"Only for women."

"Miss Harriott's name was then not changed, not yet."

"Nor was mine, then," laughing too. "Though it might have been."

"But not to Celtic 'Kane'?"

"Who can say – and you told me yourself, in the North-West only certain kinds of marriage changed names, for certain kinds of women."

"Yes, I told you…yes…." My contemplative fingers.

"And did you see Miss *Margaret* Harriott with your fingertips as well, Mr. Kane?"

Sometimes she shifts her repartee that way, meaning whatever she means, and I am forced to scramble if I wish to retain our comfortable, to us acceptable, blind exchange. As I do, I do; though on occasion I wonder why she will never dig deeper. Almost I think I wish it.

• 4. The first time I saw Margaret Harriott there was no possibility for fingertips. On the frozen North Saskatchewan River, the winter afternoon light so silver where the cliffs broke away raw across the river to bend east and steam wisped up through the ridged ice like intermittent spirits, breathing. My eyes were still superb in December, 1847, careful and swift as a painter's must be to catch the instant, and keep it, and I saw her coming towards us in the second sled quicker than Young John Rowand – though no quicker than his wife Mary, to judge from her face.

Young John Rowand's Mary. Whatever her real name was, a Cree "daughter of the country" as such "reputed wives" were then called by white men or the legitimized sons of white men who took them to live with in the fur territories. Cree Mary – what other mothering name could she have had? – was laying spruce chunks on the fire while I sketched her, leaning forward at the waist like any lady into what leaned away from her as pale flames strangely silver against snow. Her classical nose nudged a bit, beautifully, askew, her skin warm as fondled brown stone. Under her hooded fur I could discern the body of a slender Greek but sadly, as always, her face must suffice me.

"You better get in the teepee," Young John grunted behind me. "Out here you'll freeze your fast fingers."

• 5. "Young" John was the son of Chief Factor John Rowand, the "King of Edmonton," and nearly as enormous as his father: 300 pounds nurtured on thirty-six years of buffalo meat and dripping. But even walking on snowshoes as long as my body, he had come up through the creek bush soundlessly behind me. I lost my pencil line for an instant, though he had startled me before with his silence, his enormous shape beaked suddenly over my shoulder.

I had only one skill, as mysterious to him as to the Indians who crowded about me when I drew – See, powerful medicine, it makes your face appear out of paper! – but Young John considered my skill supremely useless; he spoke to me only in order to help keep alive, as he thought, a helpless man in inexplicable high favour with the supreme Sir George.

"She's so –" but I dared not utter "beautiful," not to his bearish, glowering face. "My oils are hard as rock, right beside your fire or I'd –"

A shout from below on the river, the voice of their son. And the distant ring of sled bells as all the camp dogs about us burst into their apocalyptic howl of enraged greeting. I don't know why I was looking at Mary then, but I saw sharp as if I'd painted it how her smooth face froze. She had recognized the second sled coming around the bend of the river: a cariole, and in it a white woman.

Young John was rumbling at Mary, Cree too rapid for me to decipher any words except "Fort Pitt," but then he broke off; he too had recognized the cariole woman.

• 6. Margaret Harriott. Not bothering to lift her arms in her furs to greet us, the sled long as a sarcophagus thumping her over the broken and shelved ice. At least seven days out of Fort Pitt with four men who could speak nothing but Cree or doggerel French carrying her around like the untouchable, cocooned insect she was for them, Chief Factor John Edward Harriott's daughter to be deposited with her father in Fort Edmonton. Going there for Christmas, going there to become a bride, going there to have her wedding portrait painted by me. Fortunate girl.

Young John's Metis companion, the hunter François Lucie, had emerged from his teepee and, with the boy by the river below, was hallooing mightily, arms wide. But Young John barely acknowledged the whistling, dancing whips of the drivers as the three sleds slid by. He merely flicked his hand at Mary, who immediately vanished into their teepee, and then as he himself stooped to enter, said over his shoulder to me,

"Tell François to take you back, to the Fort."

• 7. The HBC flag that snapped on the flagstaff over Fort Edmonton's inner square was precisely the same throughout the fur territories. By December,

1847, I was twenty months into my wanderings and I had learned, exactly, how everyone inside a Hudson's Bay fort lived within the Company's particular customs, its own peculiar laws. The reasons for that were simple enough: in 1670 King Charles II of England gave a charter to an enterprise designed to make money for its shareholders, in a land he had scarcely heard of and certainly cared nothing about. That solitary purpose remained for each fort factor: make money for the Company and you will make money for yourself. I was, therefore, surprised when I came through the river gate of Edmonton into its Inner Square.

More than surprised – utterly amazed. Not by the exploding dog fights, which are usual enough when new teams arrive among the hundreds of local beasts and which only indiscriminate beatings by the drivers will subdue – no, amazed at the livid white face of Miss Margaret Harriott screaming, above the dog bedlam, at her father:

"Wedding? I come for Christmas – *my wedding?*..."

And John Harriott standing like a bent sheep in the fort where he was, supposedly, absolute despot. While his wife Nancy shouted back at the furious girl, their voices bouncing from log walls and palisades,

"...plenty of time...after New Year's...what is all this..."

Questions and answers shouted or not given, what were they about? Did Miss Harriott not know? Had she not been informed of her own marriage? The Company clerks and maids and workers stood motionless about the square and on the Big House balconies, clouds of excitement snored in the frozen air; a regal spectacle acted out before every servant, a celebration of arrival indeed!

• 8. Two nights before the ravenous dogs of Edmonton very nearly devoured the Reverend Robert Rundle. Rundle was the first missionary Simpson ever permitted to enter his territories and he, as was usual for him, was carrying one of his small fluffy cats in his arms across the inner court to his quarters when he stumbled and fell among the dogs.

Not a hair of the cat was recovered, and often I had seen in the eye of a Company worker the same gleam with which several went out of their way to tell me that story: I with my papers and many little pencils was surely a fluffy indulgence of Company royalty. Fort Edmonton was not, of course, the court of the Emperor; that followed Sir George wherever he went in his immense flotilla of canoes with his irrefutable decrees, met him at every Company establishment as bowing factors and always available harems (and occasional children, some sometimes acknowledged; born as he was, Simpson understood well the inevitable vagaries of illegitimacy), harems of Indian or Metis (his preference varied) beauties of endlessly accommodating, delicate brown.

And for continuing services rendered in a remote posting, the Edmonton Rowands and Harriotts were known to be his favourites; definitely the families of the Princes Royal. Therefore, when I set up my easel the next morning to paint Margaret dressed in her wedding splendour of lace, I existed merely as a servant hired for his eyes and fingertips, nothing else.

"Father, you tricked me!"

Harriott had the surface evasions of a decent man who, when sober, knows his shortcomings only too well. This early in the day he could only plead like maudlin melodrama:

"My beautiful daughter! I so wanted to explain all this to you before, but letters are so very difficult –"

She was not beautiful. Handsome perhaps, as seventeen can be under high emotion. Obviously the best the English governesses at the Red River Academy could do, but she would never be shaped into a "lovely, tender exotic" for the highest possible connections: there was too much the tough sturdiness of her "bit of brown" visible in her. And in her voice.

"Daughter!" she burst through his words. "I've seen you five times in my life, and now you arrange this overnight marriage to a man more than twice my age who's been – "

"Your mother died," he interrupted quickly, "in that horrible mountain snow! You know that story, how could I keep you? The Company sent me, year in, year out, from one wilderness post to the next, how –?"

"You needn't have married a child bride."

"What?" His tone hardened then. "My Nancy – no Company trader could ask for a better wife."

"You married Old John Rowand's daughter at sixteen because he told you to, and this – arrangement – for me with his son, who everyone knows has wives and children behind every bush on the Saskatchewan, this is his plan as well!"

"Margaret!"

"Because I'm white enough to dignify him? Because I'm, God knows! a virgin?"

I couldn't believe it. Was this how the imported governesses trained old traders' daughters in that "little Britain in the Wilderness" of a Red River Academy? She had gone too far, even for Harriott, her face blazing with her unconfrontable facts.

"You will not speak that – I am your father!" Harriott's tone became that of the chief factor explaining the day's orders to his voyageurs. "Among us, a father makes the best possible arrangements for his daughter's marriage because he best understands our situation. Young John has the best possible connections in the entire Northern District, with all the governors, with Sir George himself. With you for his wife, you will rise to the very top of the Company."

"Like his father," she spat at him.

"Yes! Like his father!"

"Because I'm 'white' enough?"

"Yes, that helps!"

And then she truly astounded me because she had a more powerful word than "virgin" to use:

"How 'white' was my mother?"

For a moment Harriott could not speak. He pulled at his greying sideburns, so carefully trimmed for Christmas celebrations – or the anticipated wedding. Like many traders he drank too much, but he had not been sufficiently obsessive about money: he had a library of several books, he was no Simpson or Rowand; this, his only child from his first marriage, whom he had always disposed of as seemed necessary, was his best hope for a comfortable Company old age.

"Old John," Margaret said in a tone so abruptly sweet as her lips curled – if only my brush could catch that twist, a superb transformation! – "has had a Cree wife for forty years. Though he's never actually married her. And he's considered to be just below the Emperor himself. Vacationing alone now, as always, doing what he pleases in the 'imperial palace,' in Montreal."

"Such marriages," Harriott said, relieved at her apparent change, not at all sensing her sarcasm, "'in the way of the country' were fine, long ago, but their time…my dear, please, consider our situation, yours and mine. The Company's land is so large, large! Sir George insists his leading men must now have wives as white as possible, and properly married – there's a Methodist minister living here in Edmonton right now! – it is the determined policy of the future, my dearest Margaret, don't you see? You have travelled it, summer and winter, this endless land!"

He was waving his arms wide. To fill the sitting room with all the prairies and mountains I had struggled to cross, all the ranges and plains and hills and forests and rivers and grass and glaciers I had seen vanishing into continuous distance wherever I turned. And I knew that no lifetime of copying Old Masters in Rome or Amsterdam could ever help me actually see such a land. No painter can choose vision by another's eye, much less love.

"Your children will have all of it," Harriott pleaded. "This is your inheritance, this land, think of it! Larger than Europe!"

"Yes, think of it," Margaret said, strangely abstracted. "What if…when I marry…like my mother I go –" and there she stopped. She did not say "mad." "…like my mother…I…walk away."

Harriott groped for liquor. Perhaps at that moment Margaret's voice, words, were like her mother's. A month before, when our brigade was struggling towards Edmonton on snowshoes through the high snow of the Athabasca Pass, the men showed me a desolate valley and told me the story of how seventeen years before Elizabeth Harriott had left this tiny girl carefully wrapped in blankets on the snow there, and wandered away, vanished into her own particular wild. Not even her body was ever found.

• 9. Another person besides me heard this astonishing conversation in the Rowand sitting room. Mrs. John Rowand, Senior, though to my knowledge she was never openly called that. It was of course her room, and she must have been there all along, for she certainly did not enter after me, but I only saw her, suddenly, when Harriott took up his bottle and ran.

How could I not have seen her? Seated on the floor, her ancient head beside the fireplace bent into the firelight over a needle and leather. The woman Old John would later describe on her death certificate as "my reputed wife, the mother of all my reputed children." In English she was called Louise Umfrieville, a woman of the Saskatchewan, as much brown as white, though until she saved John Rowand's life and he "married" her she had lived Cree.

Harriott did not seem to notice her as he left; nor did Margaret.

• 10. Margaret Harriott was considering me. Or perhaps she was glaring; certainly her eyes burned in that loggish room of dull, frosted windows. I had not actually achieved much on my paper, barely a quick outline of features, the planes of posture on the chair. Too much to see, to hear.

"Do you often paint brides, Mr. Kane?"

"If I am commissioned, I...." I responded too quickly, stupidly, and stopped; she had no interest in a revealing honesty from me.

"Brides who refuse to be brides?"

I could only work, furiously now. "Well...in Europe, painting, I found most young ladies agree with their fathers."

"Most."

"Most...a few...may convince their father he is telling them to do what he wants...."

"When actually it is what they want."

"Yes."

"Perhaps I would agree to be a bride, if you agreed to be the bridegroom?"

"I?" Luckily I was holding a pencil, not a full paintbrush. "I don't...."

"Our educations are, I think, compatible, and at this moment I know you better than I know John Rowand."

"We...we've scarcely met...."

"Exactly. You heard my father: marriage in the 'Empire of the Company' is an arrangement between the prospective son-in-law and the father of the bride."

"Well...I'm flattered, I...."

"So, would you care to speak to my father?"

And finally I could laugh; the fundamental subject of every sitting room with any social pretensions, anywhere in the English-speaking world, here discussed not by gossiping aunts but by the possible principals themselves, direct confrontation – it suited the smoked log surroundings! And so I blundered on,

"But I hardly have the connections…it took me two years to persuade Sir George Simpson for permission to travel in his brigade! And the great inheritance your father so eloquently – I can offer…really, nothing!"

Margaret Harriott let me bumble on in my gaucherie, my uncomprehending reason against her precise irony. But finally she did relieve me, her voice abstracted, gentle:

"Presumably I already have all the inheritance possible, Mr. Kane. From my mother and my grandmother."

Obviously she did. Sitting thus, she was the Queen of Edmonton without attachment to grotesque Young John Rowand. Was if she wanted to be. Certainly more so than Frances Ramsay Simpson no matter where Sir George might have her carried, his cousin and wife enduring the ongoing illness of rich monotony in Lachine, the lovely China rapids just beyond which in 1532 a deluded Jacques Cartier thought he could already see the coming spices of the Far East. My painting of Kakabeka Falls facing her on the dining room wall, reminding her of her endless canoe-brigade honeymoon in 1830, a slender child dragged along three thousand miles of roaring fur-trade rivers with their people staring without words but with knowledge at her, a grow- ing awareness of the driven five-foot-two mechanism of a man she had in complete ignorance, except for his wealth, agreed to marry. But there was another painting, one I made just for her, that Sir George never permitted her to see. Not even after he was dead.

If you paint by commission, you never own what you paint. But then, if you're lucky, you never have to see it again either.

"You want to see Young John, he's outside there."

I was in Fort Edmonton, in the sitting room of the Big House. The soft, almost expressionless English words of the old woman by the fire.

And so he was: even from the second-floor window of the Big House her huge son towered above a herd of shaggy Blackfoot ponies twisting about half-terrified in the yard below; around the flagpole. He was choosing one, rejecting another as the Blackfoot argued their qualities; I had not noticed the din of trading outside until that moment.

Margaret had stood up too, but she did not look through the parchment window at her possible husband. She stood before my sketch with her slim body of white wedding lace poised – as if alerted to a bug. I hastened to explain:

"I'm a bit slow, tomorrow you'll...."

"What are these...pillars? Throne?"

"Your father wanted a...you know, regal. And, personally, if I may...it is appropriate."

"You find me 'regal'?" For a moment she looked at me wide-eyed as if she might possibly be interested in who I actually was.

"I'm a painter, I paint what is asked for, I...." I laughed, "My English father always said, you'll excuse his language, 'You dance with the bloke who brung you!'"

Her black eyes were deep enough to vanish me.

"I was born here, in the western mountains, here," she said with a peculiar emphasis. "I grew up on the Saskatchewan, at Fort Carlton where my mother's father John Peter Pruden was the chief trader. A Scot of course, working forever for a Company pension. My grandmother died when I was nine, my grandfather just called her 'Anne,' he lived with her for thirty-seven years, why would he know her real name? I spoke better Cree than English when I was dispatched by cart to Red River after she died. Perhaps I still do.

"Mr. Kane, do you actually think Cree royalty is best presented on a Victorian throne with a vague background of Corinthian columns?

"You accommodating ass."

• 11. The facade of the post office they built in 1852 on Toronto Street still exists. When I was alive it was just around the corner, north, from my office on King, and I had to pass its four elegant Greek columns at least twice a day;

fortunately they are Ionic. There are parts of my journey I never wrote down in any way, nor coded into my impossible notebook spelling, nor told. Not even to my good wife Harriet, née Clench. Nor of a painting I made that was destroyed by the short despot who commissioned it.

It may be I could have told these stories; if I had been a better painter.

• 12. But my eyes were what I had, and they were for hire. Whatever I had, it could always be bought and paid for. I saw Margaret Harriott once more before her wedding on January 6, 1848 – at the Fort Edmonton Christmas banquet where I was given the honour of carving the dried moose nose. I danced with several "dusky beauties" as they called them then, dried wild flowers woven in their wild black hair, but Margaret never so much as glanced at me or said a word, neither then nor when I stood as witness to the wedding ceremony conducted by the still catless Reverend Rundle. Why me? Perhaps someone anticipated I might someday be famous. Margaret did not acknowledge my existence even when I had to stand within inches of her, her husband bulging black and bearded over her. Her shoulders bare, my hands clenched together behind my back, hard clenched.

In any case, to paint her I did not actually need to see her again; all my life I had an excellent visual memory of a certain formula kind.

I often wish I had had the perception to paint – or at very least sketch, I did hundreds of every possible animal, scene, person – but I never sketched Louise Umfrieville, Mrs. Rowand. Her sitting room was full of chairs and thick, furred sofas, but she sat on the worn stones beside the fire, sometimes feeding it with split logs, her right hand forever poised as a swift, silent needle. She never spoke a word that I heard to run the household; with Old John gone once again, she too had decided to let her daughter Nancy order the house, as Nancy's husband old Harriott ordered the business of the Fort.

What did she say to me, beyond telling me her son was among the horses? What was her name?

I comprehended too little of names and my own aging then. Despite what I thought of as my omnivorous, insatiable eye, I know now I was always looking for what Sir George had instructed me so explicitly in his letter – to draw

"…buffalo hunts, conjuring dances, warlike exhibitions or any other scenes of savage life with a view to their being coloured and framed, and of equal size so as to match each other…." The European obvious: the picturesque. Which could be hung on a proper wall in a room in a rich house, no matter what possible world of image, make it small and fit for such a wall, all one size for landscapes, all one size – larger – for portraits of savage manliness, especially as seen in chiefs and warriors. And for youth, those beautiful, strong young women with their incomprehensible skin. Cunnawa-bun in her embroidered elkskin dress, her beads snaking in spiralled layers around her neck and over her breasts moving as I danced around her, as she danced so gravely, moccasined feet together in one spot while she turned, dancing, always to face me, her fluid skirt shaped by her long legs, fringes dancing. Cunnawa-bun, "One Who Looks at the Stars," she told me. Holding her white swan's-wing fan by its exquisite porcupine-quill handle above her eyes while I painted her, sat motionless, patient, looking past me with a slight smile; so near in unfathomable distance.

A father's or a husband's name attached to her would mean nothing. And hanging in a room on a wall….

How was I so ignorant as not to ask "Louise" her name? Perhaps she would not have told me – why should she? I could not see her, then. Though I do now; each decade more clearly. She endured in the enormous four-storey "Rowand's Folly" of John's house, a soft mound on the floor of the largest sitting room in the North-West. Her despotic "reputed husband" never took her anywhere, even if she had wanted to go, no more to Montreal where their second son Alexander was a medical doctor than to Hawaii in 1842 when Simpson took him along on his travels around the world. An inexplicable incarnation of much Cree and little English, always useful, always used, always there.

To me, remembering, she is the incarnate spirit of that place; of the people of the Saskatchewan. Over whom Sir George imagined himself the emperor. As I laboured to finish John Harriott's commission, she told me two things.

One was: "Margaret's mother, you know she had bad luck. She went a little bit crazy, that's okay – but in a bad place, that's bad luck. Lucky thing, she left that baby wrapped tight in a blanket, the men brought her here, ten days sucking a leather tit soaked in buffalo blood. I'm too old then, but there's lots of women here, lots of good milk."

The other: "Hunnn, maybe two coyotes crossed her path and she didn't notice. They say her mother was her father's cousin, but they got married anyway, had a baby anyway. Cree people don't marry that way, a man marry his uncle's girl, your uncle is really your father, then you're marrying your sister. Real bad luck."

Luck. I understand now the story she was telling me concerns Cree "medicine," power that can be experienced as either good or evil, depending, but actually English has no word that can deal with it. Just as Cree has no word for English "sin." I should have understood her then.

And would have; if I had dared to be a better painter.

• 13. Two days after the wedding, on January 8, 1848, a party of thirteen people started from Edmonton for Fort Pitt two hundred miles down-river. Young John Rowand had been named head of that Company establishment, and so he led the three carioles and six dogsleds out onto the river-ice trail.

A cariole is intended for one person only, a thin, wide board curled up at the front with a straight back to lean against; the sides and top covered by green buffalo hide with the hair scraped off, dry and white like parchment. When I slid myself down into the cariole I was to ride, it seemed I had slipped into a beautifully bound book. Or white coffin.

Later I painted a picture, without sketch, of our long caravan around two bends in the river, the standing spruce piled over, weighed low by snow and the dogs running furiously as they always do at first. Each cariole is painted with sprays of flowers, every team decorated in celebration, their collars and cloths fringed and embroidered with fantastic colours, feathers waving, tiny bells ringing clear above the sleds' swish and thump. "A Wedding Party Leaving Fort Edmonton" now hangs occasionally in the Royal Ontario Museum in Toronto. Standard landscape size, nineteen by twenty-nine inches. I am stretched out in the last cariole, my wilderness hair streaming. Margaret is in a sled so far ahead it is indistinguishable from her husband's.

I also painted a picture of François Lucie, his former hunting companion, complete with plumed buffalo hat, embroidered sashes, and rawhide parfleche.

On the afternoon before the wedding he took me hunting and showed me how to "make a buffalo calf." Our Fort Pitt caravan passed François' camp a few minutes out of Edmonton. It still stood on the same spot where I had tried to draw Mary bending at her fire. There she stood, between François and her young son (by Rowand) in front of Francois' teepee; she did not raise her hand in greeting as the wedding party passed, though the other two did.

The buffalo were extraordinarily numerous that winter; sometimes they nearly surrounded the Fort, grunting, farting, and sometimes they broke into an inexplicable run of dusting snow and thunder. Several came so near pawing for grass they were shot dead from the corner palisades. At night the wolves howled outside the walls and sang us to sleep; they were after the horses herded inside for protection, a horse being much easier to hamstring than a buffalo, and perhaps tastier too.

As for hunting, rather than blaze away at a wary buffalo from a distance, dull sportless work at best, François who hunted for the Fort showed me how a herd can be approached close enough for excitement. Two men "make a calf" when one covers himself with a wolf skin, the other with the light brown skin of a buffalo calf. They crawl through the snow on all fours until they are within clear sight of the herd, and then the "wolf" pretends to pounce on the "calf," which begins to bellow as in fear.

I played the wolf and François the calf, and his terrified bellowing was so perfect that a buffalo cow immediately turned from the herd and ran towards him. However, an enormous bull near her seemed to understand the trick, he tried to stop her by running between her and us, but she was too agile, she dodged him and charged so that François had to throw up his hide and shoot her. The bull ran up, smelling her all around where she had fallen. We had no interest in him, in this season only the sweet meat of cows is eaten, but he would not leave. He tried to raise her up, he shoved his immense head under hers, grunting as they do, almost like a groan. He was so unmovable that in the end we had to kill him too. "Pretty strange, eh," François said, his knife in the warm body of the cow faster than my pencil on paper. "Sometimes...a bull is like that, he won't leave her. And she for sure never leaves her calf."

The bull was magnificent in full winter fur, a massive "bell" hanging under his great hump at his throat. But only his tongue was worth eating.

• 14. Why did Margaret Harriott marry a huge, obese man more than twice her age? To be eight years the mistress of tiny Fort Pitt? By 1856 her husband had left the Company, no king he, and moved to Red River to live on his wealth doing nothing.

By then "old" John Rowand was dead, of an apoplectic fit suffered while, typically, screaming at a voyageur. It happened at the York boat landing under Margaret's Fort Pitt window. When the old man collapsed, screaming, the voyageur fled and two days later was shot in what young John recorded in the Fort journal as "a hunting accident." They buried the old curmudgeon at Fort Pitt, but George Simpson, when he heard about it, had his own ideas of proper royal fur burial. He had the body dug up, the half-rotten flesh boiled away (voyageur rumour had it by an Indian who was kept drunk the whole time, and that the Fort women made soap with the gallons of fat thus rendered), had the bones sealed in a barrel and shipped, via Norway House and York Factory, and from there all the way to London (because the voyageurs – who had suffered Rowand's abuse for forty years – would have dumped it in some deep rapid as soon as their canoes left the Saskatchewan waterways), and from there back across the Atlantic and up the St. Lawrence to Montreal where over four years later the barrel was opened and the bones buried at last, November 10, 1858, in Mount Royal Cemetery. In the plot beside Lady Frances, dead then for a year.

My wife Harriet says, as I try again to forget that travesty, Frances now lying forever between rotting little George and the clutter of John's immense boiled bones, "What else could Margaret do?"

"His thick lips…his bulging, ugly face…grotesque." Behind the underground darkness of my eyes, my memory grows uglier than when I could see the light. "Eight men could barely lift his coffin, he weighed four hundred pounds when he was finally dead!"

"So, Margaret could deal with Young John I'm sure, why wish him on your beautiful Mary?" my Harriet asks.

"At least with Mary he was a hunter, that's what he really was, and maybe he'd have been lucky and died young…crashed off his horse, broken his neck…gored by a buffalo."

Harriet says gently. "He 'turned her off,' the way the white men did then, to François. Took care of Mary as well as…as necessary."

After a time she continues, "Did Margaret tell you about her new grand-mother at Red River?"

She told me nothing; she just called me an ass. But the loutish royalty of the fur trade had no recreation beyond drink and gossip: I heard a great deal resting as the mosquitoes permitted around evening fires. Gossip of the white pretension of governesses brought from England; of how old John Peter Pruden, John Harriott's ancient uncle and so both Margaret's grand-uncle and grand-father, hauled Miss Anne Armstrong with her face like the bottom of a slop-bucket to a Fort Garry altar four months after the death of his "reputed wife and mother of my children" – that is, Margaret's grandmother – before he heard the rumours that she had spent every night of the three months' voyage from London to York Factory in the captain's cabin (though that would hardly have stopped him since, though well soured, she was white); gossip of Margaret's youngest aunt, Caroline Pruden, known everywhere as the most beautiful woman in Red River, being married off to the retired money of another groping old Indian trader.

"Did Margaret have children?"

I lie quickly: "No."

And my wife grows thoughtful. "How did…could she do that?"

"Maybe two coyotes crossed her path, and she noticed."

"What?"

But I cannot explain what I do not understand.

"Seventeen years," Harriet muses, "to survive her 'grotesque' husband as you call him, and now she's the wealthiest woman in the North-West. She lives in Silver Heights above the Assiniboine River, a house certainly grander than Rowand's Folly with no old Simpson to tramp over her every year. Why do you keep wondering, 'Oh, why did she marry him?'?"

But I do. I lie on the floor, my arm over my blind eyes forever. It may well be, if you will not see, the time comes when you cannot.

Fred Stenson

Midnight

Fort Edmonton, 1828

A man enters a forest clearing. A bird falls dead at his feet. If he ignores the omen and keeps walking, what is he? A man free of superstition? Or a careless fool?

The omen One Pound One brooded over was the death of his interpreter John Welch, which took place at precisely midnight, the moment of New Year's, 1828.

One Pound One had never been the kind to carry on long after someone died. Death was too common, something to shrug off and be glad it wasn't you. So when the Chief Factor turned nervous in response to Welch's death, he was the most surprised observer in all the fort.

Wherever he went, whatever he did, his thoughts would not leave the Edmonton ice cellar. They never stopped seeing the bluish corpse that lay there on a bed of skinned and quartered buffalo, where it must remain until the frost went out and a grave could be dug.

Whatever the relationship between One Pound One and Welch had been, it was not friendship. The Chief Factor could not name Welch's children, nor did he reliably remember that of Welch's wife. He had never been inside the interpreter's cabin and did not recall ever inviting the man to his own rooms for tea or brandy.

The death obsessed him nonetheless: the ominous way it happened and the particular man it killed. These were portents and One Pound One feared they might mean his success at Edmonton House was threatened, that a golden age had been cut off at New Year's midnight, after which something lasting and dark might begin.

Why One Pound One felt this way could be traced to events in two separate places and two separate years: Chesterfield House, 1822, and Edmonton, 1826.

The first occasion, 1822, was when Welch picked a fight with a bunch of Big Bellies outside the pickets of Chesterfield House during the Bow River Expedition, a failed venture in search of beaver they failed to find. Welch had cheated the Indians in a trade, or so they said, and now he'd been caught by them, outside the fort with no friends to back him. If Pambrun hadn't come along by accident to haul him away, Welch would have likely died there and then.

One Pound One had been second officer on that expedition and so was well aware of Welch's close call. But that alone had not been enough to make him decide that Welch's life was charmed. Anybody can be lucky once. In fact, his response had been to mark a cross beside Welch's name in the list of engagees, a mark to remind him that he shouldn't count on the man's being around for long. Next time Welch cheated someone, or his temper got the best of him, he might be alone and no hero handy to save him.

The second time was in Edmonton, in the fall of 1826 when some Stoneys came to Edmonton to trade. They had traded a few peltries as a ruse, then got behind a herd of Edmonton horses which they tried to drive away.

A Halfbreed named Lussier was the quickest into the saddle after them. He gave chase so fast that the first exchange came between the pickets and the trees. One of Lussier's bullets found the back of an Indian. The Stoney slumped in his saddle but kept riding and did not fall. Lussier drew his dagger then and rode after him. Just as the horses drew even, the Stoney straightened up and fought. The Indian fought hard for his life and only when he was badly weakened from loss of blood could Lussier finish him.

That was just the beginning.

Had the Stoneys not lost a man they might have taken their horses and gone. Now that the horses had cost them a life, they wanted a better bargain for it and so they stayed.

Though not numerous enough to keep the fort besieged, the Stoneys made it so the Edmonton horses had to be guarded by day and kept in the fort at night. Still, they were able to steal a few more. Then the Stoneys got too bold and lost a second man, not killed this time but captured. One Pound One locked the Indian in the bastion.

For some reason, the presence of that Indian captive, singing and carrying on in the bastion, caused a pall of dread to come over the fort. The gossips began to moan and whisper that the Stoneys were only waiting, that they were preparing an attack. No Indians could be seen beyond the palisades but they were believed to be there, sneaking through the grass, coming for their man, ready to inflict heavy damage on his captors if they could.

About then, the business began to affect the temper of John Welch. He started with a tirade in his cabin. Smashing things and putting his woman and children on the run. When he came out into the flag square, he was yelling that no damn Stoneys were going to keep him hiding in the fort like a frightened child.

Before long, he had gathered a company and they threw open the gate and marched out. Under every bush and broken sledge, they poked and prodded, until a bayonet thrust into a haystack sent thirty Stoneys flying.

The chase was on.

Some of the Stoneys ran for the river and a few others turned and fired. In plain view of the fort, three of the Indians were shot dead, while on the Company side, John Welch fell with a bloodied breast and a shattered arm.

The company men chased the Indians toward the river, and in all the smoke and chaos, exploding fukes and crying men, Welch was left behind, unconscious and bleeding. But after a bit, he awoke, climbed to his feet, started a bloody zig-zag for the fort.

As Welch got close to the Edmonton palisade, he looked up and saw the Stoney prisoner, the one who had started the whole thing, climbing down the outer wall, escaping. Welch drew his dagger. He let out a yell. He made one last furious rush. "Like a dying grizzly bear," was how One Pound One put it when he told the story. He told it often, his favourite yarn.

There was a collision between the two. The Indian fell one way, dead. Welch fell the other, presumed dead.

But Welch did not die. For several days he lay in a swoon. Then one morning he woke up. Just like that he sat up, produced a great vomit of blood, and lived.

The whole time Welch had been lying as if dead in the fort, the battle with the Stoneys kept on. After the first exchange in which Welch was shot, the Company had chased the Indians to the river, expecting them to plunge in and swim for it. But instead, the Indians had seemed to vanish into the riverside fringe of trees and bush. Not a hair could be seen of them and a deadly return fire started up from that position of invisibility. What it was, the Indians had dug breastworks in preparation for their attack. Safe in them now, they took command of the battle.

In truth the Stoneys were never driven off. Tired of the war, or simply satisfied with the result, they finally left of their own accord, driving upwards of twenty Edmonton horses ahead of them.

What they left behind was five severely wounded Edmonton men. One Pound One was a doctor's son and the closest thing to a physician in the fort. He studied the men's wounds and, after a long deliberation, pronounced them all fatal. He could see no medical reason for any of these men to go on living for long.

What guaranteed that the story would stick with One Pound One, as one of the strangest occurrences he had ever witnessed in the trade, was this: after Welch sat up out of death's swoon and puked himself back to life, *every one of the other wounded men did likewise.* Brebant from an arrow in his chest. Pepin, the blacksmith, from a bullet in the haunch. Sinam, the Cree Indian, from a bullet through the shoulder. Even Little Assiniboine, who had been shot clean through the throat. Every one of them recovered, rose from the dead to do the Company's work another day.

One Pound One was not a superstitious man and he proved it by not expecting, after these events, that his men would routinely jump up and live after every case of wounding. But according to some other arithmetic, he did conclude that John Welch had qualities approaching magic. To recover from such terrible wounds, coupled with his earlier escape at Chesterfield, seemed to make a case for his having a fiercer grasp on life's cable than an ordinary man.

What's more, given the four who survived with him, maybe Welch had the
ability to transfer his bulldog tenacity in the matter of staying alive to others.

Though One Pound One despised superstition, and tried to beat it out of
his men each time he found bags of pagan trash hanging around their necks,
the Chief Factor was now guilty of believing in a lucky charm himself. What
he believed in was John Welch, and what he believed was that Edmonton was
a luckier place, a safer place for having Welch in it. Now, when that same
man lay dead in the ice cellar, torn asunder from chest to crotch, it was an
understandable shock, an opening to dark forebodings.

Most men would suffer such a feeling to wear off gradually, but One Pound
One could not. He lacked the patience. Going about his fort in the first ice-
cold days of 1828, he trailed his woe like a dog with a cut arse. He turned
upon himself to snarl and bite. After a week, with the nervous agitation still
upon him, he was enraged. He locked himself in his office with a keg and a
foot of tobacco and vowed he would not come out until he had decided who
to blame. By blaming, you at least proclaim that effects have causes, and if he
could just find the cause in this case, he hoped to free himself of the notion
that a cloud of black luck had blown over his territory and meant to hang there.

From the moment he started to think this way, the Chief Factor was drawn
to Christmas Day, 1827, as a point of departure. In the chain of cause, the first
link seemed on every pass to be the moment on Christmas when Ted Harriott
and his woman Margaret came clattering down the portage road from Fort
Assiniboine.

One Pound One had gone out to meet them and the first thing he noticed
was the lack of decoration on either Harriott's cariole or his dog harness. In
keeping with his transport, Harriott himself was badly dressed and stinking of
rum. The day was brilliant, so much so that you could barely open your eyes to it,
and such a golden light made Harriott look even worse. He had the pallor of
mushrooms and he looked at you from deep inside a starved face.

His Halfbreed woman Margaret looked better, sober, well dressed, pretty,
but One Pound One saw something about her too that made him shiver. Her

eyes were bright enough but One Pound One saw there was no connection between this avidity and anything going on around her. Same with her laughter which ignored the joke and sprang forth out of nothing.

Before they sat down to the Christmas feast which was already underway, Margaret insisted she must change into a better dress. She came to the table finally in such a monstrosity of bead-covered nonsense, One Pound One had to laugh. He couldn't stop himself. The thing must have weighed a stone.

Harriott, meanwhile, acted like he saw or heard none of it, that his woman's antics along with everything else was a little more than he could follow. While the officers were toasting in wine, brandy and shrub, he somehow managed to keep toasting himself in rum. He must have had a keg cached on his cariole that he went to each time he excused himself to piss. He grew steadily blearier as the evening wore on, the map of veins on his nose and cheeks ever brighter and more complicated.

What Harriott was that night – ask anyone – was dull. Not one story worth listening to. Not one joke worth laughing at. Just complimentary nonsense about how fine the meal was and how clever the decorations. When the men separated from the women to smoke, he fell silent altogether except when goaded by a direct question.

– What's the news from Assiniboine?

– What? Oh, nothing. A quiet place.

He also had a gift these festive days for avoiding One Pound One's company. The Chief Factor never caught Harriott in the act of avoiding him but he must have been. How else explain that One Pound One was able to have private parlays galore with Fisher and Harriott's uncle John Peter and the rest, but not so much as a private minute with Harriott himself?

During his talk with John Peter, not only Harriott's uncle but his woman's father as well, that old man had complained about Harriott. The grizzled trader asked One Pound One what he knew of the domestic life of Harriott and Margaret.

– Good lord, John Peter. Your daughter. Your nephew. Why ask me?

– The nephew has nothing to say and the daughter makes no sense.

Speculation about the couple was cut short on the morning of New Year's Eve. Before dawn, Harriott had his cariole loaded and his dogs hitched. He bundled his wife into the sleigh and declared himself ready to go. One Pound One had never seen Ted Harriott pass on a regale but he did that day. He was full of reasonable-sounding blather about weather and having left only one man in charge. He was still firing back this lame nonsense when he started his dogs and made his crippled jump onto the sleigh.

One Pound One was not fooled. The reason Harriott was leaving was sitting right there in the cariole, face peeping out of her swaddle of skins, absorbed in something no one else could see.

Their going should have set the mood right and everyone pretended it had. It was to give the day a rectifying boost that One Pound One had allowed the drink to pour even before the winter sun had set. This meant the usual New Year's allotment of rum was gone well before midnight, and to keep the tempest wild, the Chief Factor made up several more toasts out of his private store.

But whatever Harriott and his woman had done to the day was hard to repair. Margaret had touched a lot of the women with a lick of her strangeness. Many men had adopted Harriott's trick of getting joylessly drunk. They were all dancing of course but the jig steps had no heart in them and the fiddling was off-key. There was not much love between lovers and not much fight between enemies.

As a remedy, a sweetener, One Pound One could think of nothing but to apply still more spirits. What else was there? Far from cheering the crowd up, it had the opposite effect. A Hudson's Bay man's gauge is set at a standard measure. He cannot deal with more. Given so much to drink, the louts fell about the place, lamely trying to fight. Men and women puked until the floor was slippery. If you shut your eyes, the sound was an animal din.

Just before midnight, One Pound One supervised a final pouring and left, disgusted. He remembered Welch coming to him by the door, dog drunk like the rest, wanting to know the time. The Chief Factor had pulled his watch out, held it dangling before the interpreter's swimming eyes. The two hands were about to clap at midnight.

Then One Pound One pushed by the interpreter into the night, crossed to his house. He was sitting on the bed pulling off his boots when he heard the cannon blast. Happy New Year, he said out loud by reflex. He said it to no one because Louise and his children had stayed behind to dance.

On New Year's Day morning, 1828, the fort slept late, or pretended to. Taken as a whole, the place was like a wounded animal that crawls into a shadow to lick and suffer itself either dead or back to health.

One Pound One had taken enough drink to make his head pound, but lying in bed was not his way. He dressed and stomped back and forth. No one rose to make his breakfast so he took his foul temper out of doors, into a sparkling morning where the world was coated thick with hoarfrost.

He walked about the fort and the silence oppressed him. For company, he went inside the horse corral and stood among the beasts. Their warmth and homely noise. Grunting and nuzzling his pockets for food. But a man couldn't do that all day. He kept moving and in so doing followed trails in the snow left by the evening's revellers. A piss-yellow bore hole here. A basin of puke there. A big trampled area speckled pink and two trails of more definite red going away.

The reason he climbed to the bastion was because he wanted to see the cannon. In his search for something amiss, for someone to scold, he remembered the midnight explosion. The one responsible would have been in a hurry to get back to the midnight ladies all lined out for kissing. Likely, he had left the cannon uncleaned, in a mess.

What One Pound One saw from the bastion doorway did not cause him to shudder or his guts to heave, perhaps because of the almost comical way John Welch was lying plastered against the wall by the force of the exploding gun. Like everything else this morning, the corpse and the cannon were coated in frost, bristling white. Welch's eyes were open wide and the face with its white beard wore a surprised look, as if his parting word with life had been, Oh.

The hoarfrost made the cannon seem fuzzy and soft, even along its burst and ragged seams. The crater that was Welch's belly was likewise decorated, the blood itself having grown an old man's beard. We need a new cannon, One Pound One told himself.

He stood a moment longer and imagined what must have happened when the night's celebrants heard the blast. They heard it, they cheered, and all the men kissed all the women. But not one of them, the drunken, careless fools, noticed that John Welch never returned.

Finally then, One Pound One had his chain of events constructed. For him, the death was recorded this way:

Harriott and his mad wife came to Edmonton for Christmas and New Year's. The trader's drunken sadness and his wife's madness had set the festive days askew.

One Pound One had tried to put things right with an excess of liquor.

Drunker than their custom, the men and women of the fort leaned toward destruction. John Welch leaned so far that death reached up and took him.

Clumsily, Welch set the charge. He probably threw in extra powder for a nice big bang. He lit the taper, lowered it to the fuse. Ignition and an outward wrench too strong for the old cannon to hold. It split and engulfed his midsection in fire, shot his guts full of hot splinters travelling faster than he was as he flew toward the wall.

But the sad thing for One Pound One was that, having explained it all, having affixed the blame, he felt no better. When he left his smoking office, the rum keg empty on the table, the doomed feeling left with him, barking at his heels.

What kind of year begins with such a midnight?

Vivian Hansen

Sounding the Medicine Map

You learn to pick your sites well. These are the places that keep your secrets from flailing, directionless, in the wind. They are points along an unmapped prairie, zones intact within larger life. They are sites of permanence; demarcations of meaning that separate past from present and future, merging all into a moment: a snapshot. You never know where is your medicine. Or what it is. Or if it will be easy to see, to sight (for sore eyes?). Will it be words, like wounds that someone cites, out of a Journal of Medicine? Medicine is Power.

The site is a place on the prairie that hails "over here" upon the wind. You turn your head toward the sound: of what? A rock, a stone, Iniskim – buffalo rubbing stone that calls, not only the buffalo, but sounds out the depths of your heart, measuring your ability to sense your site. This place counts the twenty-eight ribs of a buffalo. The prairie unknown by linearity and parallel zones, despite the power lines anchored to the Bow River valley. The prairie is terra incognita, unknown, dis-membered in a chance to be dis-embodied place on a map.

Mapped? Yes. This site discerned by geodetic survey markers that confirm what 5,000 years of travellers have known: the Medicine Wheel sits atop the highest point on the prairie. You know this…because you know. The wheel is close to the river valley, buffalo jumps, and tipi rings. Its rock cairn effaces the landscape. This place, this site, is both terra firma and incognita. It is the place of the Medicine Wheel, the place where you will dust the stones with ashes. Here you will lay the dust of your friends when they need a sacred site.

These rocks existed before and after smallpox, before and after the residential schools that hurled stones at your heritage. This wheel is a stone cairn with concentric stone rings and lines radiating from that cairn. At this place, intruders will leave their spirits half in stones, for it is known as the place that holds back the spirit.

You may not know the Medicine Road, at first. Lined with rocks, it is unfamiliar, only perceived as the crow flies. Were you the crow, you would see the prairie yield a direction. Linearity is easy to follow; we have practised its forms. Not so easy to perceive is how these forms fit within a circle.

Point One: Medicine House

Abandoned now. I search for signs of life in this space. A woman lived here in 1920, a pioneer, survivor. She planted wild rose bushes, hoping for their stretched arms around the periphery of her land, sheltering her from the wailing prairie winds.

Those roses are now twigs, some still gasping for life. I step past their rows and enter the door frame of grey-brown boards that were painted a lime green. This colour of life has eroded to the sage prairie blue-grey. Only the most muted colours survive here in the protective colouration of stewed beans.

I test the floorboards cautiously, anticipating a betrayal of my weight. Peering at the floor, I realize that I cannot fall far; the floorboards are three inches above the frozen ground. I yield to a human urge to climb. The attic rises above me, beckoning my interest. Carefully, I tiptoe up these curiously sturdy steps, as though the care I take will lose the critical mass of weight necessary to crash through the boards. Relieved, I notice that they do not give way, and I am permitted access to the attic.

The remains of a baby's bed frame my looking, the springs coiled eerily, rusting in the dim light.

Point Two: Medicine Stones

A glacier stopped here for the winter, waiting too long to map its destination. The sun got to it, melting away its crags until finally it sagged, releasing its load of rocks, stones, pebbles. The stone ridges marked a glacier fortress that later lined the paths of human inhabitants. This is the valley of the shadow of death for glaciers. It is life and medicine on the prairie.

Point Three: Medicine Rubbing Rock

Imagine the prairie covered endlessly by buffalo. They too, like the glacier, stopped here for the winter. The hot sun lured out the ticks and fleas and mosquitoes that tormented beasts. Then, a rub against that rock, hollowing out the earth in the circumference around stoneflesh, leaving the wallow for centuries to come. Only the shadows of that beast remain, the hollow of its pleasure and its relief.

Point Four: Medicine Tree

Last of its kind in the valley, residue of farm site, roots stretching like an upside down pyramid into the earth. Another landmark on the way to the wheel, this tree clings tenaciously to its underground spring. Source/Sorcery.

Point Five: Pointing Root

Remains of what? A dead tree? A grave? It points to the northwest and the Site. No riddles in its treasure map. Find the root and you will see its point to the Site. Then...wind past the Medicine Tree, through a cattle-guard. Follow this dirt road past more glacial over-wintering, rubbing rocks.

Point Six: Medicine Wheel

You climb a hill to the cairn, a resting place. This is the Majorville Medicine Wheel near what is left of the ghost town of Majorville, Alberta. A Metis woman's final bed. The only way to empower her prairie dust. The wind is cold and fierce today, as I think it must be most days. You climb the cairnstones to view the site, aligning the stonespokes in your mind's eye.

I watch you pull her dust from the urn, pouring her bone-pebbles into the tiny caverns of the cairn-pile. "Cover her with a rock," you command. It is the only time you have spoken during the making of this map. There is nothing to say on the barren prairie, for so little is heard. Should you sing, the wind would be your choir. Pray and the words will sound your musing. Dance and the wind will lead you around the rocks in a stumbling two-step, not quite your own rhythm.

I find a rock etched with the mould of wind, time, and moss. It is her quilt, your Metis Mother's comforter, covering her in death with the Medicine Rock of eternity. Ashes to ashes, dust to dust, the chant easily moaned in a maelstrom of reminder. The wind woos the sibilants into caress – around the medicine site.

Thomas Wharton

Salamander

The compositor needed one more comma. He stirred the piles of metal slugs in his typecase, hoping that somehow, in spite a lifetime's meticulous care, the particular piece he needed might turn up in the wrong compartment. He dug into the deep, lint-haunted crevices of his apron and came up with two slender wooden coigns, but no comma. Coigns. He had more than enough of these space-filling slivers. He had an entire ship that could be chopped into useful splinters if need be. Already he'd been tearing away pieces of rotting plank to keep a fire going throughout the increasingly cold nights.

The first sixteen-page forme of the book was ready to be locked in place. If he delayed much longer, the day's light would be on the wane and it would be more difficult with each passing moment to observe the fine details of his work. He glanced out the porthole of the cabin for the first time that day. A small square of the world presented itself to him, the same restless but unchanging tableau he had looked at every day since he was first marooned here: a bit of barren coastline, wet black rocks occluded not and again with a burst of spray and beyond them, a truncated swell of leaden sea. The northern summer was almost over; the days were getting shorter, and would do so with greater rapidity, he foresaw, than they did in his native city, far to the south and washed by another sea.

He had no choice. The forme would have stay as it was, imperfect. He consoled himself as well as he could with the thought that it was a very small matter, a comma. Even if it had been a z, never mind an a or an e, he doubted he would have been able to continue. As it was, very few readers would notice the absence of what was likely the most invisible of all the markings meant to mark the rhythms of *human speech. Slipping one of the wooden coigns into the empty space where the comma was meant to go the compositor swiftly locked up the chase, set it on the bed of the press, secured a slip of paper between the tympan and the frisket, and began.*

On the last day of April, in the year 1707, the Royal Observatory at Greenwich recorded an eclipse of the sun lasting precisely seventeen minutes and twelve seconds. The eclipse delivered a profound shock to the scientists at the observatory; such a phenomenon was not scheduled in their astronomical tables. Even worse, the moon was still visible in another part of the sky.

The eclipse, seen across much of Europe, was responsible for the cessation of several battles raging that day, including one on a grassy plain in Hungary not far from the Danube River, between the armies of the Hapsburg and Ottoman Empires.

When the shadow of the eclipse fell across the earth, my grandfather, the Slovak nobleman Count Konstantin Ostrov, was kneeling before the body of his youngest son, who had just been struck by a sharpshooter's bullet. Ludwig, not yet twenty-one, had drawn his sabre against the Turks for the first time only a week ago. His dying words were, *Go home, father. To Irena.* Having kissed his son on the lips and closed his eyes, the old count turned his gaze away. Through the smoke of the guns he saw the two armies standing motionless as if enchanted into stone, only their rival pennants alive and snapping in the wind. He saw the black sphere rolling across the orb of the sun. And last he saw the frail, ghostly crescent moon, adrift in the darkening sky.

The symbol of his enemy, the crescent moon, rendered ineffectual by an apparition without name. What could it mean? My grandfather swiftly decided that this riddle had been designed expressly for him.

Drawing his sabre, he cut from his son's head the warrior topknot that all Ostrov males wore, tucked it into his belt, and rose shakily to his feet. Over the years the aging count had watched all three of his sons die on the field of battle. Each time he had cut off their topknots of lustrous black hair as mementos, and gone on fighting. His scarred, lamed body had grown old and stiff in the defense of his homeland. Now at last the time had come, he vowed

as the eclipse achieved totality and a spectral night descended. Time for him
to cease fighting. He would not seek vengeance upon the Turk. He would
honour his son's last request, return home to his one remaining child, his
daughter Irena, and devote himself to his long-abandoned dream.

As a boy, my grandfather had loved puzzles.

Crossword puzzles and that newfangled craze called the jigsaw puzzle, cryp-
tograms, mathematical oddities, riddles and philosophical conundrums, optical
illusions and magic tricks: they all beguiled him and all, the count came to
believe, were related to each other in some secret way. Together their solutions
suggested a vague shape, like the scattered place names on a mariner's chart
that trace the edge of a blank and unknown land. The philosophers of the age
were asking why or how God, a perfect Being, had created an imperfect world.
A world which at the same time the new science was taking apart and showing
to be a complicated, intricate machine. Perhaps the answer to such questions
could be found in these seemingly innocent diversions of the mind. Was not
the mind itself a composite engine of animal imperfection and clockwork order?

Yet if there were a single solution to the infinite puzzlement of the world,
the young count had been forced to abandon the search for it. In the tradition
of his forefathers he had taken up the sabre and spent his life on horseback
defending Christendom from the Turks.

This celestial enigma my grandfather saw as the call to return to his lost
boyhood kingdom. Accordingly he resigned his commission, carried his son's
body from the battlefield in state, and retired to his ancestral castle on a
precipitous island of rock in the River Vah.

The count had *trompe l'oeil* doors and windows painted on walls, filled
rooms with ingenious clocks and perpetual motion devices which he would
spend hours disassembling and putting back together, forced his dinner guests
to solve riddles naming the dishes to be served before they were allowed to
eat. Beginning with a prisoner taken in the battle, a mute Turkish boy who
had six fingers on each hand, the count populated his castle with servants he
called human puzzles: giants, dwarves, three-breasted women, contortionists.
Many of the menial tasks in and around the castle were, however, performed
by ingenious devices or by automatons that the count named *robots*, from the

local word for compulsory labour. There was a mechanical manservant who polished boots and a mechanical maidservant who brought fresh bedsheets. Count Ostrov dreamed of a castle in which there would be no living servants at all, but he never succeeded in having an automaton fashioned that could cook his roast pheasant hearts just the way he liked them.

Secluding himself on his island, the count soon discovered that his intellectual solitude was threatened by another kind of invasion: that of the bureaucrats. Following the latest round of Wars, Councils, and Peaces, the empire of the Hapsburgs, like a vast blood-stained puddle, had changed shape yet again. As a consequence, all boundaries and hereditary titles were under review. Count Ostrov found himself besieged by government functionaries toting satchels bulging with documents, rolled-up maps under their arms, maps which they spread out on his huge oak desk to show him what the Imperial Survey Office and the Superintendency of Frontiers had jointly decided: the River Vah now formed the new boundary between the Arch-duchy of Lower Moravia and the Principality of Upper Hungary.

In consequence, they told the count, *although your forests, fields, and vineyards are all situated in Moravia, this castle stands precisely on the border, and thus falls into two administrative districts.*

Which means? the count growled, stroking his moustache.

Which means that Your Excellency is now subject to the duties, excises, levies, and fiduciary responsibilities pertaining to both states.

The count argued that by this logic, his castle did not in fact exist, as an entire castle, in either Moravia or Hungary.

Therefore, he countered, *I should be exempt from taxation or any other kind of meddling in my affairs by any government.*

The document men plunged into their law tomes and surfaced with an obscure ninety-year-old lex terrae stipulating that a fugitive could not be shot at by soldiers of two countries as long as he stood precisely on the border. *For if he be wounded in a leg that stands in one realm,* the statute read, *some of the blood he sheds will of necessity flow from that part of him residing in the other, the which transfer of vital humour falls under the Unlawful Conveyance of Spiritous Liquors Act.* Such a man, in other words, remained suspended in legal and political limbo for as long as he took not a single step in either direction. And so it appeared that by analogy the count's argument for autonomy was sound. Yet the document men insisted that an exemption of this kind could only take effect in the improbable circumstance that there were no separate, self-contained rooms in the Castle Ostrov.

Just as the several parts of a man's body blend together seamlessly, they reasoned, *so your castle would have to be a space in which, for example, no one could say exactly where the gaming room ended and the chapel began.*

At that moment Count Ostrov had the great revelation of his life. Not only would he fill rooms with enigmas and brain-teasers of every description, he would transform the castle itself into a giant puzzle, a devious labyrinth, a kaleidoscope in three dimensions.

Dry goods, cookware, clothing, furniture were gathered from their respective niches and redistributed throughout the castle. Ancient walls were knocked down and centuries-old doors taken off their hinges. Fixtures were unfixed, immovables became movables. Rope bridges were strung between balconies and parapets, winding passageways built that circled back upon themselves or led to impassable walls of stone. Then came the tables, chairs, and beds mounted on tracks, the mezzanines that lowered themselves into subterranean crypts, the revolving salons on platforms filled with halves of chairs, divans and settees whose other halves would be found along far-flung galleries amid a clutter of incompatible household objects.

The crowning achievement, however, was the library. The count hired a Scottish inventor who designed a system of hidden tracks, chains, and pulleys to create a ceaseless migration of books. Without warning bookcases would sink into the walls or disappear behind sliding wooden panels. Others dropped through trapdoors in the ceiling or rose from concealed wells in the floors. The entire castle in effect became the library, and no private space was inviolable. A guest at the castle might be soaking in a luxurious bath, or attempting the seduction of a servant, when, with a warble of unseen gears, a seemingly solid partition would slide back and a bookcase would trundle past, the count himself often appearing in its wake, absent-mindedly hobbling after the shelf from which he'd plucked the volume he was absorbed in reading.

In the nearby villages the people wondered what the count was up to. An astronomer who had been invited to the castle on one occasion told anyone who would listen that in the complicated movements of furniture and walls the count had mirrored the orbits of the moon, stars, and planets. An old cavalry officer from the count's regiment disagreed. He insisted that the seeming chaos of the castle in fact reconstructed the various stages of the last victorious battle against the Turks. The count himself of course preferred not to reveal what particular system, if any, had provided the model for the workings of his puzzle castle. One thing for certain was that it was all devilishly complex, and made more so by the count's insistence that, although the rooms merged, there would be no such intermingling when it came to social classes. The count's bed, and Irena's as well, roamed through the castle at night, but the count saw to it that neither of them came near the areas reserved for the servants. The servants themselves had to remain as unobtrusive as possible when they went about their tasks. They learned to walk behind moving pieces of furniture in order to remain concealed, to take circuitous routes that kept them well away from where the count and his guests were to be found. Irena was another matter. More than once, she had helped the household staff conceal some mishap that would have brought the count's wrath down upon them.

After long months of embarrassing blunders, collisions, accidental re-emergence of discrete rooms, and numerous other difficulties, the kinks and snags were smoothed out and the count sent at last for the imperial functionaries. When they arrived he challenged them to stay a fortnight in the castle and to find during that time one room that they could declare to be completely and autonomously dedicated to a single function.

The document men spent several days in the castle, feverishly scribbling floorplans in their notebooks and crossing them out, following the tortuous peregrinations of servants who had to scurry from one end of the castle to the other to complete some simple task such as cooking a pot of porridge. The count supplied each of his official visitors with a whistle to summon help when they got lost, which they did with gratifying frequency.

On the last evening of their stay, the document men gathered in the kitchen/study/wardrobe and with solemn resignation laid out the official forms of exemption. With a signature, the Castle Ostrov was about vanish from the avaricious grasp of rival empires like a popped soap bubble. Or rather, the count reflected, his homeland would emerge at last on the map of Europe. The Castle Ostrov would itself become the free and autonomous republic of Slovakia.

But just as the count was drawing his quill pen from the inkpot with an affected nonchalance, one of the document men cried out for him to hold his hand. He had idly plucked a book from one of the passing shelves and now held it aloft.

This Memoirs of the Sibyl at Cumae *is nothing but a block of pine, painted to resemble a book.*

The document men scattered through the house to confirm the truth and returned in triumph. The wandering shelves were full of dummies, impostures. The only real books in the entire castle were all crowded together under the oak panels of the count's massive ancestral bed. That was obviously the true library, and as it was located entirely on the Moravian side of the border, the Castle Ostrov did not qualify for exemption from official existence.

My grandfather cursed his own possessiveness, which had led him to keep his precious library hidden within easy reach. As a man with aspirations to an intellectual life, he felt ashamed of the expedient trick he had tried to play. Of course the books in his wandering library should be real. If there was to be trickery it would have to be of a more subtle kind. The contents of the books would also have to embody riddles, enigmas, paradoxes. Accordingly the very next day he began making plans to rectify the oversight, sending agents throughout the Continent, into England, and even across the Western Ocean in search of works of metaphysics, of speculative chemistry and abstruse geometry, of ancient hermetic wisdom.

The books were examined and arranged by the Count's only surviving child, his shy, book-loving daughter Irena.

Writing this now, I envision my grandmother as a thin, rather plain woman of twenty-four, cursed with a stutter that her father believed had chased away every suitor who had visited the castle thus far. The truth, I think, had more to do with the young men themselves. They were dragged by their avaricious fathers to the castle in the hope of a hefty dowry, but not one of these potential husbands read anything other than the suits and numbers on playing cards, Irena invariably discovered. They talked only of hunting, horses, and warfare. Irena's usual response was a stifled yawn. When it came to his only surviving child, the count found himself powerless to enforce his will, and so Irena remained unmarried.

After the early death of her mother, Irena became the chatelaine of the castle, responsible for all the practical, daily affairs of the household which the count neglected in his consuming obsession. Irena was never seen without a book in hand, and in the evenings the count would often find her standing near a lamp or a candle, stealing a quiet moment of reading before resuming her unending duties. *My little moth*, he whispered to her affectionately when he found her reading. Only Irena was permitted to examine the books when they arrived, arranging them on the shelves according to her father's diabolically complicated bibliographic system.

Almost every day crates of books arrived from near and far. One day while unpacking a crate sent from their Italian agent, Irena discovered that one of the books, its cover engraved with the title *A Conjectural Treatise on Political Economy*, had been hollowed out inside and another, smaller book lay nested within. She opened the cover of this inner book, and found within its cavity yet another book even smaller, and within it, another, and yet another within that, reminding her of the clever dolls-within-dolls crafted by the local peasant women. Only with the aid of a magnifying glass was Irena able to decipher the single sentence which made up the entire content of the tiniest volume: The great do devour the little.

Dutifully Irena took this object of ingenious trickery to her father, assuming he would reject it as he had the false wooden books. To her surprise, the count reacted with delight.

It's a joke, a pun, a riddle, he cried, *and yet not even the hairsplitters from the imperial court could disqualify it as an actual, functioning book.*

Irena handed her father the printer's catalogue, where his books, both finished and projected, were described.

"Listen to this," the count said.

We are presently engaged in creating a book more wondrous and magical than any yet seen or read by mortal eyes. The pages of this "book of mirrors" will be reflective, allowing passages from different parts of the book to appear together. The order of these ingenious pages will also change as the book is being read, so that a reader nearing the ending may find himself back at the beginning, or somewhere altogether different from where he thought himself to be.

"What printing house sent us this?" the count asked excitedly.

On the last page of the catalogue Irena discovered the microscopic publisher's imprint, under the device of a salamander amid flames.

"Vitam Mortuo Reddo"

N. Fludd, Printer and Bookseller

Venice

"Write to this Fludd," the count ordered his daughter. "We must bring him here."

After a long sea voyage in the count's antiquated merchant argosy, and a cold, miserable journey upriver on a comfortless barge, my grandfather, Nicholas Fludd, arrived one rainy night at the Castle Ostrov.

I can see him at the gates, nervously drawing his travelling cloak more tightly around him, watching apprehensively as the count's servants haul his printing apparatus, crate by crate, into the castle. He was a young man, not yet thirty, although the creases on his face were prematurely enhanced by the ink and grease of his craft. An Englishman by birth, he wandered Europe, settling for a while in one city and then moving on to another, printing what were known then as chimeras, exquisite one-of-a-kind novelty books for private customers. His last commission before leaving Venice should give you an idea of the sort of thing he specialized in. It was, or so my father informed me, a collection of ballads about haughty noblewomen ravished by brawny stablehands and handsome young priests. When the book was opened, card-paper dioramas would spring up, depicting the amorous equipment of the various Don Juans whose exploits filled the pages. The book was only half-finished when he left for Castle Ostrov, but the devout, retiring widow who ordered it paid in him full nonetheless, declaring that the blank pages happily left much for her own imagination.

It was for such creations that Fludd had been hounded by Venice's much-feared Council of Ten. Responsible for the moral health of the city, the Council regularly employed spies, saboteurs, arsonists, and assassins to safe-guard and maintain that health. In Fludd's case they simply refused to allow anyone to sell him paper. For a while he tried making his own sheets with old rags and straw, but the quality was so poor that most of his trade dried up anyway. His last desperate act was to embellish his catalogue with descriptions of invented books, books he had not printed and certainly had no intention of printing, as he knew that they were simply impossible. *Let the Council waste their time tracking down these non-existent books*, he reasoned. *In the meantime I'll begin preparations for a night-time departure.*

The count's offer of employment arrived at this moment, and Fludd seized the opportunity to slip from the council's grasp. The only problem was, the magical book that changed the order of its pages, the book that the count wanted, was one of Fludd's imaginary creations. It existed only as a catalogue description. He was not the printer of marvels he had represented himself to be. He was an impostor.

And so here he was, leaping straight from one pot of trouble into another.

Irena met him at the door with the traditional offering to favoured guests, a glass of *slivovice* and a kiss of welcome. The colourless plum liquor burned pleasantly through his insides for a moment, but the chaste touch of Irena's lips left a brand on his cheek that took hours to fade. She herself seemed disturbed by this merely formal gesture.

My father has shut down the castle's machinery for the night, she stammered in halting English, leading Fludd along an immense front hall glimmering with hundreds of candle flames. *He wishes you to be comfortable.* The young woman's pale aquamarine eyes reflected the fitful light like those of an owl.

Even after Fludd was shown to his room and had undressed and sunk into the depths of the vast, chilly bed, he kept putting a hand to his cheek in amazement. He wondered what fire burned behind the thin, pale features of this plain young woman.

The next morning Fludd awoke to find his bed shuddering underneath him. Fearing some natural calamity, he parted the curtains and discovered that he was moving down a curving passageway and into a vast circular hall panelled with mirrors. The old count was there, dressed in the uniform of a hussar and standing at a lectern, reading a Bible passage to a group of servants. When he had finished, he shut the book, dismissed the servants and beckoned to Fludd, who was still peeking out from between the bedcurtains.

Your excellency, I haven't got my clothes, the printer said.

A panel in the ceiling slid open and Fludd's clothing was winched down to him in a wicker basket. By the time he had hurriedly donned his shirt, waistcoat, breeches, and stockings behind the curtains, the lectern had been replaced by a small round table and the count was sitting in a massive oaken chair, attacking his breakfast. He greeted Fludd with a hearty grunt and offered him a less opulent and noticeably shorter chair. The printer sat down, disoriented and still dazed with sleep. A wheeled tray rolled up beside him, from which he numbly took a platter heaped with pig trotters, spiced eggs, and an assortment of braided, looped, and knotted pastries. The tray clattered out the way it had come.

As Fludd mumbled a quick grace over his food, another panel in the ceiling slid open and a servant in a coarse-striped waistcoat with blue glass buttons appeared on a descending platform, vigorously scrubbing a pair of knee-length boots with a brush. He caught Fludd's eye and with a lopsided grin that spoke of resignation in the face of madness, disappeared through another panel in the floor.

As he hacked and chewed his breakfast, flakes of pastry lodging in his drooping moustache, the count described to Fludd his plans to create new books and modify already existing volumes.

We'll start with the book of mirrors, the one listed in your catalogue, the count explained, *and after that I'll tell you the kind of thing I want, and you will make it a reality.*

Fludd nodded and kept silent.

The books would be the count's property, of course, although he conceded to the printer the right to imprint the colophon of each book with his sign of the salamander in flames.

How about assistants? the count asked. *Do you need assistants?*

I usually work alone, Fludd said. *But I would certainly welcome any....*

I've got just the fellows for the job, the count said, tapping a silver fork against his gilded china plate.

To be honest, Fludd ventured, *I'm more concerned about where I am to begin work. It seems to me I could be most productive if a room was set aside....*

The chime of a clock reverberated through the hall. The mirrors on the walls slid up to reveal alcoves in which the members of a chamber orchestra sat, tuning their instruments.

Time, the count said, checking the gold watch that hung on a chain around his neck. *Give it time, young man. You'll get used to the way we do things around here.*

He glanced down at the floor, checked his watch again, and clicked it shut. Fludd looked down beneath his feet, saw transparent glass tiles, and beneath them, the giant second hand of an immense clock filling the entire floorspace of the circular room. The count snapped his fingers and the musicians began a sonata.

You're wondering what I'm doing here, the count said. *What all this seeming madness means.*

Fludd smiled and flushed hotly at this direct response to his thoughts. The count waved a hand expansively around the room.

I thought at first that I was creating this castle of riddles in order to outwit the state. Now I understand what I have really been doing. The universe itself is a vast book of riddles written in a peculiar language, a language that I am attempting to speak.

As Fludd discovered, there were sections of the castle where one function appeared to dominate over others. This was the case with a vast elliptical hall which had probably been a ballroom but was now a gathering place for most of the roaming bookshelves, although other furniture also passed through from time to time. The count had Fludd's press, his binding tools, his vats of ink and reams of uncut paper installed here, and sent him four servants to assist with the work.

One was from the count's collection of human puzzles, the mute Turkish boy, Selim, who had six fingers on each hand. His skills with the lute and the harp were remarkable, and were adapted with little difficulty to composing type. Soon the boy could fill and lock up a chase in half the time it took Fludd.

The other three assistants were automatons of painted porcelain and joints of bronze that, when wound with a key, walked, moved their arms, and nodded their heads. The three automatons were dressed as cavalry officers and were named by the count for his three dead sons. Jozef and Stefan wore curling moustaches and martial grimaces. Ludwig, the youngest, who had died on the day the count beheld the mysterious non-lunar eclipse, was clean-shaven, smiling, and sported an apple-bright spot of red paint on each cheek.

The Swiss clockmaker who created the automatons had promised that they would not only walk and move their arms, but also possess the power of speech. It turned out that they were able to speak when spoken to, in voices like the hum from the inside of a beehive, but only returned fragmented echoes of what had been said to them. Undaunted by this disappointment, the count sent for a Leipzig physician who claimed that the human soul was lodged in the hair and fingernails. It was well known that these extremities continued to grow after death, and this observed phenomenon, he reasoned, could only reasonably be attributed to a residue of the vital force which had been harboured therein. The idea that one's coiffeur might be the seat of the soul was very popular with court ladies everywhere, and made the physician's reputation. The count brought him to the castle and supplied him with the three warrior top-knots he had cut from the heads of his dying sons on the battlefield. The faded hanks of hair were mortared into oily dust and mixed with an unguent to grease the joints of the porcelain soldiers, in the hope that any spark of vitality remaining in these battlefield mementos might be transferred to the automatons. The experiment was an utter failure. The three automatons showed not the slightest spark of vitality and, until the arrival of Fludd, the count had Jozef, Stefan, and Ludwig stowed away with the other unneeded lumber of the castle.

Regardless of their deficiencies in the art of conversation, Stefan, Jozef, and Ludwig could stand at the press for hours, inking the formes, tirelessly lowering and raising the platens, taking away the printed sheets and adding fresh ones, until their springs finally wound down and had to be cranked up again. Fludd delighted in speaking with the three wise men, as he called the automatons, finding more sense in these returned sounds than might be expected from mere echoes.

Irena Ostrov, Fludd whispered to Ludwig one day, and leaned close to catch the buzzing reply.

Rain. Trove.

Fludd smiled. At that moment he was applying the impress of his printer's device to the last page of a book.

Salamander, he said in a louder voice.

Alam, came the reply.

Selim's head went up when he heard the word.

Alam. *Does that mean anything?* Fludd asked the boy. Selim nodded. His slender fingers danced across a tray of italic type and in a moment he handed over his composing stick. Fludd read the backwards phrase.

ALAM IS ALL THE WORLD, MY LORD.

I am not your lord, Fludd said angrily.

My grandfather, despite his eccentricities, proved himself a true nobleman in his attitude to Fludd and his work. After the easy amiability of his welcome, he soon reverted to his military ways and began dictating to the printer what it was he could and could not print. His visits to Fludd's workplace coincided with execrations at the cook and orders to his valet. Fludd began to realize what he had given up by accepting this appointment, and what he had in effect become. A servant.

The count summoned Fludd to his bedside one morning, and asked how the book of mirrors was progressing. In response Fludd produced a single blank sheet.

I'm still working on the composition of the paper, he said. *This stage has proved more difficult than I expected.*

The count was visibly displeased, but in building his puzzle castle he had learned to be a patient man.

Leave it for a while, he told Fludd. *Try something else to get yourself warmed up. Feel free to play around, be inventive. And we'll see what happens.*

Fludd woke from a brief catnap at his bookbinding table, aware that something had changed. In another instant he realized that the castle had stopped. Over the past few days he had become so habituated to relentless motion that this stillness sent a tremor of dread through him, as though he had just been told someone had died.

He rose from his table, agitated by the silence, and was surprised to glimpse Irena down one of the library's narrow aisles. She was kneeling on the bare floor, immersed in a tiny pocket-sized volume, her gown like a frozen waterfall of pale blue silk around her. The look on her face was one of such guileless wonder that Fludd felt the stirring of an unfamiliar emotion. He was aware for the first time of a quality unknown to him and embodied in this shy, pale young woman. He had met many women in Venice and not one would have allowed herself to be caught unawares like this, reading in silent rapture.

She glanced up, saw who it was, and for the first time, smiled.

One of the gears wore down and threw everything off schedule, she said calmly, without a trace of her usual stammer. *It happens once in a while.*

Love is always a conspiracy against some part of the world, and both Fludd and Irena soon became aware they had been lovers from that first troubling kiss. The printer concealed his feelings and immured himself behind a wall of paper, but in his spare moments he printed and bound a small octavo volume entitled *Desire*, which contained only the name Irena repeated endlessly in eight-point cursive Garamond. He hid the book on a bottom shelf, between two volumes of Jn Plintovic's *Persian Tales*, which he had seen her reading.

Irena did not find the book, but she came more and more often to visit Fludd while he worked. She often dismissed the servants who were bringing him coffee or meals and carried the trays in herself. One night she brought candles to replace those on his work table which had burned down to stubs. As her voluminous silk gown brushed past the candelabra it caused a stir of air which blew out the sputtering flames and plunged the room into blackness. Irena apologized and said she would call a servant. Fludd told her there was no need. A moment later she saw a fuzzy patch of faint green light bobbing in the darkness, coming nearer to her.

What is that? she asked, backing away.

She saw his face swim closer to hers. The greenish glow came from a piece of paper he held in one hand.

I'm making a book you can read in the dark, he said. *I coat the paper with a tincture which renders it so sensitive to impression that it absorbs not only ink but light.*

Now she could see his hands and his forehead as well, which also faintly glowed. By the light of the paper Irena and the printer found their way to a torchlit corridor.

I've been wondering about the motto on your books, she said. Vitam mortuo reddo. *I cannot translate it because my father forbade me to learn Latin.*

Why?

He is a fierce patriot. He says that Latin is the language of official documents, of the emperors who carved up his homeland and gave the pieces to one another as gifts.

Vitam mortuo reddo, Fludd repeated. *It means* Life restored from death.

I see, Irena said. *When you print a book, it's a kind of immortality for the writer.*

I believe that's the idea.

And the salamander in fire?

My father, the printer from whom I learned the craft, used it as his device, as did his father, and his father before him. I don't know how the custom first began.

She asked him not about Venice but about London, of which she had heard many marvellous stories. Was it true, as she had been told, that in London the people of highest and lowest class mingled together in the streets and greeted one another without ceremony as fellow citizens? He said that it was true everyone mingled in the streets, but that was more a consequence of a vast population in a small area than any great, egalitarian love for one's fellow man. And yet it was certainly a fact, he admitted, that the city was full of surprises. You could find anything there.

I feel at home in this castle, he added, *because in a way it is very like London, where nothing keeps its place for long.*

If only that were truly the way of things here.

What do you mean?

Here the walls and ceilings and floors move, she said, and the people stand still.

She wanted to hear about other lands and other customs, and so he told her about his flight from London and his wanderings over the continent, the cities he had seen, the endless variety of humanity. How he had printed books wherever he went, how eager the people were to read, and how the authorities always disapproved, often violently so. Venice was not the only city he had been forced to flee in his career.

She said she could not understand why he persisted against such opposition.

By multiplying the number of books in the world I multiply the number of readers, he told her. *And the ranks of the book-burners thin out just a little more each time.*

The *Persian Tales* were favourites of Irena, as Fludd had guessed, and at last she happened across the little volume filled with her name. She was terrified and overjoyed at the same time, so much so that she took the book away, concealed in the folds of her gown, for the first time in her life shattering the perfection of her father's system by leaving an empty space on one of the bookshelves. She opened the book whenever she could steal an unobserved moment during her daily rounds.

By the end of the day she had returned the book to its place and decided upon her fate. With a wax impression of one of her father's keys she unlocked a trapdoor in a remote passageway. She crawled down a ladder into the dank viscera of cogs, gears, and pulleys driven by "atmospheric engines," as the Scottish inventor called them, which used channelled steam from boilers to power the workings of the castle.

In the evening Irena brought the printer coffee on a silver tray. As she passed the three automatons named for her brothers she tickled Ludwig's jutting porcelain chin. Selim, the Turkish boy, was dozing on a settee, wrapped in Fludd's threadbare velvet coat. Irena placed the tray on the printer's workbench. Beside the coffee decanter lay the small octavo volume of *Desire.*

Irena opened her mouth to speak and closed it again. Fludd stared up at her, frozen in fear and hope.

When the clocks tell a quarter past three tonight, Irena finally managed to stammer without looking at Fludd, *my bed will pass yours.*

That night, as the chime of the many clocks echoed through the drafty halls of the castle, Fludd leapt barefoot, like an Uzkhok pirate boarding a ship, from his moving bed to Irena's. She was waiting for him, naked and trembling, tears glittering in her eyes.

Will you always love me? she whispered.

After all the clocks in the world have stopped, he said.

Just before dawn, when his own bed passed by again, he slipped away, leaving a faint glow of phosphorescence lingering on the sheets and on Irena's skin.

Curtis Gillespie

Guadalajara

My younger brother became a priest in 1971, in Guadalajara, Mexico, when he was eleven years old and I was thirteen. This was not the precise moment of his ordination, of course, yet I know that what happened in Guadalajara led him to his vocation. He's never told me this, and I've never asked him directly if it were true, but I believe it to be so.

For the Christmas holiday our family had driven from Edmonton to Mexico City. We stopped in Guadalajara the day before Christmas, and right after getting settled went shopping for gifts. The market was about the most confusing place I'd ever been, a planet of commerce wedged into what looked like a sports coliseum no longer fit for the purpose, with four or five levels and innumerable rows of stalls on each level. Our mother instructed us explicitly not to wander, and we didn't much, but it still wasn't long before we'd become separated from her and our father. They were spending a long time haggling over an onyx chess set. Graham and I had our attention diverted by the sound of some noisy birds an aisle over, and when we came back our parents were gone.

Graham became frightened immediately, and I did, too, and we tried to make our way down the narrow aisle in the general direction we'd been heading before. There were people everywhere and the aisle was maybe five feet wide, flanked by rows of rickety booths selling every kind of merchandise available. Bright fabrics, coffee beans, piñatas. Vegetables, knives, spices. Squawking chickens. Crucifixes, candles, leather. We were surrounded by stalls. It seemed as if everything you would ever want or need was in that market, and yet we couldn't find who we were looking for. We had no idea where our parents had gone, or even what place they might think to look for us.

A booth owner came over when we stopped to get our bearings, and patted our heads as if we were friendly stray dogs. I saw no one our own age around.

"We're trying to find our mom and dad," I said to the man. He smiled and pointed towards a couple of different exits, obviously unaware of what our problem was.

I thought our parents might look for us where we'd come in, and that it would be easier to find that entrance from the outside rather than wading through the chaos inside, so we left the market and started along the wide sidewalk around the outer wall. Graham stuck close to me. There was an entrance every fifty or sixty yards and they all looked the same, each abundant with people, shoppers, hawkers set up by the doors, and beggars, most of them deformed or crippled in some way, with hands or caps or cups extended.

We stopped in front of one entrance and stood for a moment. Graham was looking around, but stayed behind me. It was a cloudless day, and the sun bore squarely on us, direct and fiercely hot in a way we were unaccustomed to even in summer back home. Graham had a fairer complexion than I did, and without a hat or shade he would suffer after not too long. We set off again. After a while I wasn't sure if we'd even gone all the way around or not, and we stopped and sat down just off the sidewalk, under the meagre shade of a near-dead tree.

People streamed past, but left us alone, except for a beggar. He had stumps for legs and came scrabbling up the sidewalk towards us, muttering in a pitiable voice. He rattled a few peso coins around in a tin can. I held out my hands indicating no money. Graham did the same but also spoke to the man. "I'm sorry," he said. "I wish we had some money for you." The man stared at Graham. His eyes were cloudy, as if they were coated in wax paper. He turned his head, spat freely on the sidewalk, and moved on. A few minutes later, not twenty yards from us, he barked aggressively at someone who'd refused him money.

"Let's go," I said, getting up. "We should keep going."

Graham stayed seated. "Where?" he said. "I don't want to get up unless we're going where Mom and Dad are."

I ignored him and he slowly rose. We were at one of the corner entrances of the market. Traffic was pulsing through the intersection. Across from us was a huge cathedral, with massive bronze doors and a spire groping into the hot blue sky.

Graham stood up. "Let's go there," he said, pointing to the church.

I looked at him. "The church?"

"Yeah," he said. "Mom and Dad'll go there for sure."

I figured Graham was right. Our father was not a particularly religious man, yet he respected our mother's intense Catholicism, agreeing to let her raise us in her faith. If our parents did explore the perimeter of the market, they, or at least our mother, would certainly gravitate to the church to pray for God's help in finding us.

A mass was in progress when we entered the church, so we sat on a couple of loose chairs in the cool shade of the entrance hall. I felt an air of respite within the church, a haven from the chaos of heat and population outside. We didn't understand a word of what was being said, but still knew which part of the mass it was when the priest lifted the Bible to his face and kissed it. The reading of the Gospel. I could feel Graham relax beside me. All the symbols were the same. An altar, a massive crucifix overhead, the sacristy, bowls of holy water at the entrance.

We watched the mass through to the end, and sat as people drifted out. A few stayed behind, kneeling and praying, for another ten or fifteen minutes, until gradually the church emptied leaving Graham and I as the last ones in the cavernous space. We stepped into the back row of pews and sat down. There seemed no reason to leave, no one was asking us to.

A priest, not the one who had just offered mass, but a much younger one, came out of a side door near the altar. He opened a cabinet under the crucifix and removed some communion wafers. As he turned to go back, he looked out over the church and saw us in the back row.

He said something in Spanish, his voice like a deep horn sounding across the high empty space. We remained silent because there was little we could say. He repeated himself, then stepped off the raised altar platform and walked down the centre aisle. He took a seat in the pew beside us.

"We're lost," I said.

We didn't understand any of what he said next, so we sat looking at him. He shook his head slightly and smiled for us. His teeth were yellow and he had thick short hair that nearly touched his eyebrows at his temples. He silently motioned for us to follow him. Unthinkingly, automatically, we did so. The three of us walked up the centre aisle, past the altar, through a door and into a long and dark hallway that took us to a kind of classroom with makeshift pews and about five rows of chairs.

The same priest who'd just finished offering mass in the cathedral was speaking to a new congregation, made up of people not like Graham and me. A sour smell, like old sweat, dominated the room. Those in the front row of the congregation all seemed crippled in one way or another, many missing limbs. The other seats were filled with dirty and sad-looking people. Some were muttering to themselves, not following what the priest was saying.

The young priest pointed to chairs along the side wall and we went and sat down. Nearly everybody turned to look at us. The other priest, who looked about our father's age and had a heavy beard, continued to offer mass, glancing our way now and then.

When it came time to deliver communion, rather than stand at the head of the aisle and receive communicants, the priest circulated amongst the group, perhaps forty strong, carrying the chalice, holding each wafer aloft while blessing it. Some of the congregation were blind, and they thrust out their tongues even though the priest was two or three people away. They just opened their mouths like baby robins and waited.

When he finished delivering communion, the priest transferred the remaining wafers into a shallow dish and set it aside. He poured red wine into the chalice, blessed and drank it. Then he meticulously cleaned the chalice, folded the cleansing napkin and carefully placed it over the chalice. While he was doing this the younger priest murmured in his ear. They glanced back to us.

After mass the congregation was slow to disperse and most of them made no move at all to leave. They merely sat, perhaps in reflection or just to relish a quiet moment before having to go back outside to meet the heat and the derision of the population. Both priests came over to where Graham and I sat.

The older priest stopped in front of us, the younger remained deferentially behind.

"Hello," he said in thickly accented English. "Father Herve is my name." He bent over warily and put out his hand palm up.

"Hello," I said, placing my hand in his.

"Hi," said Graham, who discreetly grabbed onto my shirt.

Father Herve turned to the other priest and back to us. "This is Father Michael." Father Michael said something in rapid Spanish. Father Herve listened but kept his gaze on us, smiling the whole time. He nodded once or twice, then asked us our names. We told him.

"And you were in the mass before, then?" he said to us.

I nodded back. "We're lost," I said. "Not really lost, but we're lost from our mom and dad."

Graham was not looking at Father Herve any more. He was watching the beggars and cripples, who were still sitting quietly in the makeshift pews. They were just talking amongst themselves. Three blind people sat together and they seemed to be waiting for something, for everyone else to leave perhaps. Their eyes looked milky and distant like those of the beggar who'd approached us on the street.

"Where did you get lost?" asked Father Herve.

"At the market," I said. "But our mom and dad might come here to pray."

Father Herve's smile broke through his beard. "Of course, they will find you. Father Michael and I will make sure of that. But let us first finish. With our people here." He waved his hand across the room. "Then we will look for your mother and father."

Graham pointed to the others in the room. "Why are they in here?" he asked. "Why weren't they at the other mass?" He looked back to Father Herve.

The priest stood upright. "They have their own special mass."

"Why?"

"Graham." I gave him a little elbow in the ribs.

"They are extra special to God," said Father Herve patiently. "We help them talk to Him."

Graham sat back in his chair. I could tell by the way he looked back at the people that he was fascinated. "Why are they so special to God?" he said.

"The Lord knows they need him more than the rest. Now, you wait a few moments more, then Father Michael and I will help find your parents." He smiled broadly for us. I liked him, and Graham seemed okay with him, too. He left and went back to the front of the congregation.

Father Herve said something softly and the group circled their chairs so that the blind people did not have to move. Once they'd settled the priests handed out a small Bible to each person, including the blind people. Father Michael said two or three words, and everyone opened the books to a certain page. The blind people held their Bibles in both hands, like plates of food, and sat still but attentive, almost sniffing the air.

Father Michael read from the Bible for about five minutes while Father Herve sat and listened. The group followed along closely, though one person nodded continuously. Another kept up a low mesmerizing drone, a kind of chant.

When Father Michael stopped reading there was a minute or two of complete silence, except for the droning man, who looked up but kept on with his noise. I could hear car horns and the noise of the street from outside. Father Herve asked the group a question, waited, and then appeared to answer his own question, explaining himself at length and using his hands to balance one side of his exposition with the other. Some in the group listened intently, others seemed not to be paying any attention at all.

This went on for about twenty minutes, with Father Michael doing the reading and Father Herve leading the discussion, of which there was little. Through all this I sat quietly, thinking about being lost, of maybe never being found, of how worried our mother and father were at that moment and what they were going to do to us for getting lost. I wasn't paying much attention to what was going on in the room, barely noticing the people through my worry, but Graham was sitting upright, eyes scanning the room. He kept looking at Father Herve and then back to the group, staring at each person in turn. A few minutes later some closed their Bibles.

When Father Herve paused, Graham, in a voice everybody could hear, said, "What are you talking about?"

The two priests looked our direction, as did most of the group.

"We go to church, too," said Graham. "We read the Bible sometimes with the other altar boys."

Father Herve smiled at us. "We should have asked you to join us. You would have helped us to pray." He motioned to a space beside him.

Instantly Graham was up and pulling his chair towards the group. Father Herve smiled when Graham did this, so I moved mine over too. We pulled into the circle and patiently sat while Father Herve introduced us to everyone else. Neither Graham nor I knew what he said, but we recognized our names. Some of the people greeted us with smiles, most ignored us. One of the blind people turned our direction but seemed to gaze at a spot over our heads. Father Herve continued for about another five minutes, then closed his Bible.

People started to disperse. The blind people waited, sitting patiently while the others rearranged the chairs. When that was done somebody said something and the blind rose from their chairs. One of them, the man who'd been droning throughout the mass and prayer session, tapped his way over to where we were still sitting. Father Herve watched him come toward us and then followed him over. The blind man wore tattered clothes, and was very dirty. He had a jagged gash about an inch long under his chin that looked like it should have had stitches a week before. He stopped in front of us and started to talk. We looked to Father Herve.

"He says," said Father Herve, with a patient but slightly exasperated look on his face, "that he feels a holy presence in the room."

The blind man let a hand reach out, probe the nothingness in front of him. Graham and I involuntarily backed into our chairs. He started to talk even more quickly. Again we looked to Father Herve.

"Don't mind him," he said. "He is a nice man. Aren't you, Osvaldo?" Father Herve patted Osvaldo on the shoulder.

Graham stood. His full height brought him only to Osvaldo's chest. "My name's Graham," he said.

The blind man groped out toward the sound of the voice. Father Herve made a small involuntary move with his shoulders, a slight call to readiness, but held off. Graham reached out, and put Osvaldo's hand in his. Osvaldo smiled and turned his blank stare to Father Herve, spoke again at some length, his voice cracking. He was a large man with enormous feet, but he had a pronounced stoop and made me think of someone who might be a circus clown.

"He says he feels your strength," said Father Herve. "But he is a flatterer. He says the same to me often, once a month at least." He let out a low chuckle. Father Michael, picking up Bibles from chairs, also laughed. He took a stack in each arm and left the room.

Osvaldo reached for Graham's hand and held it at the wrist, moving it up towards his face. He closed his eyes and ran the tips of Graham's fingers over his eyelids two, three times, letting them linger at the last brush. Graham's four small fingertips fit neatly into the man's closed eye sockets.

He held Graham's hand for a moment longer with his eyes closed. He released it and opened his eyes, fixing a look directly at Graham. Then he made a rigid almost fearful move of his eyes to me.

Suddenly he let out a hysterical noise, a hyena-like yelp. His voice filled the small room like an alarm, and Graham and I shrank from it. He kept repeating something over and over. He bent over, took Graham's hand and began hungrily kissing his fingertips, pointing to his own eyes.

"Gracias!" he exclaimed. "Gracias! Gracias!" He repeated this and another word over and over, dancing crazily around the room, picking up objects from tables, inspecting them closely before replacing them. He looked up and down the walls, out the window. Graham staggered behind him, half-following, looking very confused, briefly examining his own hands. The other two blind people stood motionless by the door, unexcited, patiently waiting for Osvaldo.

I turned to Father Herve and must have had a stunned look on my face. He leaned over and whispered in my ear. "He is not blind."

I looked up at him.

"I heal this man once a month, approximately," Father Herve continued. "He is a great pretender."

Finally Osvaldo stopped dancing around the room. He spoke to Father Herve and kept pointing to Graham as he did.

"He says that you have performed a miracle, and have made his life worth living," Father Herve translated with an air of bemusement. Graham stood there looking like a victim of shell-shock. "He called you little Jesus," said Father Herve, laughing. He patted Graham on the shoulder. "Perhaps you are, but not with our friend here." He pointed at Osvaldo and motioned to the door with a look of mock-impatience on his face. "Adios, Osvaldo."

Osvaldo picked up his cane, a dark wooden walking stick, and strode from the room chattering. The two people waiting for him followed behind, tapping their canes, click, click, click, down the hall.

There was quiet for a moment. Graham wandered back to where I stood. I was going to tell him what Father Herve had just told me, that Osvaldo was not blind, but Father Michael reentered the room. He made some motions to Father Herve and spoke again but in much less rapid terms than before. He seemed relieved. Our parents, Father Herve then explained, had come to the church door, holding our pictures. They were sitting in the pews that moment. We left the room and travelled back along the dark corridor.

"Graham," I said in a whisper, as we walked. "That guy wasn't really blind. Father Herve told me."

He looked at me, but I wasn't sure if what I'd said had registered.

"He wasn't blind," I said again. I know he heard me, but before he could say anything we came to the end of the hallway, and back out onto the altar platform.

Our mother came running up the centre aisle and met us beside the altar. She hugged us both. Our father came up, too, trailing behind at a more modest pace, but I could tell from his face he'd been crying.

"Oh, Graham," our mother said, bursting into tears. "Andrew." She hugged us so hard I couldn't get my arms around her.

Still flush with relief, our mother began to chastise us for getting lost. She didn't really blame one or the other of us, but, perhaps because I was the older child, her immediate attention was on me. I said nothing, just did my best not to cry, failing. Graham began to cry, too. The two priests stood watching.

While our mother was speaking, our father, whose tongue never could explain his heart, remained stoic. But our mother was gifted with the ability to project personal injury, which she used on us.

"We might never have found you," she said, her cheeks and hands visibly shaking. "You might have died, the two of you." Her anger began to rise through her ebbing relief.

Graham and I stood like garden trolls, and just looked at our feet. Our father stood a step behind our mother.

"Don't you ever do that to me again," she said, her voice a hoarse whisper. "Do you understand?"

"But it was okay, mom," Graham said quietly, breaking a silence I think our mother expected us to keep. Her mouth tightened into a grim line across her face. "We were safe here," he continued.

I nodded and said, "Yeah."

She was quiet for a moment and seemed to be trying to control nausea. "It was not okay," she said, her voice quivering.

"Honest, mom," Graham said. "We were all right." He looked at Father Herve, who smiled. The colour of our mother's face changed to a mottled purple. She said, "No," and then without any kind of warning slapped Graham across the side of the head, not violently, but high on the cheekbone and the temple. He winced audibly and his eyes watered. I flinched and stepped backward.

Father Herve immediately came forward, just one step. "Please," he said in his thick English. "Please, they did the right thing."

Our mother's eyes went big. Our father moved towards her, like he was going to grab her if she tried it again. But her eyes stayed round and then went opaque. She moved forward and surrounded Graham in her arms, rocking back and forth, kissing the top of his head. "Oh God," our mother said softly but urgently. "Oh God, I'm sorry, honey. Graham?"

Graham stood with his arms at his sides, his hands in little fists. It was then I saw our mother loved Graham more than me. He let her go on holding him, and only slowly returned her embrace. I stood watching her hold him. My father put his hand on top of my head and smoothed my hair, ran his big coarse thumb across my cheek. Father Herve was gone the next time I looked around. He must have retreated very silently. I didn't see him go and when I left the church I was sorry not to be able to say goodbye.

Graham has never spoken a word to me about the way our mother reacted that day. He just took it in, blended it into the makeup of his person. I don't know if it had anything directly to do with him entering the priesthood. Or even whether part of him believed he'd healed Osvaldo. Whatever it was, he was different after that day.

I am now thirty-six, Graham thirty-four. He says his love for God is stronger than ever. He had then and has now the capacity, the gift, for love, and he seems happy with the way he's chosen to use it. He and my mother no longer talk, for reasons neither seems able to explain to me. Their estrangement came on gradually, like something growing in a dark cellar, a damp mould that goes unnoticed for years and, once discovered, cannot then be easily removed.

My mother rarely asks me now how Graham is doing. The only context in which she mentions him is to tell me that she still attends mass at St. Clement's in north Edmonton, a place I have not been in twenty years. She goes there to pray for him, and to pray for herself. She kneels down in the rear pews, where we always sat as a family, and prays hard, prays that she'll find him again.

I think she tells me this only in the hope that I will pass word of her supplications on to Graham, which will in turn encourage him to make the opening move in their reconciliation. Yet though I talk to him regularly, I've never mentioned it. I have occasionally considered saying something, but, usually after not much deliberation, I decide not to. Far be it from me to interfere with the power of prayer.

Tim Bowling

The Rhododendron

Childhood has its own grave, and mine
is tombed by the purple rhododendron
blooming again in my mother's garden.

Tonight late bees engrave an epitaph
on the heavy flowerheads, and dusk
settles chalk-grains over their work.

The death of all life is sickly-sweet,
why not the years? There is no threat
in this black earth and this air wet

with the grief of stars. And rain,
each drop, stands straightbacked when
the bees have done, mourning the time

when a child breathed here and the grass
gave way to his light tread on the last
spring evening of a wonder so chaste

it was the only reality, the only truth.
A child has no patience for any death.
But once an adult, is it really enough,

this standing purple clutch of memory
washed round by darkness, night's sea
of hours on the gentle ebb, infinity

salting the petals? Time is a grave
that digs itself, and all we have
to do is consecrate it when we leave.

A grizzled black lab guards the portal
to the tomb. My mother's arms are full
with remembered weight; her low whistle

calls me back one more time to home.
But it is only my young ghost who comes,
a faded and gentle hour in his bones,

and pats the dog, and kneels in the rain
and hears the woman's steady heartbeat again
clocking the desecrating step of the man.

Family Bible
for my grandmother, Margaret Stevens (1881-1945)
and her children, the three living and the fourteen dead

My totem is black as the rains of Haida Gwaii; black
is my totem with tears of generations, a burnt block
of cedar sinewed with Latinate phrases and names
of dead infants tallied each year to poverty's pox
and polio; my totem is black and keeps a Christ
in its grain, His words, His blood, and His high cross;
black is my totem and the eyes that raised it, from
bedside tables to parlours of grief; my totem is black
and lurid with the ink of an illiterate hand, mother
to Toronto's graves, daughter to a dashed Irish dream;
black is my totem as the winter rains of Haida Gwaii.

Let the spiders nest in the rot of its wood, in
the soft pit of faith that sways in the wind,
under the garish streak of the mask of pain,
under the slash of light, that naked bulb
above the childbirth-bed, cast on the three
sets of twins uncried at the slap, cast on
the multiple coughs in the crib, cast on
the woman whose body is rain, and rains
through her days, her months, and her years.
Let the crows light and caw, let them sound
out the storms of the steaming kettles
that filled her kitchen as she inked the pages
and hummed the hymns, let their black wings
wreath the rented door while the undertaker
takes her teenaged girl unprettied to her
piece of earth. Let my totem eat the storm,
black into the burnt block, rain into char;

let it suffer the names of the little children
in a night without stars, as she did, turning
tear-streaked again to her husband's warmth.

Then let the sun break red over Haida Gwaii.

Notes on Contributors

David Albahari was born in 1948 in the Serbian town of Pec. He was the founder and, for years, the editor-in-chief of *Pismo*, a magazine of world literature, and is an accomplished translator of Anglo-American literature. He is the author of *Words Are Something Else* (1996), a collection of short stories, and *Tsing* (1997), a novel. He resides in Calgary. "By the Light of the Silvery Moon" was published in *Alberta Views* (January 1999).

Bert Almon has taught at the University of Alberta since 1968. He is a native of Texas and a citizen of Canada. His writing students have included Monty Reid, Aritha van Herk, and Norman Sacuta. In 1995, he won the Stephan G. Stephansson Award for *Earth Prime* (1994). His poetry publications include *The Return and Other Poems* (1968), *Taking Possession* (1976), *Poems for the Nuclear Family* (1979), *Blue Sunrise* (1980), *Deep North* (1984), *Calling Texas* (1990), *Earth Prime* (1994), and *Mind the Gap* (1996). Bert lives in Edmonton.

Douglas Barbour is a poet and critic living in Edmonton. He teaches Canadian literature, modern poetry, science fiction and fantasy, and creative writing in the Department of English at the University of Alberta. He has published many books of poetry and critical studies, the most recent of which include *Visible Visions: Selected Poems* (1984), *Story for a Saskatchewan Night* (1989), and *Michael Ondaatje* (1993).

E.D. Blodgett was born on February 26, 1935. For over three decades, he has taught at the University of Alberta, where he lectures in comparative literature. Among his many publications are a monograph on Canadian short-story writer Alice Munro and translations of *Carmina Burana*. He has published several collections of poetry, including *take away the names* (1975), *sounding* (1977), *Beast Gate* (1980), *Arche/Elegies* (1983), *Musical Offering* (1986), *Da Capo: Selected Poems* (1990), *Apostrophes: woman at a piano* (1996), *Apostrophes II: through you I* (1998), *Transfiguration* (1998, with Jacques Brault), and *Apostrophes III: alone upon the earth* (1999). He received the 1996

Governor-General's Literary Award for Poetry for *Apostrophes: woman at a piano*. He lives in Edmonton.

Tim Bowling was born in Vancouver, British Columbia and was raised in the nearby town of Ladner, where he worked for many years in the commercial salmon-fishing industry. Now living and writing full-time in Edmonton, he is the author of two collections of poems: *Low Water Slack* (1995) and *Dying Scarlet* (1997).

Nigel Darbasie was born on the Caribbean island of Trinidad; he moved to Canada in 1969. Many of his poems have appeared in literary journals across the country. *Last Crossing*, a collection of his poetry, was published in 1988. Nigel lives and works in Edmonton.

Caterina Edwards has published two novellas, *Whiter Shade of Pale* and *Becoming Emma*, and a novel, *The Lion's Mouth*, which is being published in French. Her play *Homeground* was performed professionally and published by Guernica Editions. She has also published many short stories in literary magazines and anthologies. With Kay Stewart, she has edited two collections of autobiographical writing by women: *Eating Apples, Knowing Women's Lives* and *The Second Bite*. She lives in Edmonton.

Curtis Gillespie is the author of *The Progress of an Object in Motion*, which in 1998 won the Henry Kreisel Award and the Danuta Gleed Literary Award. He lives in Edmonton.

Hiromi Goto was born in Japan and immigrated to Canada with her family when she was three. She now lives in Calgary. Her novel *A Chorus of Mushrooms* (1994) was the 1995 winner of the Commonwealth Writer's Prize Best First Book Canadian Caribbean Region, and the 1995 co-winner of the Canada-Japan Book Award. Her short stories and critical writing have been published in numerous magazines and anthologies, including *Ms. Magazine, Making a Difference: Canadian Multicultural Literature* (1996), and *Due West* (1996). She is an active member of the Calgary Women Colour Collective.

Linda Goyette grew up near Windsor, Ontario. In the late 1970s, she moved to Edmonton and began working with the *Edmonton Journal*. She presently works as a columnist and is considered to be the sharpest pen in Alberta journalism. "Imaginary

Alberta" first appeared in the *Edmonton Journal* and is published in Goyette's book *Second Opinion* (1998).

Kristjana Gunnars was born in Reykjavik, Iceland and came to Canada in 1969. She writes poetry, short stories, and novels; she is also an accomplished literary translator. Her published work includes *The Prowler, Zero Hour, Settlement Poems 1* (1980), *The Substance of Forgetting* (1992), *Guest House and Other Stories* (1992), and *A Night Train to Nykobing* (1998). She lives in Edmonton and teaches creative writing and literature at the University of Alberta.

Vivian Hansen is a native Calgarian. She has published poetry, fiction, and non-fiction in such magazines as *Legacy, freefall, Synchronicity,* and *filling station.* Some of her reviews and essays appear in *Mattoid* and *Forum.* Her first chapbook of poetry, *Never Call It Bird: The Melodies of AIDS,* was published with Passwords Enterprises, and her work appears in *Worldly Treasures: Stories of Our Grandmother* (1999). "Sounding the Medicine Map" was broadcast by CBC Radio in 1998.

Claire Harris lives, teaches, and writes in Calgary. She was awarded the Commonwealth Poetry Prize for her book *Fables from the Women's Quarters* (1985). Her other works include *The Conception of Winter* (1989), *Travelling to Find a Remedy* (1987; the Writers' Guild of Alberta Award and the First Alberta Culture Poetry Prize), and *Dipped in Shadow.* "Correspondence" is an excerpt from her forthcoming book-length poem *New York/Untitled.*

Robert Hilles was born in Kenora, Ontario in 1951; he later moved to Calgary. He has taught computer programming at the DeVry Institute of Technology since 1983. His books include *Look the Lovely Animal Speaks* (1983), *The Surprise Element* (1982), *An Angel in the Works* (1983), *Outlasting the Landscape* (1989), *Finding the Lights On* (1991), and *A Breath at a Time* (1992). His volume *Cantos from a Small Room* (1993) won the 1994 Governor General's Literary Award for Poetry. His latest book of poetry, *Breathing Distance* (1997), was shortlisted for the 1998 Milton Acorn People's Poetry Award. His next collection of poetry, *Somewhere Between Obstacles and Pleasure,* will appear in the fall of 1999.

Greg Hollingshead was born in Toronto. He has published two novels, *Spin Dry* (1992) and *The Healer* (1998); three collections of stories, *Famous Players* (1982), *White Buick* (1992), and *The Roaring Girl* (1995); and fifty stories in literary magazines and anthologies in Canada and the US. In 1993, *White Buick* was shortlisted for the Commonwealth Writers Prize and won the Howard O'Hagan Award for Short Fiction. In 1995, *The Roaring Girl* won the Governor-General's Award for Fiction. *The Roaring Girl* has been published in Britain, the US, Germany, and China. *The Healer*, which is scheduled for publication in the US and Britain in 1999, was shortlisted for the 1998 Giller Prize, and won the 1998 Rogers Communications Writers Trust Fiction Award and the Georges Bugnet Award for Fiction. Greg lives in Edmonton, where he teaches literature and creative writing in the English Department of the University of Alberta. "Daughter of God" is an excerpt from *The Healer*.

Myrna Kostash was born in Edmonton and educated at the universities of Alberta, Washington, and Toronto. She is the author of four books: *All of Baba's Children*, *No Kidding*, *Bloodlines: A Journey Through Eastern Europe*, and *The Doomed Bridegroom: A Memoir*. She has also written for radio and stage, has done extensive teaching, and has been active on many fronts of cultural politics. She lives in Edmonton. "Unmasking the Polish Dissident" is an excerpt from *The Doomed Bridegroom*.

Anne Le Dressay was born in Manitoba and now lives in Edmonton. Her first book of poetry, *Sleep is a Country*, appeared in 1997. She has also published two chapbooks: *This Body That I Live In* (1979) and *Woman Dreams* (1998). She has taught English and creative writing at Alberta community colleges.

Carol L. MacKay was born in 1964 and raised in the rural community of Ryley, Alberta. She now writes from Bawlf, Alberta, population 300. Her stories and poems have appeared in numerous journals in Canada and the US, including *The Fiddlehead*, *Maelstrom*, *CV2*, *Antigonish Review*, *Whetstone*, and *The Alberta Poetry Yearbook*.

Alice Major has lived in Edmonton since 1981. Her first collection of poetry, *Time Travels Light*, appeared in 1992. Her chapbook *Scenes from the Sugar Bowl Café* won the 1998 Shaunt Basmajian competition. Her second collection of poems is *Lattice of the Years*. Alice is vice president of the League of Canadian Poets. The selections from *Tales for an Urban Sky* were published in *CV2*.

Suzette Mayr lives and works in Calgary. She is the author of *Moon Honey* (1995) and *The Widows* (1998). Suzette teaches at the Alberta College of Art.

Ken McGoogan has published three novels: *Visions of Kerouac, Calypso Warrior,* and *Kerouac's Ghost.* His critical volume, *Canada's Undeclared War: Fighting Words from the Literary Trenches,* won the best non-fiction book award from the Writers' Guild of Alberta in 1991. "Chasing Safiya" is an excerpt from his forthcoming novel *The Shaman's Fire.* Ken lives in Calgary and works as the books editor at the *Calgary Herald.*

George Melnyk is an essayist, poet, and historian who teaches Canadian studies at the University of Calgary. He is the author of *Riel to Reform: A History of Protest in Western Canada, The Urban Prairie, Beyond Alienation: Political Essays on the West, The Literary History of Alberta, Volumes One and Two,* and *Ribstones,* a book of poetry. He lives in Calgary.

Anna Mioduchowska was born in Poland and has lived in Edmonton since she was in grade eight. Her poetry, stories, and book reviews have appeared in literary periodicals, newspapers, and anthologies, and have been broadcast on CBC Radio's Alberta Anthology. One of the founding editors of *Other Voices,* Anna is the current president of Edmonton's Stroll of Poets Society. *In-Between Seasons* is the title of her poetry collection published in 1998.

Tololwa M. Mollel is a Tanzanian-born storyteller and author of over fifteen published and forthcoming books for children, including *The Orphan Boy* and *Rhinos for Lunch and Elephants for Supper!* His children's books have been published in the US, Australia, Great Britain, and South Africa, as well as in Canada, the latest titles being *Kitoto the Mighty* and *Shadow Dance* (both published in 1998). His short stories for adults have been published internationally and broadcast on the BBC World Service. He lives in Edmonton.

Peter Oliva was born in Eugene, Oregon and grew up in Italy and western Canada. He has published articles and stories in such magazines as *Brick, Descant, Eyetalian,* and *Quarry.* His first novel, *Drowning in Darkness* (1993), won the Henry Kreisel Award for Best First Book and was shortlisted for the Bressani Prize. The book was broadcast on CBC Radio and was also published in Spain. His new novel is *The City of Yes* (1999). Peter lives in Calgary.

Joseph Pivato was born in Tezze sul Brenta, Veneto, Italy. His major writing interest is exploring the experience of Italians in Canada. In addition to many articles and conference papers on ethnic minority writing, he has written *Echo: Essays on Other Literatures* (1994) and edited *Contrast: Comparative Essays on Italian-Canadian Writing* (1985 and 1991) and the *Anthology of Italian-Canadian Writing* (1998). Joseph lives in Edmonton, where he teaches comparative literature at Athabasca University.

Peter Prest lives and teaches in Calgary. His poems have appeared in numerous literary magazines across Canada. He has published *At This Time of Day* (1995).

Roberta Rees lives in Calgary, where she teaches creative writing for women. Her work has appeared in various literary journals. *Eyes like Pigeons* (1992) was her first book of poetry. Her prose-poem "Hoar Frost" was published in *Saturday Night.*

Monty Reid was born in Saskatchewan and now lives in Camrose, Alberta. His published work includes *Fridays, Karst Means Stone, The Life of Ryley, The Dreams of Snowy Owls* (1983), and *Bunker Sonnets* (1998). His volume *Flat Side* won the Stephan G. Stephansson Award for Poetry in 1999. Poems published here are from his forthcoming book *Disappointment Islands.*

Norman Sacuta's poetry and fiction have appeared in a number of literary magazines, including *Grain, Matrix* and *Prairie Fire*, as well as in such anthologies as *Jugular Defences: An AIDS Anthology* and *Due West*. He lives in Edmonton and works as a writer and editor.

Fred Stenson is a freelance writer living in Calgary. He has published two novels, three books of short stories, and three books of non-fiction. His last fiction title was *Teeth* (1994). "Midnight" is an excerpt from his forthcoming novel *The Trade.*

Richard Stevenson is the author of ten full-length collections of poetry. His most recent books include *From the Mouths of Angels* (1993; winner of the 1994 Stephan G. Stephansson Award), *Flying Coffins* (1994), and *A Murder of Crows: New & Selected Poems* (1998). Richard listens to jazz and teaches Canadian literature, creative writing, and business communication courses for Lethbridge Community College.

Fred Wah has written sixteen volumes of poetry and prose-poetry. He was awarded the 1985 Governor-General's Literary Award for Poetry for his collection *Waiting for Saskatchewan*. His other work includes *So Far* (1991), *Alley Alley* (1992), and *Diamond Grill* (1996). He lives in Calgary and teaches English at the University of Calgary.

Thomas Wharton was born in Grande Prairie, Alberta in 1963. His first novel, *Icefields*, was published in 1995. "Dream Novels: Excerpt from a work in progress" was published in *Canadian Fiction Magazine* (1996) and reprinted in *Best Canadian Stories* (1996) and *Canadian Fiction Magazine, Silver Anniversary Anthology* (1997). Thomas lives in Edmonton and works at the Department of English at the University of Alberta. "Salamander" is an excerpt from his forthcoming second novel.

Rudy Wiebe is the author of several short-story and essay collections, including *River of Stone: Fiction and Memories* (1995), and eight novels, including *The Temptation of Big Bear* (1973) and *A Discovery of Strangers* (1994), both winners of the Governor-General's Award for Fiction. His other works include *The Blue Mountains of China* (1970), *Double Vision: An Anthology of Twentieth-Century Stories in English* (1976), *Getting Here: Stories* (1977), and *West of Fiction* (1983). His most recent book is *A Stolen Life: The Journey of a Cree Woman* (1998, with Yvonne Johnson), which won the Viacom Canada Writers' Trust Non-Fiction Prize and the Wilfred Eggleston Award for Non-Fiction. "Watch for Two Coyotes, Crossing" appeared in *Saturday Night*. Rudy lives and works in Edmonton.

About the Editor

Srdja Pavlovic is a Montenegrin writer, literary translator, and journalist. He is one of the founders of the bilingual literary magazine *Stone Soup*, where he works as contributing editor. He is also a contributing editor for *Mak* literary magazine. His publications include an ethno-monograph, *Mongolian Pictograph* (1989), and a collection of essays on politics and literature, *Western Seesaw* (1997). He has translated and published the works of Brayten Braytenbach, Ken Smith, Jehuda Amichai, Umberto Eco, Jean Baudrillard, Hanif Kureishi, Michael Ondaatje, E.D. Blodgett, Fred Wah, George Melnyk, Monty Reid, and Douglas Barbour. He came to Edmonton in 1996, where he is working toward completing his doctoral thesis in the Department of History at the University of Alberta.